I0655206

LOVER BOYS FOREVER

An Erotic Anthology

Edited By

Mickey Erlach

Herndon, VA

Published in the United States by STARbooks Press, PO Box 711612, Herndon, VA 20171. Printed in the United States

Many thanks to graphic artist John Nail for the cover design.

Mr. Nail may be reached at: tojonail@bellsouth.net

Herndon, VA

STARbooks Press Titles Edited by Mickey Erlach

Boys Will Be Boys – Their First Time

Boys Caught in the Act

Cruising for Bad Boys

Pretty Boys & Roughnecks

Boys Getting Ahead

Video Boys

Gym Buddies & Buff Boys

The Boys of Chi Omega Chi Kappa –

Freshman Initiation

Alpha Boys

Lover Boys Forever

Contents

NEVER A DULL MOMENT
By Rob Rosen

Rob Rosen (www.therobrosen.com), author of the novels *Sparkle: The Queerest Book You'll Ever Love, Divas Las Vegas, Hot Lava, Southern Fried,* and *Queerwolf,* has been published in more than 175 anthologies.

I was asleep in bed. Well, napping, anyway, being lazy on a peaceful Sunday afternoon. The house was silent, the sun blasting through the still-drawn curtains. And then, I heard the noise, a scraping, a squeak. "Joel?" I managed, in between a raucous yawn. "That you?" Only, there was no answer.

I started to fall back into slumber when I heard it again, louder this time, coming from somewhere out back. "Joel?" I said again, louder this time, propping myself up on my elbows. But still there was no answer, so I jumped up, heart rate quickening as I tied the drawer strings to my pajama bottoms tighter. Shuffling down the hallway, I made my way to the living room. "Joel, you home?" I half-croaked

I tilted my head up, my ears listening for the sound again, trying to figure out where it was coming from. And then there it was, metal scrapping wood, emanating from the kitchen, toward the rear of the house. Tiptoeing now, I quietly headed that way, reaching the kitchen just as the door flung open, a man rushing in, mask over his face, a bat in his hand. "Fuck," he spat, stopping in his tracks a mere foot away from me.

"Fuck," I echoed, hand over chest, legs instantly quaking at the sight of him.

"I saw you go out," he added, bat raised up high.

"That was my boyfriend," I replied, frozen to the spot, waiting for his next move.

He paused, hand gripping the wood. "Gay, dude?" he asked, as opposed to what one would expect, namely hand me your wallet.

"Hence the whole boyfriend thing," I replied, my eyes locked to the bat. "Who'll be home soon."

He nodded, clearly calculating his next move. "How soon?" Then he moved in closer, closer still, the bat even higher now, his mask puffing out in front of his mouth.

"Soon," I managed. "Very soon. Any minute." My bare chest was rapidly rising and falling now, belly as well, nearly panting as I stood there watching him.

His head tilted down. He was eyeing me, face suddenly pointed midsection. "Show me," he said, voice thicker now, laden with something new.

"What?" I replied, inching in reverse. "My wallet, watch? What?" I repeated.

He chuckled. "Your cock, dude," he said. "Show me your cock." The bat swung in a circle above his head. "Or else."

I gulped. "He'll be home any minute," I said again, barely above a whisper, a trickle of sweat dripping down my forehead.

"Then show me your cock fast, dude," he amended. "Or else."

Again I froze in place, the silence around us nearly deafening, save for his heavy breathing, not to mention my own. "And then you'll leave?" I managed, hands on the pajama strings.

He chuckled. "I have the bat, dude," he said. "Meaning, no promises. Just show me. Now."

I nodded, the gulp repeating. I untied the drawstrings, my pajama bottoms instantly falling to the floor, cock exposed. Balls exposed. Bush exposed. All of me exposed.

"Can you please leave now?" I asked, voice breaking as I stared down at my nudity.

"Nice dick," he replied, instead. "Wanna see mine?"

Now it was my turn to pause. "Um, no," I said.

He chuckled. "That wasn't a very convincing no, dude."

"No," I repeated, louder this time, more forceful.

He shook his head, his free hand slowly zipping down his zipper. "Oh, too slow, dude. Besides, you showed me yours, my turn to show you mine."

"You made me show you mine," I countered with.

His pants came unbuttoned next, the white of his briefs exposed. "Semantics." And then he pushed down on the denim, the briefs lowering with them, blond bush revealed, then the base of his cock, which just as quickly sprung out, hard as the bat he was still wielding. "Guess it wanted to come out and play."

Again I gulped, my eyes suddenly glued to it, at the wide, bulbous head, already leaking, at the shaft, curved to the right and slightly up, thickly veined. Suffice it say, my own cock stirred and instantly started a rise on its own, eager to meet its playmate. I stared from it to his and back again. "This doesn't change anything," I said.

His chuckle returned. "No? You sure about that? Looks like you're outvoted, two to one."

I tried to cover my burgeoning prick, but there was only so much I could do. "My boyfriend ..."

"Broken record, dude," he interrupted. "Besides, maybe he'd like to play, too."

"No he wouldn't," I protested. "Please, just take whatever it is you came for and leave."

He shrugged. "Suit yourself. Wallet please." I went to lift up my pajamas, but he stopped me. "Nope. Let's see that aft side of yours as you get me your wallet. Make it a win/win."

I grimaced and kicked them off as I made my way back to the bedroom. He followed close behind, whistling at me as I walked in front of him, dick swaying to and fro as my heart galloped through a furlong. Back at my bed, jeans on the floor from the previous night, I bent down to retrieve my wallet. His hand quickly flew out and grabbed my pole from between my legs. Again I froze as a jolt of adrenaline shot up my spine. "The wallet," I said, handing it back to him.

"In a minute," he replied, crouching down for a sniff of my ass as he continued to jack my prick. "Damn, that's a nice hole, dude. You got yourself one lucky boyfriend."

I forced back a moan as his hand rose up and down. "Who won't be happy finding you here."

He released his grip and spanked my ass, the sound pinging all around us. "Then let's make sure he doesn't," he told me, roughly grabbing my arm after he snagged my wallet, and then dragged me from the bedroom, back through the living room, and over to the kitchen door, all while I fought for escape. But he was bulkier than I by a good fifteen pounds, and all I managed to do was work up a sweat. "Out," he said, flinging open the back door.

"Let me get some clothes on first," I replied, eyes wide as I watched him remove the mask, revealing the handsome face behind, eyes as blue as the sky outside, bluer even.

He grinned, revealing a row of blindingly white teeth. "Now where would the fun be in that?" he said, shoving me out as the door slammed behind us. "Besides, you can't get far like this, I figure."

"Far?" I coughed out, shrinking from him as he again lifted the bat. "Where … where are we going? You have my wallet already. Can't you just leave?"

He grabbed my prick, which was still semi, still swinging, balls hanging low in the warm summer air. "It's not stealing, you know, if it's payment for a job well done," he replied, cryptically, the grin rising on his face as my belly lurched. Then he pushed me forward, toward the rear of my property, to the line of trees and out of sight of any prying eyes.

Seconds later, we were in the woods, silent save for the leaves crunching beneath his sneakers and my bare feet. It was cooler in there, a row of Goosebumps forming up both my arms as he marched behind me, slapping my ass if I dared slow down. Eventually, he did stop, though. "What ... what now?" I squeaked out, watching as he set the bat down and kicked off his sneakers.

I started to run, but again he grabbed my arm. "Dude, I was all-state in track, and I lettered in football. You run, and, trust me, you'll be down on the ground in no time flat. Got it?" He released my arm.

I nodded. "Got it," I replied, rubbing my now-aching limb.

Then I watched him as he grabbed his T-shirt, hiking it over his head, torso revealed, mounds of muscle, tan skin, a matting of blond chest hair nestled in between two pert, pink nipples. A six pack with an extra set of cans steadily rose and fell, faster as he reached for the top button of his jeans, the zipper again sliding down. The jeans fell and were kicked off, leaving him in nothing but his socks and tenting briefs. My Adam's apple rose and fell as the last vestiges of his clothes slid down, got kicked off, his cock again free, slick with precum.

"Sit down," he said, pointing to the forest floor.

Again I nodded, crouching down before my ass was flush with the ground, leaves tickling my balls, cock rising at the feel of it. He watched and waited for it to go full-on erect, the head quickly thick as a plumb. And then he sat across from me, feet up, legs wide, bent at the knee so that I could see his asshole, his balls, his prick, all at once. His finger rose again, pointing to my crotch. Meaning, in a flash, I was sitting like him, two holes winking at one another.

"My boyfriend is probably home already," I told him. "He's probably worried, calling the police."

He chuckled and grabbed for his cock. "He probably figured you went for a jog, just like he did. Maybe in an hour, he'll call the cops. Maybe two," he said, spitting down, the saliva dripping over his hand and his prick, glistening in the sunlight that managed its way through the trees. "I'll be long gone by then." Again he pointed at my crotch. "But clearly not forgotten." Then he lifted his index finger and gave it a mid-air loop. "Front is nice. How about the back side again?"

I grunted and got on all fours, legs wide, balls dangling, ass jutting out. He hopped up and kneeled by my side, his hand caressing my shoulder, the small of my back, my right butt cheek, and, lastly, my hole. And now that he was preoccupied, it was my chance at last to make my move.

I rolled over and then quickly whipped around him, catching him off guard as I pinned him to the ground, grabbing for the bat before pressing it to his windpipe. "Varsity wrestling," I informed him, grunting as he choked, a gagging tear streaming down his cheek. He tried to get out from under me, but I pushed harder. "I wouldn't if I were you."

He stopped thrashing, the only sounds – that of both of us panting, the leaves crunching beneath his back and my knees. I stared down the length of him as I fought to catch my breath. His cock was remarkably still solid, a fifth limb jutting straight up. I gave it a smack with my free hand, sending it reeling as he moaned and arched his back. My hand reversed, slapping the underside, the moan even louder this time.

"Let me up," he panted, another tear joining the first.

I grabbed his dick, which pulsed in my grip. "You're already up, asshole."

He groaned and stared at me. "Yeah, so what are you gonna do about that?"

Again I pushed down on the bat. "Seems we're at a standstill," I told him, eyes locked. "I let you go, you come after me. Or I keep pressing down on your throat until you pass out." I forced a smile. "Or possibly accidentally kill you."

His groan returned. "Or you can get me off, and I'll let you go." Then he, too, forced a smile. "Call it a draw."

"You're getting off is a draw?" I asked, another smack on his shaft, another moan from him, another back arch.

"Fine," he panted. "You can get off, too."

Though his logic seemed somehow flawed, I removed the bat from his throat and quickly moved away, tossing the weapon far into the distance, evening the playing field just a tad. Because at least he couldn't go for it and me at the same time, I figured. "Fine," I reluctantly agreed. "But I call all the shots."

He shrugged. "Just so long as we both, um, shoot, then I couldn't give a flying fuck." He rubbed his neck and sat back up. "Where would you like me, dude?"

"Up against the tree," I told him, pointing to a wide, old oak that stood directly behind him.

He nodded and moved toward it, his back against the wood a second later, panting as he watched me, cock still steely stiff, aimed my way. I closed the gap between us, my hand crashing down on his chest, on his belly, across his cock. Each smack elicited a groan from him, a fluttering of the eyes. "Fuck, dude," he moaned, legs buckling as I grabbed for his balls for a hard tug and a cruel twist. "Fuck yeah."

"Turn around," I told him, watching as his ass came into view, covered in the same blond down as the rest of him,

7

muscular, alabaster white. My cock pulsed at the sight of it. Thwack went my hand on one cheek, then the other, back to the first, the red quickly rising to the surface. His head titled up, legs even wider, ass further out, hole again visible. I craned my neck down, hocked a loogie at it, watching my saliva drip down. And then in a finger slid, his hole clenching down around it before allowing the intrusion, a second digit soon joining the fray, both of them reaching deep inside, all the way to the back.

"Fuuuck," he exhaled, the sound swirling around us like a swarm of wasps as he grabbed his cock, pumping away at it.

"Show it to me," I told him, a third finger buried inside now, a triple onslaught.

He grunted and pushed his cock back through his thighs, piss slit staring up at me as he continued to jack, one arm leaning against the tree for support. I crouched down, dick in hand, face up close to it all. Ass, balls, prick, the heady aroma of musk and sweat obliterating the forest's scent in an instant.

Faster my hand went inside ass and faster my other hand went on my dick, both of them in sync, both pumping away. Him too, pumping and moaning up a storm from the other side of things. "Close," he rasped over his shoulder.

"Wait," I told him. "On your back."

I retracted my fingers. He fell backwards, prone in a heartbeat. I knelt by his side, grabbed his cock and took up where he'd left off, while he grabbed mine and did the same. His dick was so thick in my grip that it was nearly impossible to keep a hold of it. Still, I worked it for all it was worth, watching, waiting for the inevitable.

Then he moaned again, so loud as to scare of a pair of doves off an upper branch. One last time his back arched, mouth in a pant as his fat cock exploded in my hand, an eruption of come that flew up and back, splattering on his belly and chest, dousing him in pungent white. A moment later, my cock, too, shot, his hand lightning fast on it as a stream of come spewed out, joining with his before both wads dripped over his side. And still I jacked his prick, making him writhe on the forest floor.

When the last drops of jizz were coaxed out, I stood up, sighed, and walked back to my house, not turning around to watch what he'd do next. Instead, I entered through my kitchen, locked the door, and headed for the shower, washing the sweat and come and forest debris off me. I played the scene back through my head as the hot water flooded over my body, allowing myself the briefest of smiles.

When I came out of the bathroom, my boyfriend was walking in through the front door, a grin on his face and a large bouquet of flowers in his hand. He walked up and handed them to me, a warm, wet kiss placed on my mouth. "Happy tenth anniversary, dude," he said, his hand tweaking one of my nipples, eyes locked tight on mine, so much blue as to take your very breath away.

My smile grew mega-watt bright on my face, a rush of tenderness rising up from my chest. My hand caressed his cheek, his neck. "Happy anniversary, Joel," I replied, my hand lingering on his throat. "What happened here? You've got a bruise."

He shrugged, reached out his hands, and pulled me in tight. "Little accident around back, hon," he replied. "Never a dull moment around here you know." His smile mirrored my own.

I couldn't help but laugh. "Amen to that, Joel," I said, the kiss repeated, again and again and again." Amen to that."

FRIENDS AND LOVERS
By Michael Bracken

Michael Bracken is the author of several books and nearly 1,000 short stories. When he isn't writing, he's sleeping.

Eddie and I were best friends throughout high school, thrown together in detention during our first week as ninth-graders for a pair of heinous offenses against the school system that I no longer remember and rarely separated from that point onward. I was the skinny new kid, having arrived in the small northern California town with my parents only three weeks before the school year started; Eddie was a town lifer, the pudgy only-child of a waitress and a laborer at the lumber mill.

We did everything together – shot pool down in fish town when we should have been at Wednesday night Bible study, drank stolen bottles of Schlitz and smoked pilfered Virginia Slims under the bridge as often as we could, and wore the ink off the pages of three pornographic magazines we found stashed in his grandfather's garage. I didn't tell him then because I didn't think he would understand – I'm not certain I understood myself – but I was more interested in the men in those photographs than the women.

I lost track of Eddie the summer after graduation. He enlisted in the Army, intending to make a career of it to avoid spending his life in the lumber mill or on the fishing boats, and went off to boot camp while I moved halfway across the country to attend a university in Austin that seemed to employ more people than even lived in the town I left behind. I found a home in the English department – a place where skinny guys like me didn't stand out – and lost my cherry to a graduate assistant after a long evening spent discussing *Beowulf* and smoking fat little spliffs in his one-bedroom walk-up.

11

After graduation, I joined the university's public relations department, traded my student hovel for a small loft apartment and, a few years later, traded up again for a two-bedroom fixer-upper not far from campus. I drifted in and out of relationships for the next two decades, with none lasting more than a few months.

The lumber company transferred my father midway through my second semester, and I lost my only incentive for returning to the northern California town where I'd attended high school. Because I made no effort to maintain contact with my former classmates, I was surprised when I opened my mailbox one evening in the spring of 2000 and discovered an invitation to my graduating class's twenty-five-year reunion. By then my fixer-upper had been fixed up, my neighborhood had become trendy, and my house was the envy of neighborhood latecomers.

I removed my jacket, loosened my tie, and settled onto one of the two director's chairs I kept on my porch. I read and reread the invitation, examined the schedule of events, and pondered the wisdom of using vacation time to return to a place that held few particularly good memories. There was only one reason to take the time and spend the money: I wanted to know what had happened to Eddie, and I had no way to know if he would be there or not.

Three weeks later, after spring became summer, I flew into San Francisco, rented a car, and drove north along the coastline until Highway 1 became Main Street. The town hadn't changed much. A McDonald's had joined the locally owned cafes and restaurants, the lumber mill where my father had once been a senior manager had closed, and Main Street had two more stoplights.

I had reserved a room at a motel north of town, across the creek from the bowling alley where Eddie and I first encountered Pong. My second floor room overlooked the Pacific Ocean, held a king-size bed, and had the same decor as every other low-budget chain motel room across small town

12

America. I probably could have stayed in a newer hotel, but I had booked my room in the only place I could remember by name.

After I unpacked, I napped for an hour, then showered and dressed for the evening, an adults-only affair in the banquet room of a restaurant that hadn't existed twenty-five years earlier, and the first of a weekend's worth of activities that included a family-friendly picnic the following day in the state park three miles north of town.

At the registration table, I realized that some overly ambitious former classmate – probably a bored housewife for whom the reunion was the highlight of her social calendar for the decade – had included our yearbook photos on the name badges. I grimaced when I saw the longhaired, pimple-faced young man I had once been, then silently thanked fate when I realized the elephantine mouth-breather on the far side of the registration table had been the head cheerleader, a buxom blonde who had more balls between her thighs our senior year than the football team's center.

After pinning the name badge to my jacket, I stopped at the cash bar for a glass of Pinot Grigio. Then I circumnavigated the banquet room, stopping now and then to stare at name badges and speak briefly with people I barely remembered and who barely remembered me.

Then I saw Eddie.

He was speaking with two pot-bellied ex-jocks, not looking in my direction. His shoulder-length black hair had been buzzed into a flattop liberally sprinkled with salt, and the doughy young man I had known then had become a thick, muscular adult. I had changed as well, adding weight and muscle tone thanks to the exercise room and lap pool in the university's student center, and I regularly visited a stylist who not only trimmed my hair, but also maintained the highlights that masked the encroaching gray. I didn't approach Eddie immediately, instead waiting until he finished his conversation and the two jocks moved on.

He turned, saw me approaching and smiled. Without glancing at my name badge or even hearing my voice, he said, "I didn't think you'd come."

Eddie gathered me into his arms, gave me a bear hug that spilled my wine and threatened to crack a few ribs, and then held me at arm's length and looked me up and down. "Time's been good to you."

"You, too," I said, and it was true.

When Eddie saw that my Pinot Grigio had spilled, he took my elbow, led me to the bar, and asked what I'd been drinking. Then he ordered a replacement for me and for himself a Jack and Coke.

After we had our drinks, Eddie raised his in a toast and said, "To misspent youth."

I touched my wine glass to his tumbler, and we both drank.

We spent the rest of the evening reminiscing, oblivious to our former classmates milling about, and we remained long after they returned home or headed to their motel rooms. When restaurant staff closed the banquet room, we moved to the bar.

We talked about cruising Main Street with Bachman-Turner Overdrive blaring from the 8-track player, about hours spent playing pinball at the miniature golf course south of town, and about more hours spent immersed in digest-sized science fiction magazines we bought at the liquor store. We talked out about our parents – mine retired and living in Seattle, his still working and living in the same house where he'd been raised.

I told him about life in Austin, a liberal pimple on the conservative ass of Texas, and he told me about his military career and his role in Desert Storm after Iraq invaded

14

Kuwait. There was a delicious irony in that, after a childhood spent as a corporate vagabond, I had opted to settle in one place for the entirety of my adult life and Eddie, having spent his entire childhood in one place, had seen the world through military service and had continued traveling after retirement, purchasing a small motor home and towing a Jeep behind it as he cruised the back roads of America.

Despite all the places he had traveled and all the things he had experienced, Eddie was the same person I had known all those years ago, the same person I had called my best friend, and our conversation flowed as if mere hours had passed since we'd last been together. We were so entranced with one another that we remained long past last call and the bartender finally had to escort us out the door before barricading it behind us. We walked around the restaurant to the dark back lot where ours were the only two cars remaining, his a WWII-era Jeep with a tow bar sticking up in front of the grill, mine a rental with no discernible personality.

I probably should have shaken Eddie's hand, maybe given him a hug, but I'd had a bit too much Pinot Grigio and I wasn't thinking. Eddie had been my best friend for four years, someone I had cared about more than any other person in my life other than my parents, and someone who, I was reluctant to admit, I actually loved. So, I grabbed his face with both hands and planted a kiss on his lips.

Eddie didn't resist, but he didn't return the kiss, either.

Realizing what I had done, I stepped back, horrified at what he must have thought, and then turned and hurried to my car. I drove away without looking back, and I spent the rest of the night chastising myself.

I arrived at the reunion picnic just before noon the next day, arriving late because I was unsure how to deal with the conflicting emotions seeing Eddie had stirred up and finally decided to confront them head on. I found Eddie sitting alone at one of the picnic tables gnawing on a ham sandwich and nursing a beer.

"About last night ..." I started.

"Don't worry about it," he said around a mouthful of sandwich.

"But ..."

He held up his hand, palm toward me, a silent command to stop talking. After he swallowed, Eddie said, "I knew. Even back then, I knew. You don't have to apologize."

"You did?"

"I didn't know the words for it, but I knew." He held up his beer bottle and used it as a pointer. "There's more where this came from in that cooler over there."

After I grabbed a beer, I was stopped by one of the reunion organizers, a woman I had barely known when we were high school students. I then visited with more of my former classmates, met their spouses and children and grandchildren, and deflected questions about my own marital status and prospects for parenthood by saying I was happy with my career and hadn't yet met the right person. Many of my former classmates were happy to tell me about their lives and the insignificant things they'd accomplished in the years since graduation. Few of them seemed to notice than I shared little in return.

Someone had brought lawn darts, and I found myself taking third place in an impromptu lawn darts tournament. Someone else had set up a volleyball net on the beach, but the only people playing where the children and grandchildren of my former classmates. The afternoon disappeared in a flurry of activity that included gathering the Class of '75 in one place for a group picture while the sunlight was still favorable.

After posing for the group picture, standing in the back row with Eddie's arm around my shoulder, I bade my farewells and told Eddie I would be leaving town first thing the next morning.

"Where are you staying?" he asked.

I told him.

"Mind if I stop by on the way back into town?"

I had no idea why he would want to, but I told him he could.

I had been in my room for nearly an hour when Eddie rapped on the door. I opened it and found him standing outside with a cold six-pack of beer, a bucket of warm potato salad, a paper plate filled with lunchmeat, and half a loaf of bread that he had liberated from the reunion committee.

"Dinner's ready," he said with a smile as he pushed past me into my room.

He piled everything on the room's only table. As we ate, we continued the conversation the bartender had interrupted the night before as if nothing had happened after being escorted from the bar. When he finished his second beer, Eddie kicked off his shoes and stretched out on the bed.

Before long, I stretched out beside him and our conversation drifted from past to present and covered all the intervening years. After another hour, Eddie finally revealed himself to me, telling me how difficult it had been to remain in the service after he finally admitted to himself that he was in the closet.

"I think about you all the time," Eddie said. "Dream about you, fantasize about you, wonder what might have been if I hadn't taken so long to – if I had just admitted to myself – if ..."

"I've wondered the same things," I admitted.

"You surprised me last night in the parking lot," he said. "I should have told you right then how I felt."

"Tell me now."

When Eddie rose up on one elbow and looked down at me, I knew what was going to happen and I wasn't about to resist. He kissed me, gently at first, his lips just brushing against mine. He kissed me again and again, on my lips, my cheek, my earlobe, my shoulder, the hollow at the base of my throat. When his lips returned to mine, his kiss became more urgent and soon our tongues met in a fiery dance of desire. At the same time, our fingers fumbled with buttons, buckles, snaps, and zippers. Our clothes hit the floor at a steady pace.

And when we were both naked, we paused and looked at one another. We had seen each other unclothed many times – in the locker room showers after gym class, skinny dipping in the river, while preparing for bed during sleepovers at his house or mine – but we were no longer undeveloped and inexperienced young men. We were adults, with men's bodies and more experience than either of us was ever likely to admit.

Black hair covered his barrel chest and abdomen, and his crotch was a wild and untamed forest from which the thick tube of his cock rose majestically. I ran my thin fingers through his chest hair, teased his nipples with my thumbs, and then let my hands stray lower until I wrapped one fist around his cock. I slowly stroked the entire length, from the hard pubic bone at the base to the spongy soft mushroom cap of the glans.

Unlike Eddie, I don't have much body hair, and I keep my nether region neatly groomed. Though neither as long nor as thick as his cock, mine didn't have to compete with surrounding shrubbery for attention, and one of Eddie's strong hands enveloped it. I was too excited, and it only took a few powerful strokes of his fist before I came.

My cock spasmed in his fist and a thin stream of warm cum covered my abdomen. Eddie released his grip on my cock and let it flounder against my abdomen. I started to apologize, but he stopped me with a smile and said. "You always did like to be first, didn't you?"

Eddie slipped off the bed, dug a lubricated condom packet from his pants pocket, and then rejoined me. Ever since that night with the graduate assistant when I realized what I was and why I had felt the way I had about Eddie, I had dreamed of this moment.

He didn't disappoint me. He tore open the condom packet and unrolled the condom over his thick cock. Then he knelt between my widespread thighs, lifted my legs and bent me nearly in half. He pressed the tip of his condom-covered cock against the tight pucker of my ass hole and then pushed forward. The lubrication allowed him to enter me easily and smoothly, and he buried the entire length of his cock inside me. Then, resting much of his weight on my thighs, he drew back and pushed forward as he stared down into my eyes.

Previous lovers had all taken me from behind, and being able to watch Eddie's face as we made love filled me with unexpected pleasure. I reached up and cupped his face in my hands, stroking his cheeks with the balls of my thumbs as I held him.

As he pumped into me, my cock regained its former stature and his hairy abdomen rubbed against the head with each of his powerful thrusts. Eddie began pumping faster, driving deeper into me with each thrust, and I felt myself approaching a second orgasm. I moved my hands from his face and gripped the cheeks of his ass just as we came.

His face contorted as he came, and he stiffened above me just before filling the condom with his cum. And then I came, too, covering my belly with a second load of spunk.

For several heartbeats neither of us could move. Finally, Eddie withdrew, slipped from the bed into the bathroom and discarded the condom.

When he returned, he lay behind in and spooned me until I fell asleep in his arms.

When the alarm woke me Sunday morning, the other side of the bed was empty. Eddie had cleaned up the mess we'd made of the picnic food, and all that remained of him was the lingering scent of his aftershave and our coupling. He hadn't left a note, hadn't told me how I could reach him, and hadn't even asked how to find me in Austin.

I checked out of the motel that morning, returned to San Francisco, the airport, and home. I never expected to see Eddie again. Maybe it was better that way. Maybe one powerful memory of the night when I realized Eddie felt the same way about me that I felt about him would be enough to sustain me for years to come. Maybe we finally had the answers to all the unanswered questions we had been carrying with us for twenty-five years.

For the next several weeks, I compared every man I met to Eddie – Eddie as a young man, Eddie as an adult – and none of them measured up nor were they invited into my bed.

Nearly two months after the reunion I returned home from the university to find a motor home with California license plates and a Jeep in tow parked in front of my house. I pulled into my drive, walked to the porch, and found Eddie sitting on one of the director's chairs drinking from a sweating can of beer. He reached into the cooler at his feet and pulled out another can. After he handed it to me, I settled onto the other director's chair. As I popped the top of the beer, Eddie said, "Nice place."

"I think so."

"It's a little frou-frou, though," he said. "Could use a man's touch."

"Yours?"

Eddie nodded.

He's been here ever since.

SEAN
By Michael Turner

Michael Turner lives in South Wales, UK with his partner and a mad Springer Spaniel. He divides his time between writing, painting and walking the dog. E-mail him at galadann100@gmail.com.

It was Monday. I hate Mondays. They are the natural low points of the week, signaling, as it does, the end of the weekend, the end of fun and frolics and the return to the grindstone of work.

The morning dawned dark and overcast; the sky full of dark ominous clouds heavy with their unshed rain. The sky mirrored my mood – black and thunderous.

I yawned and stretched, reaching over to the other side of the bed. My heart jumped into my throat as I realized he wasn't there. The space occupied by his masculine body was empty, cold. Reality hit me like a runaway steam train.

I sighed and slowly, like a sloth, climbed from my warm, pit of a bed into the cold dark world.

Shivering, I ran into the bathroom, pulled the cords on the electric wall heater and the shower and jumped into the hot spray of water.

Thirty minutes later, I was out of the front door and on my way to work.

Alighting from the bus, which was full of the usual commuters, the suits and skirts of the corporate world and the soiled overalls and torn jeans of the blue collar workers mixed together in a mismatch of human life, I made my way through the center of town toward McDonald's, the neon yellow of the grand 'm' shining in the drab day as bright as the sun, acting as a lure to all those weary, hungry lost souls.

I hurried through the large fat drops of rain that were just beginning to fall from the thunderclouds that covered the

21

city from horizon to horizon, like a black dome covering the rooftops.

As I walked through the double doors, the heat hit me like an oasis of warmth in a city of cold. The glaring strip lights hurt my eyes as they adjusted to the brightness of the room.

The room itself was open plan in the typical McDonald's way. To the left was a flight of stairs that led to the second floor of the restaurant and next to that the baby changing room. Nestled snugly under the stairs was a corner complete with tables and chairs designed to resemble mushrooms and a TV showing cartoons even at this time of the morning.

The main body of the room spread out to the right. The ubiquitous plastic table and chairs lined the walls and formed two islands in the middle of the open space. On the walls, in a very Romanesque-Greco style, were paintings depicting chipped and cracked terracotta urns and jugs. Throughout the open space, rubber plants reared their heads, their greenery lending a false air to the room.

At the far end stood the counter complete with its electronic tills and stainless steel so highly polished you could see your reflection. Behind the counter were two members of staff trying to look busy; I suppose that at eight-thirty in the morning with only a few customers, there can't be that much to do.

Further back in the kitchen, another two members of staff, dressed in the black T-shirts and tight trousers that passed for the uniforms in this particular branch were hard at work preparing the world famous breakfasts that graced every McDonald's counter this time of the morning.

"Two hash browns and a cup of tea," I replied in such a flat, dead tired tone of voice a zombie would have been proud to the unspoken question thrown in my direction by the girl who served me.

It was lucky that I was half-asleep otherwise I might have said something about her appearance. It was awful and most certainly not something you wanted to come face to face with on a dreary, bleak Monday morning.

She was of average build and height with a pair of long legs that filled out the trousers of her uniform in a way I could only consider would be flattering to heterosexuals. Likewise the T-shirt tucked in her trousers and cinched tight by the black leather belt that she wore outlined her breasts entirely. Yet another sight that would put a good poof like me off my breakfast.

However, the *piece de resistance* was her face. If I had to guess, I would say she had put her make-up on in a darkened room with a trowel. Talk about thick! If you were to scrape her lipstick off it would keep the whole chain of Body Shops in lipsticks for a year at least, not to mention her mascara and eyeliner. It was repulsive.

I paid and retrieved my breakfast from this walking Max Factor advert. I'm not really sure if she could talk for all she said to me was "One pound fifty three." No please or thank you and as she hadn't strung a sentence together I couldn't really judge.

I retreated to my favorite table on the side of the restaurant hidden behind a huge rubber plant potted in a large cracked urn and in prime position to watch the door for any decent eye-candy that walked in.

I tucked into my breakfast well aware of the fat and calorie content and that I was doing my heart and arteries no favors. I didn't care. I loved hash browns, and there are worse things in the world for you to eat.

After a few minutes, I pulled the novel I was reading from my bag, turned to the marked page, removed the bookmark, and began to read as I ate. Now if there is one thing I cannot stand is being disturbed when I'm reading. So when someone began to clean my table I prepared a verbal assault and readied for battle.

I looked up, my face as black and impenetrable as the thunder clouds outside, my eyes flashing lethally and began my verbal tirade. "Just what the ..."

That was as far as I got. My mental preparations abandoned me, and my mouth fell open leaving me looking like a fish. My breath seemed to have stopped in my throat, and my heart ached. I felt sick as my stomach turned and the butterflies that don't normally reside there began an air display the Red Devils would have been proud.

Standing before me and looking at me with an alarmed expression, was a man who was simply gorgeous.

"Sorry," I stammered as he regained his composure. "You startled me."

"Not as much as you startled me," he said in a normal voice. I had expected him to be pissed off, but he took it all in his stride. Perhaps it's some kind of secret McDonald's training for handling grumpy assholes or maybe he was just an easygoing bloke, to this day I don't know.

What I do know was that at that moment I felt myself going down the old familiar slippery slope of lust. The slope I had vowed I would never go down after the last attempt. So much for vows.

He had been talking to me, and I had missed everything he'd said. This was a great start. First, I shouted at him and then I didn't listen. He would think I was a right twat.

To be fair, it wasn't really my fault. As I have already said, he was gorgeous and I have a weakness for gorgeous men.

He was dressed in the ubiquitous McDonald's uniform, which made him look wonderful. The shirt was stretched taut across his expansive shoulders and his arms which showed the bulge of his biceps every time he moved. His shirt was open at the neck and I could tell that he either had none or very little chest hair. The blue material was molded to his torso revealing the outline of his broad pectorals. He wore a tartan waistcoat, which while it hindered me in my investigation of his chest did outline his flat stomach and trim waist.

But by far the best part lay below his waist. To say his blue uniform trousers fit him snugly would be an understatement. They were like a second skin so tight did they fit. I could tell just from a glance that he had thick, muscled thighs to die for.

The material was stretched to the limit so tight over his groin I could see the outline of his cock and balls, all nestled comfortably toward his left leg.

He was like me in his looks – to a certain extent. We were both around the same age with dark brown hair and eyes. That was where the similarity ended. He was taller than I, about six feet, with a full head of thick shining dark brown hair, which was pulled back away from his hard, handsome face in a style that was *en vogue* and held in place by gel.

"Sorry?" I asked as I finally realized he'd been asking me a question.

"Do you want a top-up?" he repeated, his superb mouth breaking into a grin as he realized I'd been checking him out.

I stared into his almost perfect face with its hard chiseled jaw complete with a dark beard line and full sensual lips. "Yeah," I replied.

He reached forward to take my cup and as he did so, his lips parted slightly leaving a moist impression. My cock jumped as I imagined those sensual lips closing over my cockhead and sliding their silkiness over my length.

His touch jolted me back to reality. His one hand was on my shoulder while the other was wrapped around mine, still holding my cup. I could feel the heat coming from him so close he was standing.

"Are you all right, mate?" he asked as he leaned forward, concern furrowing his forehead and making his deep brown eyes sparkle.

"Fine," I managed to mutter as the pain from my cock, expanding into a region that was too tight for it, began to register in my brain.

"I'll get you that top-up."

As he turned toward the counter, I was faced with the best view I'd had so far on that bleak and dreary Monday morning – his ass.

Like the front of his trousers, the material at the back was stretched tight and had slipped up his crack revealing a small, firm, boyish butt with taut finely rounded ass cheeks, which undulated provocatively beneath the tight material.

My mind went into overdrive as I imagined roughly grabbing the collection of hard looking muscle and forcing my swollen cock between his firm cheeks past his tense sphincter muscle and into his tight little hole.

I imagined plowing my manhood into his aching hole, my long brown shaft creating friction and pleasure for us both.

My dick throbbed again and I could feel my load churning in my bollocks, which were pulled tight and trapped in my trousers.

Before I knew it, he was back with my top-up, the concerned look still on his face.

"I've had a word with my manager," he began, "he says you're to come with me to the restroom," he flashed that cheeky grin at me again, "until you feel better."

Was it my imagination or did he place too much emphasis on the word come.

"That isn't necessary," I protested.

"He insists," he said, then in a quieter voice, "I insist." He placed his hand gently over mine.

I don't know why, nor will I ever probably, but something compelled me to follow him across the room and up the stairs.

The mounds of his curvaceous butt rocked gently in his tight trousers directly in front of my face as we climbed the stairs, and I couldn't help licking my lips as I thought of them locked around his pink hole.

We crossed the upper floor and passed through a drab brown door marked "Private. This door is alarmed."

So much for that I thought. Either they don't have one, it doesn't work, or it's been switched off. I mentally shrugged. I really didn't care. My only concern was keeping my newly found Adonis in sight.

He held the door open, and we passed through into the region of McDonald's that no self-respecting customer ever sees.

Here the fake plants and wipe clean plastic was gone. The corridor was breezeblock painted yellow, bare except for a notice board, which we quickly passed, turning into a room.

The room itself wasn't overly large with the same plastic tables that graced the restaurant below. On the far wall was a group of lockers the same as you would expect to find in a school changing room. Opposite them, a large open window looked out on the street below and to the right of that two boring brown doors.

He turned around and leaned his cute backside against one of the plastic tables folding his arms across his muscular chest at the same time looking me up and down, a thoughtful expression on his face as if he was weighing up some decision.

"I bet I know what would make you feel better," he said softly as he spread his legs slightly revealing his cock bulging against the thin material of his trousers.

Whether he did this intentionally or not I don't know but I appreciated it all the same. "Come here!"

As if in a trance, I did as I was told and walked toward him.

"Your treatment needs to be in three parts." He paused licking his sensual lips.

I held my breath as he unfolded his arms and slowly with exaggerated care reached out and grasped my cock, which was thickening down the leg of my trousers. Slowly and gently, he caressed my manhood, his thumb running over my cum-slit time and again.

Throughout this, we had been staring at each other; his deep brown eyes were locked on mine, holding them as if in a vice, and every time he elicited a gasp of pleasure from me, they flashed with a life of their own.

I broke the hold he had over my eyes and closed them as I shuddered with the pleasure of his hard hand playing with my dick, his fingers firm through the material of my trousers, running up and down the length of my swollen rod.

He began fumbling with my belt and soon had my trousers down around my knees, working on my cock through the thin material of my briefs.

I opened my eyes. His arresting brown orbs and the broad cheeky grin, which was spread across his handsome features, captured them immediately.

I grinned back and in that moment when I was off-guard he launched his attack. He pushed away from the table and grabbing my hips, swung me around so that I was leaning against the table.

Before I could catch my breath, he was pressing against me, his hand still holding my hips. I was trapped between the hard plastic of the cold table and the hard flesh of his hot cock, which I could feel, pressed firmly against my thigh.

He smiled that disarming grin and slowly lowered his lips to mine, kissing me hard on the mouth. It occurred to me that anyone could walk in at any minute, but after a second's doubt, I returned his kiss, slipping my tongue between his lips and Frenching him for all I was worth.

He pushed his tongue deep into my throat, moving like a live thing in my mouth. His crotch was pressed hard against me, and I could feel the throbbing of his thick dick as he ground it against mine.

I ripped off his shirt as I introduced myself. "I'm Luke, by the way."

"Sean," he said, his voice muffled through the material as his shirt went over his head.

I undid his belt and yanked his trousers down. In a matter of seconds, he was almost naked; his trousers and a pair of skimpy Versace briefs gathered at his knees.

His cock slapped his stomach as it was released from the confines of the thin material, and I caught a quick glance of it before he began dry-humping my stomach. It was at least eight inches in length, long enough to reach his belly button with ease, and so thick a horse would have been proud of it. The meaty shaft was crossed with thick veins, pulsing with blood, but by far, the most intriguing part of his rod, was his cockhead. Large and wide it almost looked out of place on the end of his brown shaft. It was an angry, purple-red as more and more blood diffused through his uncut swollen member. Gaping wide, like a fish, was his cum-slit which led all the way back to his heavy, low hanging balls complete with their dense foliage of blond hair.

Sean grabbed my own erection, placed it against his in his large paw of a hand, and began pumping up and down, wanking us off together. I could feel the heat coming from his elongated weapon, hot enough to melt the Polar ice caps and speed up global warming by a century.

Sean abruptly broke away from me leaving me feeling lost and devoid of his warmth. The dismay I felt must have shown on my face because he smiled his cheeky grin trying to reassure me.

He stretched over to a locker, opened the door and reached in. He rummaged about for a few minutes, playing with his cock as he did so, keeping his pulsing beast hard and solid. When he pulled his hand from the locker, he brought with him a condom and a tube of lube.

"You do the honors," he said, tossing the items to me.

I desperately wanted him to fuck me, so I wasted no time in tearing open the condom packet and rolling the thin latex over his huge dick meat and smearing a good amount of lube over his hard shaft. It felt good to be holding his cock. It was different from how I'd imagined it to be. I thought it would be rock hard, but it was quite malleable but with an inner core of strength, like a steel girder which had been wrapped in duvets.

He kissed me once again and then, without another word, spun me around and threw me over the table, trapping my cock between my stomach and the hard, unyielding plastic.

I spread my legs wide offering him my aching hole. He rubbed the tight valley between my ass cheeks with his thick, eight inches, his cockhead stroking my pucker tentatively, sending a shiver like pure lightening up my spine.

Suddenly there was a searing pain as he plunged in, his eight inches of solid meat tearing through my ring and traveling up my chute with the speed of Concorde. I yelped loudly. "For Christ's sake take it easy," I snapped over my shoulder.

"Relax," was all he said as I felt his hairy balls slap my ass. "Christ, you've got the tightest butthole I've fucked in ages." I could feel his desire hammering through his long shaft, the thick, sleek skin conveying his message clearly.

"Fuck, it hurts!" I said, sucking in air, trying to accommodate the pain.

Sean laughed and flexed his pelvic muscles causing his manhood to grow even harder in my hot, warm chute. Curiously, the pain began to subside and along with it the fear that he was going to rip me in two. For that, I was glad. It meant I could enjoy the feel of his dick embedded in my butt and the ride that was to come.

His hips began pumping with a quick, fierce rhythm, his cock driving between the mounds of my twitching buttocks. Time and again, Sean pulled out until only his cockhead remained in me and then his powerful hips would thrust forward, his latex sheathed sword plowing into my heaving gut.

I sighed and yelped and squealed and moaned and cried out in sheer ecstasy as Sean buried his rigid, pulsating shaft into me. Sometimes, he would leave his dick impaled in me and grind his hips. That felt so good! I would squeeze my ass tight, making him sigh with pleasure.

My cock trapped painfully between my stomach and the unrelenting plastic of the table was rock hard and oozing amounts of precum so copious as to outdo Niagara. I could feel his muscular chest rubbing against my back, his hairs tickling me, the friction causing the sexual heat between us to rise to greater heights.

Every time Sean rammed his cock into me, his hairy balls would slap my ass cheeks and he would let out a groan, which slowly turned into one continuous moan. His manhood

31

hammered my tortured rectum and as his dick tightened it set off the chain of reactions that led to me blowing one of the biggest wads I'd ever dropped.

My jizz blasted from my cum-slit and having nowhere to go pooled beneath me on the table. I could feel the heat coming from the wet liquid as the smell of man sex rose to pervade the air.

As I came, I tightened my ass muscles, and that was enough to set Sean off. With a roar a lion would have been proud, he held me tight as his cock filled the rubber with his thick man cream.

I could feel his dick spasm in my ass chute as he continued to pump, his hips powerfully thrusting his manhood into me, my ass muscles squeezing tightly, milking him for all he was worth.

Sean collapsed onto me as his orgasm subsided. He wrapped his arms around me and held me tight as he whispered breathlessly, "That was fucking amazing!"

His cock squirmed in my gut as he softly kissed the back of my neck. My body felt weak as he vacated my throbbing hole.

"Feeling better?" he asked as I stood up and turned around, his cheeky grin plastered on his face.

My knees trembled with the effort of standing up and I slumped into one of the nearby seats, the plastic cold on my hot, well-used ass.

"You bet!"

# # # # #

Two weeks later Sean moved in with me, and we began a relationship that was to last eight long, happy and joyous years. We shared in each other's hopes and aspirations, lived our dreams to the fullest, experienced all that we wanted to and generally lived life – milking the marrow out of life as one of our friends said.

It was a Monday morning then as well, and Sean was in work. I had gone in to the restaurant as I did every morning when he was working early.

I was sitting at my usual table eating my usual order of hash browns when a deep voice said, "You al'right?" I grinned recognizing his voice immediately.

I looked up straight into his gentle caring eyes and smiled.

"We've been invited to Tom and Zak's tonight," he started, "I told them we'll be there at ... "

I never did find out what time we would be there. It happened so suddenly. One minute he was standing there, smiling at me, telling me of the plans he had made for us, the next minute he turned ghostly white and grabbed his chest. His eyes rolled back, and he fell to the floor.

The rest of the staff were running toward us as I knelt by his writhing body, calling for a doctor.

In the ambulance, I held his hand tightly. "Hold on, Babe," I said time and again, repeating it like a mantra. "We're almost there now. Stay with me, Sean."

The paramedics worked frantically trying to save him. I was horrified at his appearance. Ten minutes earlier he had been laughing. Now he was blue and had seemed to age perceptibly. The features I knew so well had distorted into that of an old man.

"Sean ... Sean?"

His eyelids parted and a ghost of a smile passed over his lips. His soft eyes flashed as he looked at me and filled with warmth.

His smile grew stronger. "I ... love ... you," he said between labored breaths. His examined my face as if trying to memorize every detail. Then they closed, and he sighed.

The paramedic who had been working on him, fighting so hard to keep him breathing, lowered his head.

"Is he ...?" I barely whispered. He nodded.

The church on the day of the funeral was packed. It seemed as if everyone Sean had ever known had come to pay their respects.

Six close friends of Sean's, all members of the rugby team he played for, carried his casket into the hallowed building, I and members of his family following behind.

I waited until everyone had passed his casket. Finally, I stood there staring down at him, tall and muscular, alone with my thoughts.

He looked strange to me, not like my Sean at all. He was wearing a suit I had rarely seen him in and the shirt was a color I know he would have hated. He looked unnatural. His face looked like peach parchment and was devoid of the merriment and spark of life that made everyone he knew love him.

I reached into the coffin and held his hands for the last time. "Goodbye, my love," I whispered. It might have been my imagination, but I thought I saw his mouth twitch in a brief smile of recognition.

I no longer go to his restaurant in the city anymore; the memories are still too painful. Instead, I spend my time sitting at the river in all winds and weather wondering why the only good thing in my life was taken away from me so suddenly.

BROTHER SIMON'S HABIT
By Michael Turner

I have sinned! Oh, God forgive me, I have sinned! I have sinned against His most glorious Name!

Guilt fills and wracks me. Guilt courses through my veins, flowing through every organ and every limb of my being. Guilt exudes from every pore and surrounds me, a halo of obscene presence around my body.

My heart aches – heavy and overwrought as I am.

How could I? How could I have perpetrated such a heinous crime against man and against my God?

I am guilty. I am doomed to Hellfire everlasting. My body will burn in the Devil's fire, his nymphs and satyrs cavorting around me in a parody of my sins. My flesh and bones will roast on the Devil's spit and wither away; my soul shall be ripped open and tormented for time everlasting, my entire being: my body, my soul, my mind, all will be tortured beyond endurance, and still the tortures will go on.

Yet shall I have deserved my punishment?

The Holy Gospels say it right, the realm's laws say it right, the abbot say it right and mine own family, should they know, would say it right.

Yet is it right? I think it harsh. Yet when I took my vows did I not agree to abide by God's laws, to obey the Holy Word?

I am only human after all. The mind may be strong, but the flesh is weak. There are so many earthly temptations the Devil can choose and pick his weapons ... and there is only one defense ... Faith.

That is the nub of my problem ... Faith ... I don't have enough ... My faith is not strong enough.

Recently I have found myself doubting every aspect, wondering if it's all true. That is how it all started.

Wandering in the fields and the woods surrounding the abbey alone with my thoughts, my mind wandered to my time up north.

Three years ago, I was a monk in a large northern abbey. The abbey had controlled many acres; its grounds providing employment to many of the local people. It had been through Brother James, the Supervisor of the Granges that my fall from grace had began.

When I had seen him lift up his habit, tucking it in his belt, his thick thighs visible to all, in order to join the peasant people in the river helping them regain their drifting boat, I had lost my heart. With the lower folds of his habit tucked into his girdle he had waded out like a water god of old, the cool-looking river water splashing his sturdy thighs.

I smiled as I recalled the scene. Two weeks after that first idea of attraction had entered my mind, we became lovers in the full sense of the word. We would spend all our free time together.

Brother James found an old abandoned hut near the edge of the woods that surrounded one of the abbey's granges, which we made our own. It was there the abbot himself caught us.

Three days later, James was heading further north to an abbey, and I was heading south to this abbey. I hadn't seen him since.

That was three years ago. Since then I've been a model of behavior. My current abbot knows of my past indiscretion and as such keeps a close eye on me. But to reward my good behavior, he has recently made me Supervisor of the Granges – the exact same position my James held.

As such, I am now required to travel the local area checking on the granges, which belong to the abbey. Granges are small farms, which are managed by the lay brothers and overseen by one of the full brothers.

It was on one of these granges I met Ripley. He was overseeing the gathering of the harvest on the Batstock Grange about an hour's ride to the west of the abbey.

I'd set out at dawn in order to be early and had come upon the field where they were working as the sun burst over the tree-tops of the nearby wood.

The light illuminated the field, bathing it in soft, early morning sunshine and silhouetting the shapes of the workers. At first, I couldn't tell who was in charge. All I could see were groups of men standing about drinking from earthenware jugs.

As I rode into the field through the open five-bar gate, one of the men detached himself from the nearest group and approached me. "Morning, Brother."

"Good morning," I responded as I climbed down off my horse. As I turned to meet the man, my breath caught in my throat and I began coughing.

"You all right?" he asked stepping forward. I nodded. If only he knew it was he who had caused my coughing fit? I felt my cock stirring within the confines of my loose robe and prayed when, not if, I become erect it wouldn't be too obvious.

The man before me was striking, his body stunning. He was about six feet two and looked to have seen thirty-three summers, with a shock of hair black as the deepest night, parted on the right sweeping down over his left brow, the ends teasing his dark eyebrows. His light brown eyes complemented his dark hair perfectly and twinkled at me. They seemed so full of innocence that I wondered if he knew the power he possessed.

His face had fine bone structure, high and noble cheekbones setting off his powerfully chiseled jaw that, even at this time in the morning, had a dark growth of hair. His

37

lips were full and red and reminded me so much of James I wanted to grab him and kiss him there and then in full view of everyone.

As my coughing subsided, the man stuck out his hand and introduced himself. "Ripley."

"Brother Simon," I replied taking his hand and shaking it. He had a firm grip, and as I looked, I could see the muscles in his forearm, which was covered in fine dark hairs, ripple underneath his taut skin. "And you are?"

"I run this grange, Brother."

"Then you are a lay brother?" I enquired for he certainly didn't look like a lay brother, and I had never set eyes on him at prayers. I would have remembered. He was wearing a pair of old leggings, which stopped just short of his ankles and were held up with a piece of rope tied tight around his narrow waist. The upper half of his body was covered in a coarse short-sleeved top, open at the neck revealing an amount of bare flesh for me to look at.

"No, Brother," he began softly, his voice rich and deep. "The Abbot put me in charge two years back as a trial like." I must have looked confused for he raised his eyes skyward as if asking the Lord for help before he continued. "We work the land all year round and are as close to nature as you brothers are to God. He wanted to see if we could make them any more profitable if one of us were in charge."

"And have you?"

"Aye, Brother Simon," he said, a big smile breaking over his face, revealing a set of perfect white teeth rare for a peasant, and transforming it into one the angels would have been proud of. "Doubled this grange's income last year. Abbot was very pleased."

That smile was beautiful. It was a beam of pure light and joy. A signal to the heavens and mankind that God's creation can be, if not ideal, then almost perfect. I nodded and, because of his smile, knew I had lost the battle to control my erection.

It was at this point, as my stiffened member was at full mast beginning to tent my habit that Ripley glanced down. To this day, I know not what caused to him to look, but I was glad he did.

The change was sudden and all the more remarkable for it. The gentle twinkle in his light brown eyes changed and became a glint laced with wickedness. He turned and quickly looked at the other men in the field who were returning to work and, seeing no one looking, turned back to me, a wide smile parting his sensual lips.

Ripley lowered his head, his shock of hair hiding his face. Then he raised it slightly, the hair parting, so I could see his eyes and their wicked, evil yet delightful gleam. In this way, he looked at me; coy, bashful and shy, like a youth just learning of his devastating good looks. Once again, he broke into a huge grin and slowly reached for his groin.

His grin changed to a smirk as he saw my shock. Grinning up at me from beneath his falling hair, he smoothed his stomach and then massaged his groin, the heel of his hand kneading into his recesses as if he was making bread.

I stood transfixed, watching as he cupped his growing flesh in his hand, pressing and caressing himself in front of me, unconcerned with anyone else seeing us.

Brazenly, he reached out and grabbed my erection, his fingers wrapping around my hardened member trapping it between his hand and my habit using his body to shield his actions from anyone glancing our way. I could feel the heat from his hand penetrating the material as he gently squeezed me, putting pressure on my hardened manhood.

Breathing deeply, my eyes closed with the pleasure he was creating. I could feel the desire radiate from my extended and hardened muscle, coursing through my veins filling my body with lust – another carnal sin, which deep down as a monk sworn to chastity I knew I must resist.

I'd broken my vows once and had been absolved, this time I knew there would be no forgiveness – if I were caught. My decision had been made in a split second. I was going to sin again. I had decided to give myself to him.

And then, he suddenly stopped. He released my member, stopped manipulating himself and raised his head. "Shall I show you the sights of the grange?" he asked, a boyish, cheeky smile on his face.

Naturally, I agreed.

Ripley led me around the edge of the field toward the woods, which grew on the far side. As I followed behind, I tried to make out his body but the looseness of his clothing hid everything from sight. I did know he had broad shoulders and a narrow waist, but that was all.

The cool interior of the woods was a welcome relief from the sun that had been getting progressively hotter as we had talked. All around us stood trees with trunks so thick and gnarled, they must have been old when the Romans walked the country. The undergrowth of this ancient, yet living forest was tangled and overgrown, the paths and tracks strewn with leaves and sticks, twigs and fungi.

Ripley led me down little used tracks and paths, the overgrown scrub catching at my habit as if some force of good was trying to hold me back from the sin I was about to commit ... again.

I gasped as we broke from the dappled shade of the trees into a small clearing, the sunlight lighting the far side of the lush green grass.

Ripley turned to me. "So Brother, do you prefer to sodomize or be sodomized?" Ripley looked at me intently.

To tell the truth I'd always liked it when James filled me; I preferred it to filling him. But I especially liked it when

James pulled apart my cheeks and filled me ... and then rode me hard.

My face must have betrayed my thoughts because Ripley stepped forward and grinning, grabbed my hand. "Feel this, Brother," he said, placing my hand against his groin, his warm brown eyes holding mine, "this is going to split you apart and fill you up."

I groaned as my fingers tightened around his erect member. "That's it, Brother," said Ripley, "squeeze it, feel it. Feel the core of inner strength," his fingers tightened on my shoulders as he whispered, "Feel the muscle that's going to rip you apart."

His firm lips found mine, pressing hard, forcing open my mouth, so he could invade with his tongue. I returned Ripley's kiss just as passionately as he offered it. I felt his hands grab my buttocks and followed his example. To my delight, I found two mounds of superb tight muscle. I probed deeper into Ripley's mouth as I pulled him hard against me, his stiff member pressing hard against my own.

After a while, Ripley pushed me away and made me sit on a nearby fallen log. "Ready for some fun, Brother?"

Without waiting for an answer, Ripley began taking off his clothes. Once again, the superb beauty of the man took my breath away. As he stood before me topless, his hands on his hips, he looked exquisite, like one of Michelangelo's sculptures.

Ripley's shoulders were broad and wide. Bunched with muscle, they looked powerful enough to lift me and bend me to his will. His upper arms were as wide as one of the surrounding tree's branches and crossed with veins as blue and as winding as a river. His fingers, where they splayed on his hips, were long and fine and looked to be very supple.

His expansive chest was formed from two slabs of square, heavy muscle topped with two of the most suck-able nipples

41

I'd ever seen. It was smooth, not a hair in sight. The deep depression between his broad plateaux of muscle led down to his flat well-developed stomach, the ridges looking like a small mountain range.

Ripley flashed his cheeky, boyish grin once again and started to undo the rope holding his leggings up. I watched avidly – waiting for the moment when he would drop the material and would reveal himself to me.

I didn't have long to wait. He turned his back on me and slowly started to lower his trousers, wriggling his butt as I imagined would a whore.

I watched in great anticipation as he slowly lowered the material, the tops of his ass mounds coming into view.

All of a sudden, Ripley let the material go, his leggings falling to the floor in a heap around his ankles. And there it was. One of the best sights I'd ever seen – Ripley's ass faced me.

The tight mounds, which I had earlier held in my hands, glared openly at me. Two melon-sized spheres formed the collection of hard looking muscle, lightly covered in soft brown downy hair.

Ripley's taut peach of a bum astounded me. Those finely rounded butt cheeks hid his tight manhole from view, guarding the entrance to his virtue the way Cerebus guards the way to Hades – where no doubt I would soon be going.

I mentally shrugged and decided if that was where I was to go then so be it. With this gorgeous man standing bare ass naked before me, I didn't care. I licked my lips wondering what it would be like to sink my tongue between the firm cheeks and into the hair-lined crack.

As if Ripley had been reading my thoughts, he bent over and pulled apart his ass-cheeks, his long graceful fingers splayed wide on his firm buttocks. I lost my breath again as his small, tight pucker came into view. The object of my adoration stared at me and, looking back, I would swear it had winked at me.

It was at that moment Ripley stood up and turned around. "Like what you see, Brother?" He breathed softly.

How could I not? I thought. Before me stood a man naked as the day he was born with a body like Hercules – well-developed chest, shoulder and arm muscles, thighs as thick as the surrounding trees and sporting a long, thick penis, which was cocked and obviously ready for action.

Ripley took a few steps forward until he was standing right in front of me, his groin level with my face. Bobbing before me, sticking straight out from his flat stomach was his hardened manhood.

I licked my lips. Bouncing around before me, it was so tempting just to take it in my mouth and suck. Instead, I examined Ripley's throbbing member. Seven inches of solid man-muscle began at its broad base, narrowed slightly to form his long shaft and flared again at his glistening head, which was an angry, purple-red colour.

His member was criss-crossed in blue veins like tributaries to a river, and he was circumcised, which I found strange yet intriguing. Was Ripley a Jew or was there some other reason for his missing cover?

At that moment, a pearl of pre-cum oozed from his cum-slit. Reaching out, I took hold of his member, surprised at the weight. A groan escaped his lips as my thumb ran across his head wiping away his discharge.

I leaned forward and planted a kiss on the very tip of Ripley's elongated manhood. I could taste the sweetness of the pre-cum I had just wiped away and decided there and then that I wanted to taste this man's creamy flow of life-giving seed.

But not now. Now I needed him to take me and ride me hard. I needed him to pound away the guilt I was feeling, the guilt of committing carnal sin. "Fuck me!" I said squeezing Ripley's dick and looking up into his spaniel-brown eyes.

He grinned back at me and gently stroked a finger down my cheek. "Well, well," he smirked, "that ain't no language for a brother to use."

"I care not. Just, please, fuck me."

Throwing back his head, he laughed to the sky, a kind of silvery peal. I squeezed his dick again to remind him I was still there.

Reaching down he grasped me beneath the arms and raised me to my feet, pulling me hard against him. Our lips met once again, and he kissed me longingly, his hand cupping my butt cheeks.

"Ready?" he asked when he surfaced for air, flashing his charming, boyish smile at me. I nodded in answer to his question.

Turning me around, Ripley made me kneel over the trunk of the fallen tree I had previously been sitting on, the grass still damp beneath my knees from the morning's dew.

Ripley knelt behind me, and I shuddered like a newborn colt as I felt his hands on my thighs raising my habit. The material felt rough as Ripley pushed it further up my legs until it crested the rise of my buttocks exposing me to the day and to the man I hoped was going to pleasure me beyond belief.

Once my ass was in sight, Ripley didn't waste any time. As great as my need was to be fucked by this man, his need seemed greater. His fingers dug into my hips as his manly knee gently nudged apart my thighs before they travelled softly over the firm flesh of my butt cheeks.

Grabbing my buttocks Ripley dug his thumbs into my crack pulling the firm mounds apart until the guardian of my portal was winking at the brightness of the daylight.

Without hesitating, Ripley smeared goose-fat from a pot he had produced onto my fuck hole, which was aching with anticipation and dread. It had been three years since anything thicker than my fingers had been up me, so I knew this would hurt.

I felt the heat radiating from his cock as he moved forward, slipping his great member between my cheeks, his cockhead lightly touching my guardian sphincter. "Ready, Brother?"

I nodded in answer.

Ripley began his assault on my pink, aching hole. I did my best to help, forcing my hole open trying to help him gain access. James had been wider then Ripley, so I knew I could take what he had but for the last three years, my butt had been virginal.

Ripley increased the pressure against my ring, forcing the tip of his dick into my rosette. Again, Ripley increased the pressure, his muscular hips pushing his dick forward, the head of his cock forcing apart the walls of my hole.

The pain was excruciating. Sparks of pain like bolts of lightning shot through my body as instinctively my hole tightened and tried to shut out Ripley's invading monster.

Through the mist of pain, I could feel the hot glands of his cockhead forcing open my sphincter and passing through into my most sacred of chambers. Sweat broke out on my forehead, and my breath came in huge great gasps as I tried to accommodate the width of flesh that had just broken through my defenses.

I snorted and tossed my head like a stallion as Ripley began his journey up my back passage, his flared cockhead pushing aside the walls of my chute burying his cock inside me.

When he had buried half of his length, he paused. "Get used to that, Brother," he said, "before I split you apart with the rest."

Fear coursed through my body tightening my muscles, causing me to grip his cock hard. He let out a soft whimper and jabbed another of his seven inches into me. I panicked and wondered if he would tear me apart.

Just before hysteria set in, reason flooded my mind. James had been thicker than Ripley had and I had taken him without being ripped open so therefore I should be able to accommodate Ripley with ease. I took deep breaths and willed myself to calm down.

Just then, Ripley decided to continue his advance into my ass. The mixture of pain and pleasure, which my body felt, soon gave way to pleasure alone as his monstrous cock filled my passage.

I could feel every ridge and hollow of his cock as it moved within me. I thought it was never going to stop. I half expected his cockhead to come out of my mouth so long did it feel.

I gasped in ecstasy as Ripley changed pace from the slow, long drive he had been using to short sharp jabs. Forcing more of his seven inches into me in staccato movements filled me with a pleasure I thought I would never feel again.

This was the first man to take me since James three years ago. Suddenly all the longing and yearnings those years had produced burst from their hiding places and flooded my body like the feelings of ecstasy Ripley was creating. They seemed to attack as a cohesive force taking control of my organs at one singular moment as if they had been waiting for a command and that command had come from Ripley.

I gasped at a particularly vicious lunge by Ripley and brought all my senses to bear on what was happening. James was in the past, as much as I had loved him, he was history; Ripley was the here and now.

I decided to try and make this the best coupling Ripley had had to date, after all I might be paying the ultimate price for it later by leaving the monastery and, when I die, going to Hell; then again after all that James, and I did I was probably going there anyway.

Ripley was leaning over me, his tongue doing exquisite things to the shell and lobe of my ear as my senses came back to me. I could feel the thickness of his manhood within me from the roundness of his cockhead to the thickness of his base stretching wide my moist manhole.

I squeezed the muscles of my ass hard, taking hold of his member firmly seemingly trying to rip it away from his body. "Fuck me!" I said just loud enough for him to hear, "hard."

And that's exactly what he did. Ripley, far from being the angel I had first assumed him to be, became a devil. In one movement, he pulled his member out of me, leaving my hole gaping wide like a tunnel mouth.

It felt strange to be full of a man's hard rod one moment and then for it to be gone the next. To tell the truth I didn't like it. I wanted Ripley's massive flesh pole back where it belonged.

As if reading my thoughts, that was exactly, what Ripley did. Tearing into my ass with abandon Ripley, his hands on my hips holding me steady, rammed his length back into me, pushing his entire seven inches into me in one go.

I gasped and groaned, gripping the tree beneath me hard, tossing my head back and sucking air, in an effort to remain conscious and not be overwhelmed by the feelings of pleasure radiating out from my asshole.

Ripley paused. I could feel his pendulous sack holding his life-giving globes, bouncing against my wide spread cheeks as he ground his thick nest of silky-soft hair against me.

Before long, the holiday was over. Ripley resumed his possession of my body. Moving in me slowly and gently. While it was nice, it wasn't what I wanted. I wanted it to be as it was with James. "Fuck me, hard!" I said again.

Ripley complied immediately. Stepping up his pace, he began to pound my ass, driving his stiff manhood into me; forcing me hard against the tree log with every thrust of his powerful hips.

His swollen manhood seemed to move like lightening within the confines of my tight tunnel, so fast did it move. Pushing repeatedly through my guardian sphincter his hot, throbbing manhood plunged its way in and out of my being, coring open an entrance that I had thought sealed shut forever.

Through the cloud of ecstasy, which was fogging my mind, I could hear the slapping of his loins against my ass, loud, like a clap, as the skin met forcefully. Accompanying the slap of flesh was the slurping and squishing of my ass juices and the groans and moans of a rutting male in the prime of his life.

I knew from those moans, those sounds of bliss and elation that Ripley was nearing his climax. I was undecided – I wanted him to shoot his load into me; I wanted to feel the pulsing of his engorged member and the heat of his man-seed within me. Yet I wanted this to last forever. I wanted to have this man invading my body for as long as possible.

In the end, the decision was taken out of my hands. Within minutes, Ripley increased his pace again, his breathing becoming irregular. Then it happened. Deep within my ass, I felt his cock become stiffer and thicker and knew he was only moments away.

With a bestial roar a lion would have been proud of, Ripley flooded my tunnel. Spasm after spasm wracked his manhood as he blasted forth his man-cream. Ripley continued to fuck me, smearing his love juice over the walls of my ass, continually pumping the hot liquid into me. I could feel it blasting all hot and thick and creamy.

Moments after Ripley delivered his present I brought forth a fountain of my own. My member, hard and sensitive as it was after being rubbed forcefully against the coarse cloth of my habit, erupted, spewing my cum all over my groin and soaking the cloth.

Ripley leaned over me; the rhythmic rise and fall of his chest, and the panting of his breath in my ear enough to remind me of the pleasure my body had caused this man. I smiled as he whispered, "Did you enjoy that, Brother?"

"Yes," I panted, totally exhausted.

That was three days ago. Since then my mind has thought of nothing else. The way he made me feel so good; the coupling and what went on afterward will stay with me for the rest of my days.

But unfortunately, I have seriously sinned to the highest degree yet again. Without doubt, my soul is now lost for all eternity. Surely, there is no way possible for me to now ascend to the kingdom in the sky and take my place in the celestial house of God? God loves a sinner come back to the path of righteousness I know, but this is beyond all reasoning. I am beyond redemption.

And in fact, I have no wish to be redeemed. Reliving the events, I realize I have nothing to feel guilty about. I may have broken my vows for a second time, but what are they but man-made rules. Who says I want to return to the path of righteousness? At present, even though I have sinned grievously, I am happy and content with Ripley. I have Confession this afternoon but I shan't be divulging anything that happened three days ago.

In fact, immediately after Confession, I have to check on progress at the Batstock Grange – and I am sincerely looking forward to it.

THE MASKED BALL
By Logan Zachary

Logan Zachary (LoganZachary2002@yahoo.com) lives in Minneapolis, MN. His new book *Calendar Boys* is out, and his stories can be found in dozens of anthologies.

"Last summer at band camp ..." How I hated those words. Ever since that stupid teen sex comedy and all of its sequels, each June when I pack for music camp, I cringe. But this year, I've been asked to help teach the students and assist the faculty. This was a huge honor for such a new teacher. Usually I would get odd jobs for the summer painting houses, doing yard work or home repairs to add to the income. So when this job offer came, I jumped on it. My big question was: Who knew me well enough to hire me for the summer?

As I arrived at Camp Allegro, I juggled my three suitcases through the dorm's doorway. My cut-off shorts and T-shirt clung to my skin as I walked down the hot, humid hallway to my room. Each camp was a week long. Eight weeks of students, pimple faced music geeks from seventh grade to junior years in high school who wanted to improve their musical skills.

My mind flashed back to my weeks at camp. "Alex Peters, adjust your embouchure like this," Mr. Brad Ramsey, pressed on my mouth to form my lips into the correct position. His touch burned my skin, and I was instantly hard. He massaged my cheek muscles into a perfect seal on the saxophone's mouthpiece, how I longed for that seal somewhere else. He puckered up his beautiful mouth in such a way that all I wanted to do was kiss him. How many times had I dreamed about how those luscious lips would feel on mine?

I inhaled and still smelled his cologne, English Leather and him. I licked my lips as I remembered my favorite teacher, Mr. Ramsey. He was my first real schoolboy crush.

How many times had I jacked off under the covers thinking of that tuft of hair that would peek out over his open shirt collar? Growing up in a small Minnesota town didn't allow for a lot of gay exposure.

Inhaling deeply, I swore I could smell him. As if conjuring him from my daydreams, Mr. Brad Ramsey walked out of a dorm room next to mine and stood in front of me. "Alex, you're here." His eyes lit up as soon as he saw me. He wore sandals, jean shorts, and a loose necked T-shirt that showed his furry chest. Gray hair dotted his beautiful pelt, but it looked as soft and thick as I remember.

"What are you doing here?" I asked, setting the suitcases down with a thump. Sweat dripped down my forehead and burned my eyes. I wiped it away and squinted to look at my idol.

"I've always taught summer music, don't you remember? How many years did I teach you?"

"I attended three years of band camp." I pulled the dorm room key out of my pocket and inserted into the slot.

"See, I knew you'd remember." Mr. Ramsey pointed to the door. "You're staying next to me all summer. The dorms are hot some days, but they promised the A/C was new this year, and it would keep these rooms cold all summer. Here, let me help you." His hairy hand brushed mine as we both reached for the same suitcase.

My hand burned where his skin touched me. I let go of the case and picked up the other two. I pushed the heavy door open and entered my new home. The stale humid air hung in the room.

Mr. Ramsey followed close behind and set the suitcase down on the bed. He flipped a switch on the wall and turned the dial to cold. The A/C fan whirled into life and a cool breeze of air circulated in the cinderblock room.

"Thanks," I said.

"The showers and the restroom are down the hall two doors from my room. Did you have anything else to carry in?"

"I have one more trip, but I was going to bring that in after supper. I pulled my damp shirt away from body. "I need to unpack and then hit the shower."

"Need any help?"

Images of him in the shower flooded my mind, of water running over his hairy, naked body, his hands washing me, and my hands washing him. I could feel the erection start to grow as I started to unpack.

"I think I got it; it shouldn't take too long. I didn't bring much."

Mr. Ramsey smiled and stepped back to the door. "Well, I need to hit the shower before supper, too. Where are you eating? Maybe we can meet up? Catch up on life and grab a pizza and a few beers?"

"Cool, I should be ready in an hour? Is that too long?"

He shook his head, "Perfect, knock on my door when you're ready to go."

"Okay," I said, as he left my room. I ripped open the suitcases and jammed all my clothes and stuff into the dresser's drawers. I wanted to shower next to him. I frantically looked for my towel. "Shit, shit, shit." I left my sheets and towels at home.

I kicked the door between our rooms. I'm sure during the school year the door could open up for a student suite if needed.

"Alex? Is everything okay?" Mr. Ramsey's called from the other side of the double door.

I heard him unlock his side and open his door. I closed my eyes and shook my head, as I walked to my door. I unlocked and opened it. I forced a smile.

"Is something wrong?" concern came into his voice.

"I forgot my towels and sheets."

Mr. Ramsey turned and opened his closet. He pulled out two towels, a hand towel, a wash cloth, and a set of blue cotton twin sheets. He handed me the pile. "Will this help?"

The scent of English Leather rose from the linens, as I savored each deep breath I took. My eyes stared at the tuft of graying hair that escaped from his collar, my hands didn't register how soft and thick the cotton towels were. All I noticed was his smell and his tuft of hair.

"I can't ..."

"Just use them until you get yours. It's not a problem. I have extra."

"Thanks," I said, stepping back into my room. I closed the door and just inhaled over and over again, his scent. I doubted I'd get any sleep in these sheets to night. I kicked off my sneakers and pulled off my damp socks. I pulled off the rest of my clothing and dropped them into a pile in the closet. I wrapped the cotton towel around my body and felt my hard-on swell to full length.

I hated to get the clean towel dirty with my sweat, but I needed a fix of Mr. Ramsey. The soft cotton rubbed against my sensitive cock, and I was afraid I'd shoot a load. I stroked myself as I pressed one end of the towel into my mouth. The scent of Mr. Ramsey curled up my nose making all of my nerve endings tingle. I flopped down on the bare mattress and felt the cool air blow over my damp body. I stroked my cock up and down. The other hand reached between my legs and grabbed my low hanging balls. I rolled them like dice in my hand. One finger extended and brushed against my hole.

My head fell back on the bed and rubbed the cotton towel all over me. My balls rose, and I knew this wasn't going to take long. My finger touched my tight opening as my other hand worked the wet swollen tip of my cock. The explosion hit my chin, and I ripped the towel away before any more cum streaked across it. Wave after wave came out of me. I squeezed the head and milked out all the rest. My cock was too tender to touch and still fully erect. I waited a few minutes for my body to return to normal. I wrapped the towel around my waist and grabbed my shampoo bottle.

As I entered the rest room, I heard a shower turn off. I found an open stall and jumped inside. I threw the towel over the bar and turned the water on as hot as it would go. The cold spray turned hot in a few seconds. I stepped under the spray and rinsed everything down the drain. Shampoo foamed and flowed over me, as I washed.

A shadow walked past my stall, and it looked like Mr. Ramsey's silhouette. Peeking from behind the curtain, I saw it was Mr. Ramsey. He had a towel slung around his hips. The fabric clung to his ass and slipped into his crease. His stocky, hairy legs showed powerful muscles. He had a little extra around the middle, but not bad for a middle aged man.

I finished rinsing the soap off my body. I turned off the water and grabbed the towel. I dried quickly to be able to join Mr. Ramsey at the sinks. Pushing the curtain back, the metal loops sounded over the metal bar.

Ramsey looked over his shoulder and saw me standing there. "Nothing feels better than a good hot shower." He looked at me as I approached. He looked down at my towel. "I was looking for you, because I ... ah ... need to cancel supper tonight. Sorry." He looked down at my towel and stepped back. "I'll catch you later."

I watched as Mr. Ramsey collected his things and headed back to his room. I savored the sight of his ass as he walked away. My arousal returned quickly, and I turned to look into the mirror. That was when I noticed the streak of cum across my lap, the line of cum that clung to the towel. Had Mr. Ramsey seen that? How could he have missed it? No wonder he canceled supper.

Classes started at eight o'clock Monday morning. I stared in the low brass room, but ended up being assigned to work in the woodwind's room and help the students. Mr. Ramsey ran in and out, teaching and lecturing, helping students with the flute and saxophone. I floated around the room coaching the section leaders, answering questions, and demonstrating techniques.

The week flew by, and the Friday afternoon event was the concert for the students to show all that they have learned. After the concert, the parents took their children home, and the staff had the weekend off until Sunday afternoon, when the new batch of students arrived. And the whole week started all over again.

Despite having a room next to Mr. Ramsey, after the first day together, I didn't see much of him. The first weekend went by quickly, and I didn't have time to be bored. The second week flew by, and after the last student left the building, I returned to my room. Should I go out or call it an early night? I didn't know what sounded better as I unlocked the door. Flipping the lights on, I saw something on my bed.

A cream colored envelope rested on top of a big box. The paper was thick and carried a fancy watermark. Alexander Peters was inscribed in gold on the envelope in Old English letters.

I picked it up and turned it over. My finger flipped the back flap open, and I pulled out a formal invitation.

Mr. Alexander Peters

Your presence is requested for The Masked Ball

10:00 P.M. Friday Night in Room 213 Verdi Hall

Formal attire provided and required.

On the back of the invitation, I noticed something handwritten. "Alex, Wear only the items in the box. Do not add any extra items." I opened the box. A black leather mask sat in the center of a carefully folded black hooded robe. A small, black G-string rested on the bottom.

I picked up the satin material and rubbed it between my fingers. What did this mean? I could feel my body respond. My cock started to swell, as my balls rolled in my shorts. A mask, a robe, a G-string, and nothing else. What kind of Masked Ball was this? Like Verdi's opera, The Masked Ball, or something else. From my body's response, I figured it was something else.

I glanced at my watch and saw that I had a few hours before the ball began. I went out for supper, but found I was too excited to eat. I picked at my food, returned to the dorm, took a shower and waited. Time seemed to drag on forever. In my concern and nervousness, I had to take a second shower before ten. Finally, it was quarter to ten; I figured I could get ready. I slipped out of my sweats and slipped on the G-string, I was instantly hard as the satin pouch cupped my junk. The string rode between my ass cheeks, and I had to adjust it so it didn't cut into me.

The A/C worked well and Goosebumps rose over my body as I donned the robe. I figured sandals would be okay to add to the outfit, since I didn't want to go barefoot, but they would be easy to remove if needed. I slipped the leather mask on my face and flipped the hood down over my head. I doubted anyone would know who I was if they saw me walking across a vacant campus in the dark. I took the invitation with me as if I needed it as a ticket for admission.

The walk across campus was creepy, shadows danced around the lights that lit the walkways, the gentle night wind rustled the robe, and my almost naked state made me vulnerable.

The door was unlocked as I pulled on the handle, and I walked up the marble steps to the second floor. My footfalls echoed in the dim hallways. No one was around. As I neared Room 213, panic threatened to take over, but my cock was still hard, excited to see what was happening.

A red ribbon was tied to the door handle, and I pulled it open. The door opened silently as I entered. I walked down the aisle and saw a single spotlight shining down from the ceiling to the center of the stage. I saw a red ribbon tied to the railing of the staircase on the side of the stage.

As I walked to the stage, I didn't see anyone in the audience. All the seats were empty. I stood at the edge of the stage and saw a chair was just outside the circle of light. I looked around and still didn't see anyone. Another red ribbon dangled from the chair. I took that to mean come up on the stage. I headed up the stairs and stepped into the darkness at the side of the stage.

Still no one appeared. I slipped out of my sandals, stepped into the center light, and felt the warmth of the beam. I stood there facing the audience and waited.

Nothing.

Maybe I was supposed to sit down. I stepped back to the chair and set the invitation on it. Was I supposed to play something? Clarinet? Flute? I walked around the chair, looking for an instrument, for any clue of what I was supposed to do.

Nothing.

I stepped back into the circle of light and waited.

Suddenly, a cool breeze swirled around me, and my robe puffed up. I turned to see where the draft was coming from and noticed a shadow and then another and another. Silhouettes surrounded me and moved closer.

As they neared, I saw they all wore hooded robes like mine. I waited and felt someone touch my shoulder. The hand grabbed the hood and pulled it off my head. The sudden flash of light blinded me, and I didn't see the surge. When I opened my eyes, I was the center of a tight circle. Two hands reached forward and unzipped my robe, as the front opened, hands from behind pulled it off my shoulders.

My erection had softened once the uncertainty rose, but the stirring started again, now that I was on display. The hair on my body glistened in the spotlight; the heat of the light and the staring eyes started a sheen across my body.

Hands emerged from the long sleeves and started to caress my body. My arms, my back and my chest were the first places touched, but my ass was the next target. Fingers explored and touched, traced and pinched.

I didn't see the thick blanket until it was rolled across the floor. As my bare feet stepped onto it, hands picked me up and lay me across the center. I couldn't fight the invasion; I was to embrace whatever happened.

Fingers pulled along my G-string and sweet music started to flow from my body. I rose to full erection and felt exploration into my satin pouch. One snap, and the fabric was gone, and I was naked, except for the mask.

For some reason, I didn't feel naked. The mask covered me, my identity, and my dignity. It gave me power to accept joy and have fun. The crowd stood up and unzipped their robes. There was a mass shedding of robes, and naked male bodies surrounded me.

I thought I recognized a few of the bodies, but one stood out. I knew this one very well. I've dreamed about that hairy chest many times, and just recently saw it fresh out of the shower. The man stepped back from the group, and a few seconds later, the spot light went out, plunging the auditorium into darkness. Then the action started. Hands, fingers, lips, and tongues covered my body, explored my body, and tasted my body. I thought I smelled English Leather for a moment, and then it was gone.

Since hands touched me, I felt free to touch back. Hairy legs, a low hanging set of balls, a throbbing penis, and an open mouth. My legs were spread wide, and my cock was sucked, stroked, and celebrated.

Rolling onto my side opened me up for a posterior invasion. I had never been in an orchestral orgy. Music and rhythm flowed through the room as skin rubbed against skin. The room heated up, and my whole body tingled as if a bass beat throbbed through the building.

My climax rose to the edge and receded, only to rise and recede again. I lost count of how many things I had sucked on and how many fingers had entered my body, but the sweat flowed over me and someone slowly and steadily worked my engorged flesh to bursting. The sweetest aria into the world flowed over me and out of my cock. More followed close behind with a harmony only heard from a choir of angels. When I crawled out of the cacophony, I couldn't find my robe or sandals, even my G-string was gone.

Since I couldn't find my robe for the walk across campus, I used a curtain that covered the workings under the stage. I abandoned the curtain after my shower, once I returned to the dorm. I walked down the hallway back to my room buck naked. I noticed the light was on in Mr. Ramsey's room, and it looked like the door on his side was open.

Was that an invitation for me?

I hadn't seen him at the Masked Ball, but the lights went out before I saw much. The invited guests saw me, but I recognized a few. I stepped over to the door and unlocked my side. I placed my ear to the wood and listened.

"You can come in if you want," Mr. Ramsey called.

"I'm naked."

Silence.

I grabbed my sweats and slipped them on. Opening the door, I peeked around the archway.

Mr. Ramsey wore a leather mask as he read in bed. His hairy, bare chest rose above the blanket. He set his book down on his lap and looked at me. "I thought you were naked."

I flushed as he scanned me.

"What have you been up to?" He removed his mask and patted his bed.

So he had been involved. I wondered if he had organized the whole Masked Ball. But what did he want? He had left the event before it started. I knew what I wanted; it's what I've wanted for so many years. Did he know what I wanted? "What are you reading?" I neared the bed and turned my head to read the title: *Flowers in the Attic*.

"Guilty pleasure for the summer," Mr. Ramsey said. "It's the only time I get to read the fun stuff." He set the book down and patted the bed next to him. "Are you cold? You can join me if you want." He pulled the blanket and the sheets back and slid over.

I took his offer and jumped in next to him. My bare feet brushed against his as I snuggled next to him.

"Did you enjoy the Masked Ball?"

"How did you ...? Did you set that up?" I turned to look into his eyes, his hazel eyes.

His eyes glowed with excitement. "I did send you the offer for the Masked Ball, but it was up to you to accept or not."

"I didn't know what it was about. The G-string gave me an idea, but ..."

Mr. Ramsey smiled. "I wanted to join you, but I'm jealous, I wanted you all to myself. I always have."

"What?"

"Why did you think I spent so much time with you? Training you, perfecting you, encouraging you to be the best, and hoping you'd stay with it."

"I loved those weeks of band camp. I loved ..."

"What?"

61

"Never mind."

"Tell me."

"I'm embarrassed."

"Embarrassed to tell me you jacked off to me?"

My face burned.

"I've jacked off thinking of you, many times, I did even last night." He reached under the covers and adjusted himself.

Was he completely naked? I hadn't noticed when I slipped into the bed.

I reached over to touch his chest. The scent of English Leather filled my nostrils. He was so warm and hairy under my palm.

Mr. Ramsey settled back into his pillow, allowing me to explore and caress. I traced over his pec to the dip between and followed the line underneath. My thumb brushed his nipple, and I felt it rise under my touch. I pinched it and turned it, making it grow hard in my fingers. My other hand moved to the other side, and I turned to face him.

He looked into my eyes and kissed me, deep and hard and passionate.

I tasted his tongue in my mouth and savored it. How long had I dreamed and desired this?

I broke our kiss, hugging his body, and I moved to nibble on his ear.

He shrugged his shoulders up to protect his ears. "You're tickling me."

I rolled over his body and straddled his waist. I pushed down his body and felt a hard throbbing beneath me. I licked down his neck and played across his chest to his silver dollar sized nipples. I kissed one and sucked it into my mouth.

He combed his fingers through my hair and held my head in his hands. He pressed me down onto his nipple.

My teeth caught his pointed tip and rolled it, biting gently.

He moaned in pleasure, as did I from the manly taste that exploded in my mouth.

I pushed down his body and brought my ass up into the air.

He released my hair and caressed my bare back.

I discovered his tented boxers. His fly opened, and a thick bush of curly hair burst out. A thick veined penis jumped inside as a wet spot grew in the cotton. I pulled the elastic waistband down and freed his huge cock. It flipped up, and I removed his boxers in one swift pull. His hairy balls fell out and lay between his legs.

I couldn't wait any longer. I dove for his massive dick and sucked it deep into my mouth. His sweet, salty pre-cum oozed out of him and danced across my taste buds. I drew him in deeper and deeper. He tasted even better than I imagined. My mind couldn't believe I was doing this. How I worshiped his dick. I licked every inch of it. My tongue combed through the hair and continued down one of his low hangers. Sweat tanged my tongue, and I swallowed hard. I kissed the fleshy, hairy orb, and sucked it into my mouth. I tried to swallow it whole. It dangled in my mouth as my fingers lifted his other ball to my lips. I tried to take both into my mouth, but they were too big.

His balls slipped down my chin, and I licked up his shaft. More clear juices flowed out of him as my hand stroked his girth, milking more and more out.

He shifted his ass, and his hairy crack came into view. A tender pink pucker winked at me and called my tongue into action. I jacked his cock as my mouth found his crease. I rimmed his ass with the double tongue technique he had tutored me with.

Ta ka ta ka ta ka ... I used my flutter tongue trick to manipulate my instrument as my hand traced his cock. *The William Tell Overture* ran through my mind as I played his tight ass.

He bucked his hips, forcing my tongue deeper into him as he fucked my fist. *The Music Man* had nothing on me. I felt his excitement grow and threaten to overflow. So I slowed down to edge him close, but not too close.

I shifted my position, and my erection sprang forward and throbbed in my hand.

Mr. Ramsey started to sit up, but I pushed him down and signaled for him to stop and lay there. I grabbed my cock and started to trace his body. I slid it up his leg over his hip, across his torso and over an erect nipple.

I kneeled over his pillow and ran my dick over his full lips, across his moustache, over his Polish nose.

He closed his eyes, and I circled each socket, leaving a thin line above the brow. Back down his nose and over his lips, I glossed them and made them shine in the light. I guided it down his chin and over his chest and down his hairy belly.

I rubbed our cocks together as I leaned forward and kissed him. My balls tingled and started to pull up, I wasn't going to last much longer, despite the Masked Ball orgy.

I slid down his body and found his raging hard on; I sucked on him, swallowing him as far as I could.

His hips bucked as he pulled out of me and grabbed onto the sheets and squeezed for all he could, fighting back the climax that erupted. Measure after measure of cum shot out of his staff and sprayed over his furry belly. I stroked my cock and watched as my cream shot over his body. I flopped down on him and held him close as the intense tremors of our orgasms rolled over our bodies.

Our juices mixed over him and once the pleasure ebbed, I rose onto an elbow and licked over his torso, cleaning him with my tongue.

Mr. Ramsey could barely lay still as my lapping pushed him over the edge. Once our excitement was gone, I moved along side to kiss him. He held me close, and I rested my head on his chest. He held me tight as I drifted off to sleep, and the leather mask lay discarded on the floor. We were finally together, after all these years and so many more years in the future, hopefully forever ...

The weekend consisted of rearranging our rooms into a sexual suite for the summer. Mr. Ramsey became Brad, all my fantasies came true, and many new ones were orchestrated. Before we knew it, the weekend was over way too fast.

Monday morning started with an announcement, "Alex Peters, Alex Peters, come to the front office." My footfalls echoed down the halls as I made my way to the dean's office.

I was waved in. Dean Richard handed me a manila envelope. "It has come to my attention that you have gone above and beyond the call of duty for this music program, and I want to offer you a standing invitation to help teach any summer you would like."

I swallowed hard, unsure of who had said what and what he knew.

He smiled at me and shook my hand, "Welcome to the family. Enjoy the rest of your summer."

As I walked back to class, I wondered what was inside the envelope. I pulled the glued flap back and reached inside: My black satin G-string.

Now, I finally had stories that I could begin with "last summer at band camp ..."

HANDY-MEN
By Landon Dixon

Dixon's stories have been published in the several magazines and dozens of anthologies.

I'd known Ken for about a month when he invited me over to his place to watch a football game. We'd met at work. He seemed like a nice guy.

The game quickly turned into a blow-out, so Ken and I got to talking as we nursed a few cold ones. Until he got a call on his cellphone.

"Oh-oh," he said, looking at the number. "My mother. This might take awhile." He grinned and trotted up the stairs of the basement, already arguing on the phone.

I'm not sure why he didn't just ignore the call, like I usually do when my mother phones. But I just shrugged and picked up the remote off the couch, started scrolling through the on-screen menu of movies available for immediate rental from the cable company.

Handjob Honeys looked good to me, and I ordered it, grinning at the joke I was playing on Ken. Then I started watching the first scene: a big-titted brunette giving a point of-view oiled erection a hardy workout with both her hands. I grew some wood myself.

Then I got splinters, unzipping and pulling my cock out of my jeans and shorts. I could still hear Ken arguing away with his mother upstairs. So I pulled out a tissue, intent on squeezing a quick one out before the guy got back.

The brunette was really working that POV pole, her bare tits squeezing together with every two-handed tug. I stroked in rhythm, my dick stretching out full-length, throbbing hard in my shifting hand. I didn't need two hands to pull the prong, but I was sure going to need that tissue in a moment.

67

The brunette's plush, red lips parted in a seductive smile, one hand snaking down to work the guy's balls, other hand pumping harder and faster, swirling up over glistening cap. My own balls bubbled, my prick quivering in my quick-gliding hand, getting ready to ...

Something bumped against my cheek.

I twisted my head around. Ken was standing there, behind the couch, his hard cock in his hand, batting the bloated hood against the side of my head. "That's some hot stuff, huh?" he commented, completely unselfconsciously.

The guy had mentioned he'd gone to a private school. But even so.

I stared at his hard cock, my own cock still standing stiffly to attention in my hand, not backing down a bit. Ken made the next move, the tall, skinny, brown-haired guy swinging his legs over the back of the leather couch and resuming his sitting position next to me, not letting go of his rather impressive erection.

His eyes were glued to the pretty brunette on-screen stroking that lucky stiff, as he stroked his own dick now. Then he suddenly turned to me still staring at him, and grabbed my hand on my cock. "This'll make it more fun, huh?" he said, like a crazy man. "See who can make the other guy come first."

I jerked, jolted by the impact of another man touching my fully-engorged cock. And then I almost jumped right off the couch, as Ken pushed my hand down and off and grabbed onto my dick bare-handed himself.

It felt ... weird. But not so bad. The guy had a smooth, warm palm and soft, slender fingers that knew exactly how to stroke a cock. His hand could've been the video brunette's hand.

But there was no mistaking my hand, as Ken grabbed it up and hooked it around his hard-on. No escaping the fact that I held another man's throbbing penis in my left hand.

I kind of tingled all over, a warm, strange feeling – getting stroked by another guy, stroking another guy. Because that's what I was doing, pumping my hand up and down Ken's huge, hard erection. The thing beat in my beating hand; I could feel every pumped vein, the bloated swell of the guy's cap. I was jacking him taller and thicker, like he was me, the power of controlling another man's cock surging through my body and brain.

We stared at the TV screen, pumping each other's pricks. And, so help me, I forged another half-inch in the guy's swirling hand, my balls ready to explode down below, send steaming semen piping up my steel-hard stem.

"Pull down your pants and pull up your shirt," Ken said. "So you don't get cum all over your clothes."

The guy was taking it for granted!

He popped his jeans fully open and shoved them down with his free hand, pushed up his shirt. His balls were tight and fuzzy, his stomach lean and hard. I followed his example, the brunette really jacking on-screen, the hidden guy's cock rising, thrusting up in her hands.

Ken never let go of my cock, and when I was as bared as he was, he resumed cranking me, hard and fast like the brunette. My dick beat wildly in his fist, like my heart in my chest. I pumped him with a passion I never thought I possessed.

"Fuck!" I cried, unable to control myself. Hot sperm leapt out of the tip of my manhandled cock, fountained up into the air. I bucked repeatedly, coming like I never had before, with a wicked intensity and tremendous volume.

Ken grunted and shuddered, his own cock erupting in my hand. He blasted out rope after rope, as I struggled to keep pumping, blowing out my own perverted joy. Just like the guy in the movie, jetting hot jack right into the brunette's face as she urgently tugged.

We sat there gasping for air, our hands lightly pumping each other's cocks, squeezing the last few, shivering drops of cum out of our slits. I cooled off rapidly, the heat of ecstasy dissipating like a flash summer storm as I sat there with Ken's cock in my hand, his hand on my cock, wondering just how the hell this awkward situation was going to be resolved.

Ken showed the way, like he'd showed me the joy of mutual masturbation. The guy leaned over and started licking my cum off my chest and stomach, lapping it up like a hungry male kitten.

I bit my lip and groaned, watching his pink tongue scoop up my jizz, feeling the wet, wonderful stroke of his tongue on my buzzing skin. I instantly flushed hot as I'd been before, quivering with each dragging lap of his mouth-organ over my bared body.

He licked up every last drop of cum he could get his tongue on, painting my torso with passion. Then he raised his head and looked at me, his mouth full. His Adam's apple bobbed; he swallowed my load. He licked his plush, red lips with satisfaction.

I gaped at the guy, hardly believing what had just happened. This was way beyond innocent jack-me-off-I'll-jack-you-off male bonding. This was prancing right over the line into the shadowy world of homo-eroticism.

Leaping right over, as Ken bent his long neck down and, holding my cock, flowed his lips over my crown. "Holy shit!" I cried, making the leap of sexual faith right with the guy.

What could I do? He held my cock in his hand, my hood in his mouth. It felt so fucking hot and wet and good. The man's tongue was spinning all around my cap, his cheeks billowing vacuum pressure to suck up any remaining jizz, his hand gliding up and down my shaft, pumping me up to my former pulsating glory.

I threw my arms over the back of the couch and dug my fingernails into the leather, watching my friend – boyfriend? – go to work on my dong. My chest and stomach heaved with the need to suck air, my face gone red and sweaty, my groin bathed in velvety warmth, cock vibrating in Ken's hand and mouth.

He popped my knob out from between his soft, sucking lips and tongued my slit, tapping the soft spot, his hand rising and falling along my swollen length. Then he inhaled my hood again, my shaft this time, his head and mouth dropping with alarming, exhilarating speed. Until his lips met up with his fist at the base of my cock.

The guy had my entire dong locked up in his mouth, a wet-hot inferno. I bucked all over again, with the sheer sexual agony of being swallowed whole by that man-eater. The pressure was intense, the pleasure immense.

Ken's hot breath pumped out of his flared nostrils and flooded my groin, bathing my balls in additional heat. I quivered, my cock disappeared, devoured by the guy, immersed in the boiling cauldron of his mouth and throat; ten seconds, twenty, thirty.

"Oh, Jesus!" I gasped, ready to blow all over again.

Ken pulled his head back, popping my over-pressurized cock out of his mouth in a gush of pent-up air and saliva and pre-cum. "Feels good, huh?" he stated rhetorically. "Feels even better when you've got another guy's cock in your mouth while he's sucking yours."

I stared at him, unconsciously moving my hips in rhythm to his hand gliding up and down my slickened dick. Mutual cocksucking? Was this flaming fagdom for me? Maybe this had gone too far and had to be stopped.

But Ken had the answer, as usual. "Come on, it'll be fun."

Well, as long as it was just good dirty fun ...

I stretched out flat on my back on the big leather couch, while Ken straddled my head with his knees, his full-blown erection dangling dangerously over my face. Our pants and underwear was totally gone now, just a couple of guys in their socks and shirts about suck each other off in a sixty-niner. Typical male roughhousing, right?

Ken planted a hand on my bare thigh, his mouth on my hood, other hand gripping my shaft. I stared up at his bloated purple knob and licked my lips, my throat as dry as the time I'd first asked out a girl. Then Ken slid his lips down my dick, mouth-enveloping my entire dong in heat and wetness again. I owed it to the guy; I wouldn't be outdone. I opened my mouth and sucked his hood inside.

His ass cheeks trembled in my gripping hands. His cap was soft and meaty. I sucked on it, moving my head back and forth a bit. Nothing to it. He dropped his hips own, plunging his cock right into my mouth and almost straight down my throat. I gagged like a greenhorn.

He lifted his hips, his shaft gliding between my lips. He was bobbing his head up and down on my prick, sucking tight and hard, making my balls boil with seed. I dug my fingernails into his taut, mounded cheeks and pushed my head back and forth, resolutely sucking on the guy's dong.

I was sucking another man's cock! His prick pulsed in my mouth. I could feel every swollen vein and inch of smooth shaft with my lips and tongue. It was okay, it was all right, it was fucking fantastic! Getting and giving a blowjob. What the hell were all these male hang-ups about?

I sucked with real enthusiasm. Ken felt it, his butt cheeks rippling with pleasure in my clutching hands. He hummered my own hard-on with a practiced ease and sensual gusto. My body trembled beneath him, the hot, sweaty scent of the guy filling my head, his hot, hard cock filling my mouth.

I sucked with mounting urgency, smoothly, rhythmically, taking his glorious pipe almost up to the hanging balls, sliding back down again. I tasted pre-cum, warm and salty.

I thrust my hips up, my cock back and forth in Ken's mouth, fucking the guy's face, my nut sack tingling and tightening with imminent total explosion. "Fuck me up the ass!" Ken gulped, yanking my dong out of his loving mouth with a pop.

I gagged on his prong, pulled it clear of my lips. Fuck him up the ass?!? What the hell?!? There was no misinterpreting that move. That was pure flaming gay-

"It's just like fucking a girl, except in the ass," Ken explained, pumping my cock. That made sense.

He got me to squirm out from underneath him, kneel upright behind him. He pulled a convenient tube of lube out of a drawer in the table next to the couch and passed it back to me with the advice, "For your cock and my butthole."

I stared down at the lube in my hand, at Ken's tight, pale, mounded buttocks, my hard, jutting cock pointed right at the crack in those cheeks. Then I greased my cock, jerking with the impact of the cool, slippery liquid on my boner. I lubed a couple of fingers, reached out, hesitated.

Ken wiggled his bum at me. With his narrow waist and hips and pert little bottom, it was almost like I was looking at a girl's backside, getting ready to fuck a girl's backside. Almost. I slid my fingers in between his cheeks and rubbed his crack.

He groaned, pushing back against my digits. His ass crack was smooth, just like a girl's. I rubbed it slick with the lube, then pressed my fingers against his pucker, popped inside. He whimpered.

A shiver ran through me from head to toe. As I speared my fingers into the guy's asshole, burying one-knuckle, two-

73

knuckles deep. He was hot and tight, and wanting it bad. His ring sucked on my digits, as I slowly pumped back and forth.

I extracted my fingers and gripped my cock. I swallowed hard, pulling Ken's ass open with my left hand, steering my knob into his exposed starfish with my right. I touched cap to asshole, and we both jumped.

Gritting my teeth, I pushed my knob hard up against him, and popped through his rim, inside his ass. Shaft followed quickly, slickly, sinking into Ken's gripping anus. Until my fist touched up against his butt cheeks, my cock buried in the inferno hot vise of the man's rectum.

There was no retreat, no surrender to society's norms now. I had penetrated a man, was fucking him, pumping my cock back and forth in his ass. And he was loving it, rutting around on the end of my plunging dick. And I was rejoicing in it, the weirdness gone, replaced with a sensation of pure sexual lust, my cock doing all the thinking for me, enjoying pistoning the luscious pink sleeve of Ken's chute.

"Yeah! Fuck me harder! Faster!" he gasped.

I gripped his hips and slammed up against his buttocks, ramming deep into his sexhole, churning his tunnel. I was on fire, ablaze with passion, my cock a length of molten steel in the guy's anus. I splashed up against his cheeks, pounding into his butt.

Ken rocked back and forth in rhythm to my savage analizing. But he still managed to grab up his own prick, and stroke, keep pace with my heated stroke.

Sweat rolled down my burning face, my nails biting into the man's body, as I flung my hips to and fro in a frenzy, driving the guy's ass and myself wild. It was so fucking hot and so fucking right I wanted it to go on forever. But my cock had been squeezed and polished beyond the point of no return, my balls slapping against Ken's cheeks with a boiling urgency.

I whined, "Oh, jeez, I'm going to ... I'm going to ..."

"I'm coming!" Ken yelled, his body jerking beneath me, on the end of my butt-plundering cock.

I was jolted by all-out orgasm, my cock exploding in Ken's ass, blasting white-hot jizz against his bowels.

We shook like a pair of ragdolls, coming and coming. Ken sprayed a steaming pool of semen onto the leather couch, as I filled his sucking chute to overflowing with my sizzling man-juice.

We watch and "play" a lot of games now, every chance we get.

Just a couple of buds enjoying one another's company.

A QUEER TURN OF EVENTS
By Landon Dixon

These sex games are getting out of hand, I thought, under my half-face black rubber mask, orange ball gag secure in my mouth, arms bound at the wrists by leather cuffs, stretched up over my head by a steel chain locked onto the iron hook embedded in the ceiling.

I'd been carrying on an affair with a co-worker's wife for a couple of months, and the small, tightly-wound, taut-bodied blonde was dragging me further and further out of my comfort zone, into wild, uncharted zones. First, I'd never had sex with a married woman before. Second, I'd never had public sex before (on a park bench). Third, I'd never given a "golden shower" before. And finally, and lately, I'd never allowed myself to be trussed up naked and helpless, subjected to any sexual torture the little blonde wanted to dish out on my achingly vulnerable body and ego.

I felt a finger stroke along the underside of my vibrating erection, nail scraping the foreskin. I jumped up higher on my tip-toes, rattling the chain. Hot breath flooded the exposed lower half of my face, a tongue painting my stretched lips around the ball gag. The eyeholes on the black mask were zipped shut, so I couldn't see a thing; just feel, anticipate, agonize, fervently fear and lust. A hand slapped one of my ass cheeks, and I almost jerked my quivering arms out of their sockets.

I was bathed in sweat, dripping it down my sides and face, but shivering as if I was chilled to the bone. My body burned, though, the granite-hard erection jutting out from my loins testimony to my true feelings. A tongue tickled my balls, teeth bit into the back of my neck.

What the fuck!?

I was jolted like I'd been hooked up to a car battery and blasted full of juice. There were two of them! That naughty little blonde had tossed an equally kinky girlfriend into our steaming sexual mix. What would she think of next?

I found out soon enough, when a hand gripped my cock and tugged, a tongue swirled in behind my ear and licked, something long and hard and throbbing glided in between my buttocks and pumped. Sweet Jesus, a guy!

Two guys, it was shockingly revealed, when my blonde playmate's husband, my co-worker, unzipped the leather lids on my eyes and revealed his smiling face up close. He kissed my ball gag with his plush, red lips, as I almost swallowed the thing.

"That's Clark in behind," Travis informed me. "My not-so-secret lover."

I twisted my head around. The other man smiled at me, a tall, toned brunette with a pair of twinkling brown eyes and petulant pair of lips, dimpled chin. He was as completely and utterly naked as I was, as Travis was, pumping his hips, sliding what felt like one huge, horking bare cock in between my trembling butt cheeks; frotting, as it were.

I jerked my head back around. Travis had sealed his soft lips onto one of my hard nipples, was gently tugging, staring up at my frog-popped eyes. He was built not unlike his sexy spouse – short and lean-muscled, with pronounced buttocks and a sweet, sensuous face, soft blond hair. Only he sported a cock and a set of nuts, the cock spearing up into the air a good seven inches or so, the nuts shaved as smooth as the rest of the guy.

My illicit girlfriend was nowhere in sight. She'd decided I needed a guy's night out, I guess, with me being the one outed. Her husband sucked on my nipples, Clark licking my neck, cock-cruising my crack. Travis's rigid dick bumped bloated hoods with my straining dong, as he cupped my pecs and bounced his blond head back and forth between my equally engorged nipples.

I'd never been intimate with a man – men! – before. Sure, I'd fooled around as a kid, pretending I was a weak little girl as my buddy dry-humped me on his bed, simulating heterosexual rape fully clothed, though fully erect. That was just innocent boyish fun.

There was nothing innocent, or necessarily fun, about what was going on now. These guys meant business. The appearance of the nipple clamps and cock ring and sack tie signaled that for sure.

They both stood in front of me, looking at my stretched-up, shaking form, my twitching hard-on. As I gaped back at them. Travis picked up a pair of silver nipple clamps off the bed I'd banged his wife on many a time, while Clark scooped up the red rubber cock ring, a red length of cord that was used to rope and bind balls. The men's cocks jutted out at me, pointing accusingly, erotically.

Then they turned, embraced, their mouths meeting, their dicks pressing together. They kissed, heavily, hungrily. Hot red wet tongues jumped out and twirled together, the guys excitedly Frenching, exploring hands fondling each other's backs and buttocks. They were putting on a male-male make-out show for me, and while my mind still rebelled, my body and cock responded.

I surged with a fresh wave of tingling heat, shimmering out from my straining hard-on and suffusing my sweating body; staring at the guy's hard mounded butt cheeks, the supple smoothness of their tanned skin, the sensual repartee of their twisting tongues, the wicked thrusting of their massive pricks foreskin-on-foreskin. The times I wandered onto all of those gay porn sites hadn't just been idle curiosity, after all. I was turned-on trussed-up, willing, anxious to be treated like a sexual ragdoll by these two beautiful men.

Travis clamped my left nipple, my right. The metal clips bit hard into my stiffened buds. I shuddered when he gave a tug on the pair, stretching my rubbery jutters out painfully, pleasurably.

Clark was on his knees, at my dick. He locked the cock ring in place around the base of my dong. It bit into my shaft, cutting off some of the blood flow and feeling, ballooning my cock even more, turning it numb and yet super-sensitive. His quick hand-pump proved that. Then he tied my balls together with the cord, making a neat throbbing package, looping me at the top of my scrotum so that my nuts were lashed tight as my cock. How the hell was I going to come?!?

That was the whole idea, I found out. Keeping me achingly aroused and yearning to blast while they took their sexual time on my body, and their pleasure.

Clark got in behind me again, while Travis went down on his knees in front. The blond blew hot humid breath on my dick, the brunette sending a heated stream against my crack. Then Travis slid his wet lips over my hood, engulfing the bulb. As Clark spread my cheeks with his fingers and shot his tongue up against my asshole.

I jerked forward and aft, stunned, stung by the intimate mouth-contact on my most intimates. It was wild, weird, fucking wonderful – getting my cock sucked by one man, my ass licked by another.

Travis tugged on my cap, went deeper, opening his mouth wider, sliding his lips down my shaft with a graceful, glorious precision. He consumed my entire raging dong in one gulp; then held me there, pounding away in the velvety confines of his mouth, my hood and some shaft bent down his tight-clasping throat.

Clark bit his fingernails into my buttocks and really opened me up, baring my crack and my bumhole. He swabbed my exposed starfish with his tongue, in prelude to jamming the slippery, wriggling sticker right into my anus. He went in up to his lips kissing against my butt cheeks, burying his tongue in my chute.

And while Travis billowed his cheeks and sucked on my cock without moving his head, Clark squirmed his tongue around inside my anus, eating ass with a fearsome intensity. Then pulling back, punching in, plugging my chute with the now hardened blade of his tongue.

Travis slowly pulled his head back. My cock emerged a glistening snake from between his dragging lips. He caught the swollen tip with his white teeth, swallowed down shaft again; repeated the awesomely sensual process again and again. As I glared through my eye slits, groaned around my ball gag, thrust out in my cock and ball restraints.

Clark sunk his tongue down deep in between my legs, catching my balls on the other side. Then he dragged the wet, beaded love instrument up and along my sensitive crack, all the way up to my tailbone. He did it over and over, painting my butt cleavage with his tongue, bathing it in his saliva, tracing buzzing bliss up my ass.

Travis cock-sucked. Clark ass-licked. I took it like a man, unashamedly loving the loving the men were dishing out. Travis gripped my hips and wet-vacced my prick with mind-blowing urgency. Clark spiraled his tongue all around my puckered bumhole, slithered the appendage into my anus and pumped with body-jolting eagerness. Bound by lust, I tilted my rubber-wrapped head back and howled into my gag.

The men got to their feet, their warm-up and wetting-down complete. Travis pulled on my nipple clamps, smacked my cock around with his cock. Clark whacked my ass, heating my cheeks up even more. He reached down around and gripped my balls, twisted the trussed pair. They had to dish out some pain with all of the pleasure they were providing. I didn't blame them a bit; would've praised them orally, if I could.

But the restraints stayed in place. And now lube was added, to grease the heated action up to a whole new level. I'd never been fucked up the ass before, or fucked ass. That all changed, my sexual horizons expanding still further, exploding.

Clark crowded in behind me. I felt his slippery dong slide in between my cheeks, really felt his cap push up against my manhole. I lurched higher onto my toes, arching my body away.

But there was no getting away – I was facing from the rear what I'd always been so curious about. Clark gripped one of my hips and squished his hood against my back opening. He popped through, sunk in, busting my anal cherry with ease, pure delight. His cock surged into my anus, stretching me, stuffing me full of wild sensation. He drove his entire dong home, analizing this virgin.

He held his position, his cock pulsating powerfully inside my gripping butt tunnel. As Travis bent forward in front of me, displaying his own bronze, rounded butt cheeks, spreading them with one hand to show off his tiny pink pucker. He reached back and grasped my slab of meat with his other hand, plowed my hood up against his hole.

I jerked, ass muscles clamping down on Clark's lodged beef. I thrust forward, helping Travis burst cap into his bum, pour shaft down his chute. My cock was enveloped in blistering heat, sinking into another man's ass.

I pushed forward, Travis pushed back. I watched through tear-filled eyes, biting on my ball gag, as my enormous erection penetrated, plunged inside Travis. Until there was nothing left but my hairy, roped balls pressing up against the man's buttocks.

I had a cock in my ass, my cock was buried up another ass. I wallowed, rutted in the roilingly raw emotions. Why the fuck hadn't I done this before?!? It was so natural, so wonderful. And it got even more so, as Clark pumped his hips, fucking my butt, and Travis shifted back and forth, fucking himself on my cock.

I rattled my chain and just about ruptured my spleen, bucking my hips, thrusting in and out of Travis' anus.

We got a rhythm going, Clark pistoning me from behind, sawing away at my chute, as I pumped into Travis bouncing back and forth on my pole. The perspiration absolutely gushed out of every pore on my body, our bodies splashing together; Clark shuddering cheeks, cleaving my ass, me banging Travis's buttocks, watching them ripple and gyrate, feeling his ass suck on my pile-driving prick.

We went faster and faster, a well-oiled, wholly uninhibited sexual male-machine. Travis grabbed up his dick and stroked, shouted, shot. The guy jerked and jostled on the end of my drilling prong, jacking thick ropes of semen out of his prick again and again and again.

I was amazed, astonished. Because my tied tight cock and balls were good to keep going, and going.

And then I was rendered flat-out delirious, when I felt Clark's fingernails bite savagely into my hips, heard his groan of blissful surrender, was splashed with hot semen up my chute. He pumped and sprayed and moaned, blasting me full of sizzling sperm.

Travis stumbled off of my cock up front. Clark staggered backwards in behind me, pulling his dick out of my bung. I felt gapingly empty and unfulfilled, on full-boil and no way to blow off my steam.

The two men took care of me, like they had all along. They crowded down on their knees at my cock. Travis took a long, deep pull on the thudding appendage, looking up at me with his baby-blue eyes. Then Clark took a suck, just as deep and tight and wet. They passed my obscenely swollen dong back and forth, deep-throating, keeping their mouths occupied when the other's was full of my prick by sucking on my balls.

It was good, but it was no good. I just couldn't come, let loose. I was bound too tight.

My pleading eyes and pattering sweat were finally answered. Travis kissed Clark, Frenched the studly brunette, as he unfastened my cock ring, and Clark unleashed my nut sack.

My genitals flooded with hot, coursing blood, my quivering body with sheer, sweet relief. The men pressed their pretty faces side by side at my surging dong. Travis captured me in his mouth again, and sucked.

I bucked like a bull in harness, orgasm shocking me with seismic intensity, volcanoing out my ruptured cock into Travis' moist pulling mouth. I spray-painted his throat. He unplugged my hose and planted it in Clark's mouth. I filled him to the tugging lips with heady, star-crashing bursts.

They passed my spouting organ back and forth between their lovely mouths, bravely, sexily taking my superheated gushes of man-lust deep into their beings. I was all but passed out by the time they finally released me, let me drop to the carpet on the end of my chain.

These sex games are getting better and better, I thought, as my first male lovers rolled me over, sucked the last drops of delight out of my prick, kissing my nipples, fondling my crack, affectionately squeezing my balls.

POOL OFF
By Landon Dixon

The party was going great for the first two hours Glen and I were there. Then I spotted the tall, willowy blond with his hand on another guy's ass, rubbing cheek while he gesticulated in the middle of a conversation with his other hand.

I bit off the edge of my plastic cup, not listening anymore to the host of the party, Rene, as he droned on about the new sod he'd planted in his front lawn. Watching Glen covertly feel up that other man's ass. The other guy was a small, wiry redhead, wearing a tight pair of faded blue jeans and a green top. He acted like nothing was happening, listening to Glen in the middle of the group, getting his pert little bottom pinched and caressed by my man.

Then the redhead put his hand on Glen's shoulder and said something – naughty, no doubt. Because Glen grinned, took a look around the room, trying to see where I was.

I slipped in front of a big, fat guy wearing what looked like some of our host's sod on top of his head, shielding myself from Glen's view. Then I looked around the fat man's shoulder, saw Glen leading the petite redhead upstairs, hand-in-hand. I crushed the plastic cup in my hand, watching Glen's lean buttocks swish from side-to-side in his white pants, as he and his latest toy-boy ascended the stairs.

I should've known better than to take Glen anywhere. But I never thought he'd cheat on me this openly and humiliatingly. The more I thought about it, the more my blood boiled.

Finally, after two minutes of building up steam, I threw my crumpled cup down and took the stairs three at a time, charging after the pair.

They weren't hard to find; I just had to follow the moaning and groaning coming from behind the bathroom door at the end of the upstairs hallway. I gripped the handle with a sweaty paw, turned, flung the door open.

Glen was holding the redhead up in his arms, the guy's bare legs hooked around Glen's bare waist, Glen's cock sawing back and forth in the redhead's chute. These fuckers didn't waste any time.

Glen froze in mid-stroke, staring at me, his grey eyes gone wide. The redhead had his eyes closed, was still urging Glen on, clinging to his neck and bouncing up and down in the tall man's arms, wiggling his butt around on the end of Glen's cock.

"You fucking bastard!" I growled. Then threw myself at the pair.

It took our host and four other strapping men to pull me off of the cheaters. Rene escorted me downstairs and out into the backyard, to the edge of his swimming pool. "Here, why don't you take a swim?" he soothed. "Cool down a bit."

I shrugged off his arm, and he left me alone, returning inside to his precious party.

It was a cool, damp night, which meant I was all by myself out by the pool. I pulled off my turtleneck, pushed my pants and underwear down, kicked them and my shoes off. "I'll fucking cool down, all right!" I rasped, diving into the pool buck-naked.

I swam a few laps, fast, but that did nothing to lower my temperature. The water was warm, my blood still hot from what I'd seen in the bathroom, and now from the exercise. I flung myself up onto the edge of the dunk tank and sat there with my legs in the water, letting the rain splutter down on me, deciding what I was going to do next.

It was decided for me.

Because a man suddenly stepped through the sliding doors that led out to the backyard patio and pool. He carefully re-latched the curtained doors, then walked across the patio and to the side of the pool, opposite the one I was sitting on. He was a tall guy, with long, dark hair and a slender body. He was dressed in a blue silk shirt and white cotton pants, brown deck shoes. He nodded at me, his handsome face reflecting the glittering waters of the pool. I nodded back, self-consciously folding my hands over my lap to cover up my bare cock.

"I'm Ramon," he said from across the rectangular expanse of lighted water.

I opened my mouth to respond. Then left my jaw hanging there, as Ramon stripped off his shirt, unbuckled his pants and eased them down, stepped out of his shoes. He stood there on the near edge of the pool as completely naked as I was, a starkly stunning sight to behold. His long body was burnished bronze, smooth as polished copper, his prick dangling long even soft over top of his shaven balls. He dove, splitting the water with hardly a splash.

I watched his lean form knife through the water below the surface, watching his butt cheeks clench and unclench as he kicked with his feet. He swam the fifty feet or so from the deep end to my end in a matter of seconds, then hit the wall right between my dangling legs and flipped around, swam back in the direction he'd come, still underwater.

The guy could hold his breath longer than a pearl-diver. A talent like that could come in handy for other purposes, I mused, forgetting all about my recent spat with my boyfriend. I let my hands drift off of my lap, letting my cock rise up into the air, stiffening with excitement at the nude water follies Ramon was putting on for my benefit.

He popped up in the deep end, turned and looked at me, smoothing his shining black hair back on his head. He waved. I waved, wondering if I should go ahead and wave my dick at the guy; the thing was almost wagging as it was, my tongue hanging out.

Ramon slipped back beneath the waves he'd created, pushed off from the side of the pool and swam toward me again. I gripped the edge of the water tank with whitened knuckles, swinging my submerged legs as if they were bait for a shark bite, staring at that lithe, gorgeous body surging closer and closer to me under the crystal-clear water.

His hands touched the wall of the pool, in between my widened legs. I yearned to hook him with my feet before he swam away again. But he made that action unnecessary, when he took the bait of my wriggling toes, capturing my right big toe in his underwater mouth and sucking.

"Thar she blows!" I yelped, jolted by the warm tug on my toe.

The guy was sort of squatting down in the water, sucking on my big toe, looking up at me through the shimmering liquid. He sucked on my next toe, the next one, all the way down, and up, the line, pulling on my individual foot-digits with his soft lips and hot mouth.

It was a feat worthy of any manmaid. My cock pronged out straight up in front of me, no hiding it now, no need to hide it now. It quivered in appreciation with what the manmal was doing down below. He plunged my entire left foot-tip into his mouth – all five slender-stemmed, plumped-topped toes – and pulled on it.

I rocked back and forth with the wicked tug, loving it.

He performed the same luscious actions on my right foot, consuming the toes one by one, then all together. Then he squished my two peds together and gorged himself on the tapered pair both at the same time. All underwater!

It was an act fit for an adult San Diego aquarium. He'd been under for at least two minutes, cramming his mouth full of my feet and sucking on them. He just about pulled me over the edge with his ardor.

And then, finally, he surfaced. He took one more pull on both of my peds together and then pulled them out of his mouth and pushed them apart and burst upwards out of the water, in between my legs. I was there to meet him, jumping down, into the water, into his arms.

We clutched each other tight and kissed one another. His body was slippery, supple, hotter than the water itself. We were up to our waists, perhaps over my head. I still had a so-called boyfriend inside, after all. But a man in the arms is worth two in the bathroom.

Ramon locked his mouth onto mine, his lips warm and wet, his arms strong around my torso. My hard cock pressed into his lean belly, and I could feel his cock bobbing up, nudging at my balls. His tongue swam into my mouth and snaked around my tongue.

We swirled out slick stickers together, entwining over and over. He moved his hips back, forward, pushing his now fully-erect cock against my cock. I moaned into his mouth, feeling that swollen shaft beating against my shaft. I wasn't cooling down in the pool; I was heating up big-time.

Ramon pulled his head back, and his tongue started sliding out of my mouth. Not all the way, though, because I captured the glistening red appendage with my teeth, sealing my lips around it, sucking on it.

Ramon groaned, as I urgently tugged on his tongue as he'd tugged on my toes. He undulated his hips underwater, thrusting his cock against mine, the hardened pair of us rubbing together. It felt fantastic, out there in the pool, under the rain, mano-a-mano, dong-to-dong.

Ramon reeled his tongue back in, leaving me gasping like a fish out of water. He cupped my pecs, squeezed them, setting my chest ablaze. Then fanned the fire with his tongue, as he dipped down in my arms and flogged first one of my nipples with his agile mouth-organ, and then the other.

I groaned and tilted my head back, the lash of the man's bud-beaded tongue making my nipples buzz with delight. They went near-rigid as my cock, as Ramon teased them higher and harder than they'd ever been with his flicking and swirling tongue.

He painted my pebbly areolas in sweet rotation. Before nipping a nipple with his sharp, white teeth and biting into it, pulling on it.

I gripped the man's buff shoulders, as he stretched my nipples out to the snapping point, my mind having snapped long previous. Then he was bobbing lower, underwater, in line with my periscope. He gripped my hips and inhaled my hood.

"Yes!" I gasped, jolted up in the water by the heated impact of his mouth on my cock.

He was completely immersed again, just some of his hair stranding out on the surface. He sucked on my knob, pulling on it with his lips, mouth enveloping the chewy meat. I stared down at him in the churning waters, getting eaten alive, so wanting him to devour me whole.

He devoured me, swallowing my cock. Almost right to the waterlogged balls. Blissful sensation flooded my body, as Ramon moved his mouth down my shaft, inhaling my prong. I shook on the end of his lips, locked down in the cauldron of his mouth.

It was exquisite, exhilarating. I plunged my hands down and gripped the man's head in the water, as he moved that head in my hands, sucking on my cock. I quivered like my dick in his mouth, feeling the glorious tug all through me. The guy knew how to swim, the guy knew how to suck, like a fish to water.

He bobbed back and forth, wet-vaccing my straining dong. I clung to him, adrift on a sea of sensuality, immersed in eroticism. It was all I could do to not spout off right then and there.

He disgorged me and shot up into my arms again, gasping for air. I gave him air – from my mouth to his – kissing the beautiful cocksucker, Frenching him. He towed me sideways over to a water jet. Then positioned himself against the rushing water, cock-first.

"Fuck me!" he breathed, looking back at me, his deep, brown eyes shining.

I gripped his waist with my left hand, my submerged log with my right. He sluiced his hands back in the water and grabbed onto his butt mounds, pulling them open, giving me clear aim at his asshole. I rubbed my cockhead over the smooth, taut skin of his buttocks, the backs of his straining fingers. And then I dove in headfirst – in between his spread cheeks, impacting his asshole.

He and I both jumped. Then I jammed, shoving my cap deep into his manhole. My shaft sunk into his anus like an oil drill into the seabed, without spilling a drop of pre-cum.

I gripped both his hips and thrust inside the man, his bung swallowing up my cock. Until I was embedded in his sinkhole, buried in his butt.

"Yes! Yes! Fuck me!" he moaned. His hands were off his ass and gripping the edge of the pool now, his cock taking the gushing water jet full foreskin.

I pumped, sliding my squeezed-tight dick back and forth in his chute. Faster and faster, flinging my hips into the aquatic sexing. Until I was absolutely cornholing the guy, driving his ass, plundering his anus. The sucking pressure almost gave me the bends, the heat just about melting my snorkel.

"Fuck, yeah!" I gritted, absolutely foaming the waters.

I pounded into Ramon's bung, bouncing my thighs off his buttocks, making them and me and him shiver. My cock went numb-hard in his ass, spearing over and over and over, my flapping balls tightening, tingling ominously.

Ramon was pushed right up against the water jet, shuddering in rhythm to my frantic analizing. Then he jerked with more than my mania, and cried out. He was coming, spurting his joy into the jetting water, driven into the deep end of lust by my blistering butt-fucking.

I slammed him in a frenzy, reaming his chute with a savage intensity, tearing the guy a new one. "Sweet Jesus!" I hollered, jerking, spouting my own spray.

I almost flew up out of the pool on the end of my spurting cock, sailing ecstatically. I filled Ramon's ass to overflowing, coming and coming and coming in the frothy waters.

I met back up with Glen inside the party house. He was apologetic. But I brushed him aside with one hand while I led Ramon up the stairs with the other. A nice hot shower was just the thing to wash away all that chlorine after so long in the pool.

LOVE AFTER DESPAIR
By Donald Webb

Donald Webb resides in Victoria, BC. He has been published in numerous gay magazines and anthologies. Contact him at andon402@shaw.ca

The telephone roused me from a deep sleep. It was 10:25 a.m. I rolled over onto Steve's side of the bed and picked up the phone.

"Hi, baby," Steve said, "I wake you?"

"Yeah ... but it's time I got up. I didn't even hear you leave for work this morning."

"Well, I didn't hear you come home last night, so we're even."

"What's up?" I asked.

"Just called to tell you I loved you."

"I love you, too, Stevie. Don't know what I'd do without you." I yawned and sat up on the edge of the bed.

"You been in the living-room yet?" he asked.

"Uh-uh."

"Well go take a look."

Carrying the cordless phone with me, I walked into the living-room. The sweet scent of roses filled the air. Twelve red roses, arranged in a cut-glass vase, sat on the coffee table. A card rested against the vase. I opened the card and read the message: *Happy twenty-fifth anniversary, Baby ... I couldn't live without you! Steve.*

A warm fuzzy feeling permeated my senses and tears sprang to my eyes. "They're beautiful, honey," I said clutching the card to my chest. "I couldn't live without you, too."

Lover Boys Forever

He giggled like teenage boy. "I've made a reservation for dinner at eight ... so get your glad rags ready."

I could hear a beeping noise in the background. "Got to go, baby," he said. "They're paging me. See you later ... kiss, kiss."

After he disconnected, I sat down on the sofa and picked up the photograph of the two of us taken five years ago when we'd finally been able to tie the knot in Vancouver. It was hard to believe twenty-five years had passed since we'd first met, but it had. We often joked about being engaged for twenty years.

Memories of the day we'd first met came flooding back. It had started out like any other day. I was cleaning the apartment I shared with my then lover, Ryan, when a pounding on the door interrupted my dusting. I opened the door. Chris, my friend since high school, stood on the threshold. Using a wad of tissues, he dabbed at his red swollen eyes.

"What's up?" I asked. "What's happened?"

He walked past me and collapsed on the sofa. "Jason's dead!" he sobbed.

"He can't be," I said. "Stop fooling around, Chris. It's not funny"

"I'm not, I'm not," he wailed. "It's true!"

I took a big breath and sat next to him. "What happened? I didn't know he was sick."

"It was awful," Chris said, between sobs. "I found him on the floor when I got home from work this morning. You should've seen all the blood, Tyler, and, oh, God, he'd been mutilated. My beautiful Jason was cut to ribbons." He paused, blew his nose, and then continued. "I called 911 right away and started CPR, but it was no use. He was pronounced when they got there."

I put my arm around his shoulders. I couldn't believe what I was hearing. "Oh, God, that's terrible, honey. I'm so sorry."

"I was working the graveyard shift last night. The police think that it must've happened around midnight. Jason worked until eleven. Ryan would know – they worked the same shift didn't they?"

My lover, Ryan, worked with Jason. Ryan, Jason, and Chris were all registered nurses at Brook County Hospital. Chris worked in the surgical suite, while Jason and Ryan worked in the trauma unit. "Yes, he did work evenings yesterday," I said. "He's not here now though – they phoned and asked him to come in this morning. Do the police know why? I mean was he robbed?"

Chris blew his nose. "No they don't think it was robbery. They think Jason knew his murderer."

"What! Someone he knew. Why do they think that?"

"The police asked me not to tell anyone about this, Tyler. They don't want the details to get out."

"I'm not going to tell anyone," I said as I took his shaking body in my arms and gently wiped the tears from his face.

After he had calmed down he continued, "There was no forced entry, and nothing seemed to be disturbed. His wallet was on the bedside table."

"This sounds really weird. Why would someone he knew do that to him?"

"I haven't told you the worst part yet," Chris said.

"What could be worse?"

"They found three ampoules of Demerol on the coffee table."

"Demerol ... what's that?"

"It's a narcotic that we give to patients in pain."

"But why would there be Demerol in your apartment?"

"They're going to check, but I could see that they think he was stealing it from work."

"That's crazy," I said. "Jason would never do anything like that. He's always been against drugs. I mean he won't even try poppers."

"I know, I know. There's got to be a logical explanation"

The telephone interrupted us. I let it ring for a while, not wanting to speak with anyone, hoping it would stop. It didn't. I went into the kitchen to answer it.

"What took you so long?" Ryan asked.

"I was talking to Chris. He was ..."

"What's he doing there?" Ryan interrupted. "You know I don't like you seeing him. What's he saying about me?"

"About you! Why would he be talking about you? Surely you must've heard about Jason?"

"Yeah, I did. I know he doesn't like me ... that's why I don't want him there."

"Oh, shit. What's your problem? I don't have time for this crap now, Ryan. He's come to me because I'm his friend, and he doesn't have anyone else to turn to. Why do you always have to be so selfish?"

"Well. Yeah ... I guess. Anyway that creep got what he deserved. He was always acting so high and mighty, and now they know he's been stealing drugs," he said.

"That's terrible. How can you be so hard?" I thought for a few moments. "How do you know about the drugs?"

"The police've been here, so it's common knowledge."

"Well, I don't believe it. Not for a moment. I mean he was a straight A guy."

"I'm the one who worked with him. Don't you think I would know? How come you're suddenly the expert?"

"I have to go. Chris needs me."

"Just make sure he's gone when I get home. I have enough crises to deal with at work, without having one when I get home."

I hung up. I was furious with him for being so insensitive. *Why am I still with him?* Flashed through my mind. *It's time I moved on with my life. When this crisis is over I'll confront him.*

When I went back into the living-room Chris was pulling on his jacket. "What're you doing?" I asked.

"I have to go home and rest. I'm due in at work at eleven."

"Surely you don't have to work tonight? I'm sure they'll give you the night off if you explain."

"Explain what? That I'm a fag, and my lover has been murdered? Sure they'll understand," Chris said. "Never mind I'll be okay. Anyway it'll be good to concentrate on something else. Thanks for listening."

"Are you sure you're okay? Will you be able to get into your apartment? You can stay if you want."

"Oh yes, sure. Ryan would just love that. Thanks for asking anyway. The cops told me that they'd be finished checking the apartment by noon, so I'll go home."

Later that day, when Ryan arrived home, I was still thinking about Jason. I just couldn't get it out of my mind. I was ready for a fight, still fuming because Ryan had been so callous. Before I could say anything, he defused the whole situation by immediately apologizing. "Sorry about the earlier call," he said. Taking me in his arms, he continued, "I shouldn't have been so insensitive. Chris must be knotted. If you want he can spend a few days with us."

97

Ryan's mood swings always amazed me. He could change from one minute to the next. He had seemed so hard earlier, and now he was all soft and cuddly. "Thanks, that means a lot to me," I said. "You know he's like a brother to me. Anyway he's going into work at eleven, and he doesn't want to stay here."

"I'm sure that's the best thing for him. By the way, I've made plans to meet Steve at the gym this evening," Ryan added. "He's been after me for a while. I'll probably bring him home afterwards to meet you."

"Steve? Who's he?"

"He's one of the trauma docs. I'm sure I've mentioned him before. He's the only one on the team with any brains, the rest are all incompetent. I don't know how I've put up with them for so long. Maybe I should be looking for a new job."

"What are you on about?" I asked. "You've only been there for six months. You can't be thinking about leaving already. Why don't you give it a fair trial?"

"Oh hell! What would you know anyway? The least you could do is support me. It's not my fault if they're all assholes."

Oh, shit, I thought. *Here we go again.* Why do our discussions always end up like this? This was his third job in two years. We never seemed to have any friends. I was just beginning to get settled in the new apartment, and still looking for a job, and here he was talking about moving again. I knew that it wasn't the right time – if any time was right, to continue the topic, so I let it drop.

"Will you be expecting dinner when you get home?" I asked.

"No. We'll have a snack at the gym. You go ahead and eat. We'll probably be here by eight."

After Ryan left, I settled down with a book. I was bored and would like to have gone out for a drink, but I knew that would make Ryan mad. I couldn't even go out for a walk because I knew he would probably phone to make sure I was home.

At 8:15 p.m., I was relaxing in the recliner, in a pair of old gym shorts, watching television, when Ryan arrived home with Steve in tow. I couldn't remember Ryan talking about him before, but if he had, he hadn't told me how gorgeous Steve was. He didn't look the least bit like a doctor. He was dressed in tight black jeans and a form fitting white sleeveless T-shirt. His well-defined pecs and hard abdomen were clearly visible through the tight shirt. The earring in his left ear, intricate tattoo around his left bicep, and punk blond hair style, all added up to hunk.

"Would you believe the goddamn showers were closed? They're doing some work on the plumbing," Ryan exploded. "What a bunch of morons. You'd think they'd get something right for a change."

"Hi, I'm Steve," the hunk said, as he came over to me. "Ryan's told me all about you, but he left out all the good parts. He didn't tell me how cute you were."

I could feel myself blushing as Steve took my hand. "Hi, I'm Tyler," I said. I felt an immediate sexual attraction to Steve, so I quickly changed the subject. "Would you guys like a drink?"

"That sounds great," Ryan said, "but I think I'd like a shower first. What about you, Steve?"

"Yeah, that sounds good. I'm all sweaty, but you go first."

"Would you like a beer?" I asked Steve.

"I'd kill for one."

When I came back into the living-room with the cold beer, Steve had already stripped to his bikini briefs. I could feel myself getting hard as I stared at his tanned body. It had been quite some time since Ryan and I had fucked, so I guess it was only natural that I would react that way. He held the cold beer against his forehead, and then flopped down onto the sofa next to me. I could smell his sweaty body as he lifted his arm and took a swig from the bottle. "Ah," he sighed, "just what I needed. Ryan practically wore me out at the gym, but then I'm sure he often wears you out."

"Not really. I don't go to the gym with him. I think he's scared I'll show him up."

I could hear the shower running when Steve placed his hand on my naked thigh. "You've got a beautiful body. I don't believe that you don't go to the gym."

"Well I do, but not at the same time as Ryan. I try to go first thing in the morning."

"It shows," Steve said as he moved his hand to my abdomen. "You have great definition. And the definition down here looks pretty good, too."

I watched as his hand moved onto my dick. He rubbed me through the thin silk of my shorts for a while, and then he moved his hand into my shorts and brought my hard-on out into the open. "Oh yes, you're ready for it aren't you?" he said, as he rubbed my precum over the sensitive head of my dick.

Before I could respond, he placed his beer on the coffee table, and then swooped down on my dick, burying it in his throat in one continuous lunge. I couldn't believe what was happening. Ryan and I never tricked around. I hadn't had sex with anyone but Ryan for two years. We were faithful to one another.

"Please," I said, trying to pull his head up. "Ryan'll kill me."

"What do you mean he'll kill you?" Steve asked as he abandoned my dick. "Isn't this why he invited me home? I thought you knew that I wanted a threesome."

Before I could respond, the shower stopped running. I quickly slipped my dick back into my shorts, and ran into the kitchen. As I took a beer out of the fridge for Ryan, my mind was in a whirl. What did Steve mean? Had Ryan really set this up? They stopped talking when I entered the room. Ryan was naked and was standing in the center of the room drying his hair. His big semi-hard dick swung back and forth as he moved.

I couldn't help comparing the two guys. They were both tall and well-built, but their coloring was completely opposite. Dark hair covered Ryan's chest, while Steve only had a sprinkling of blond hair over his pecs.

"It's all yours," Ryan said to Steve. "You wanna get him a clean towel, Tyler?"

I pulled a towel out of the closet and then went into the bathroom. Steve was naked. He was proudly displaying his long semi-hard dick. And who wouldn't be proud of such an appendage, I thought. He pulled me into his arms and slipped me his tongue. I couldn't help myself. I was immediately hard again. I was overcome with the male aroma emanating from his body. He lowered his arms, slipped his hands into my shorts, and then cupped my butt in his hands. His finger slipped into my moist hole.

We could both smell my ass-juice on his finger when he pulled it out of my hole and brought it to his nose. He closed his eyes and breathed in, seemingly intoxicated by my distinctive aroma. "Suck me," he whispered. "I want to feel your lips on my rod."

I couldn't resist. Even though I knew Ryan was in the next room. I knelt before Steve and swallowed him, right down to his pubes. He was just starting to face-fuck me when I heard Ryan bellow, "What are you two up to in there?"

I jumped to my feet and quickly left the bathroom. I adjusted myself then went into the living-room to face Ryan, who was lounging back on the sofa. "Is there something you're not telling me?" I asked. "Steve seems to think that you invited him back here for a threesome."

"Oh, sweetie, don't be mad. I thought you would enjoy a little variety. He wants me badly, but I didn't want to do anything with him without you. You mind?"

Asshole, I thought, *using me to get what you want.* I wanted to tell him to go fuck himself, but I couldn't. I knew he would be impossible to live with if I didn't go with the flow, and also, I was horny. I wanted Steve. I hadn't felt so excited in a long time. I wanted that big dick up my chute. "No I don't mind," I said after a long moment. "Just remember this was your idea. Don't go blaming me later on."

"Sure, sweetie. Come over here now and give me some head," he said as he opened his towel and shook his dick at me.

I knelt between his thighs and started sucking his dick. He lifted his legs up and pushed my head down to his pucker. Even though he liked me licking his hole, he was strictly top. Sometimes he would fuck me for hours, shoot his load, and then roll over and go to sleep, not seeming to care whether I was satisfied or not. When he did that I would lie between his legs, rim him, and jerk-off. One time, when he'd been snoring, I'd slipped a finger into his hot chute. I thought about fucking him, but I was too chicken.

I was still rimming Ryan when I felt Steve's hand on my shoulder. "Oh yes, eat him. He really likes that. Put your finger in him. Go on, I know he wants it."

What's going on here? I thought. It sounds as though he knows what Ryan likes. I gently inserted a finger into Ryan – a first for me, while he was awake, that is. I watched in amazement when he ground his asshole onto my finger.

"Put another one in," Steve said.

I was more excited than I'd been in years. I was doing things to Ryan that up to this point had been forbidden. As I continued to fuck Ryan's chute with my fingers, Steve licked Ryan's cockhead, and then he sank his mouth down Ryan's shaft. He released Ryan's dick, and then climbed up onto the settee and hooked Ryan's legs behind his own legs. He pushed forward until his dick was pushed against Ryan's lips then said, "Suck my dick."

In this position Ryan was bent like a pretzel, with his hairy asshole completely open to my probing fingers. I ran into the bedroom and came back with a tube of lube and a fist full of condoms. I lubed my fingers then stuck two into him. I pushed another finger in and twirled them inside his hot chute until I could feel his prostate. I couldn't believe how flexible his so-called virgin hole felt. His rear-end twitched around my fingers as though he was trying to get away from me, but Steve had him pinned tightly to the sofa. I watched through Steve's widely spread legs as he sank his reamer into Ryan's throat, grinding his ass when he bottomed out.

Steve looked over his shoulder at me and said, "Fuck him. He wants it. He likes to pretend that he's a top, but what he likes most is to get fucked by a big cock."

Ryan's widely dilated hole seemed to be begging for my cock, so I sheathed up, and then slowly pushed my hard boner into his chute. The lining of his channel felt hot and smooth against my cock as I sank all the way in, right to the hilt. I could hear Ryan mewling around Steve's dick as I plowed him deep and fast, living a fantasy.

I bent forward and tentatively licked Steve's exposed manhole, which was surrounded by a sprinkling of blond hair, as I continued to pound Ryan. I used my thumbs to pry open Steve's sphincter, then pushed my tongue all the way inside. Steve let me rim him for a while then he said, "I want to fuck you while you're fucking Ryan."

I thought Ryan would unseat me when Steve stepped down, but he didn't. His eyes were closed as he let me fuck him. Steve covered his rod with lubed latex and then fell to his knees behind me. He spread my ass-cheeks apart, and then ran his tongue over my pucker.

"Sweet ass, baby," he said, as he came up for air. "Just like I knew it would be."

He continued rimming me for a short time, but I wanted his big dick in me. "Fuck me," I heard myself say. "Give it to me."

Steve obliged. He lubed my hole then slipped his rod into my chute, all in one long plunge, and then he held still, letting me set the pace. I repeatedly moved forward into Ryan, and then pulled out, impaling myself on the pole in my ass. The sensation was incredible. I knew I wouldn't be able to last very long. Ryan was moving his head back and forth, as though he was in some kind of trance, while at the same time he jerked on his reamer.

"Oh fuck," Ryan cried. "I'm coming. Shoot your load."

His asshole clamped down on my shaft, his legs stiffened, and his neck arched backwards as he climaxed. His thick cum covered his chest and neck. Steve turned my head and planted his lips on mine. My own orgasm soon followed Ryan's, brought on by the overwhelming stimulation. When I shot, I could feel Steve's dick pounding out his own load up my chute.

After we had discarded the safes and were lying back on the settee, I have to admit, I was a little scared at how Ryan was going to react, after all; I had fucked his ass. He seemed at ease though, so I hoped that it meant there was going to be a new phase to our relationship.

"I wonder how things are going with Chris," I couldn't help voicing. "He was so down when he left earlier."

"Oh, fuck," Ryan said. "Did you have to bring that up? I don't want to talk about it."

"The cops were asking all kinds of questions at work today," Steve said, ignoring Ryan's outburst. "It's as though they think someone from work did it to him."

"Those cops are so stupid. You don't really think they'll be able to catch the murderer do you?" Ryan asked.

"Oh come on, Ryan, they're not that stupid," Steve said.

"They were asking me if I saw him leaving with anyone, but I didn't see anything," Ryan said. "I was too anxious to get home to my sweetie. I was home by eleven-thirty. Isn't that right, Tyler? You remember me getting home then?"

"Sure, you woke me up when you got into bed and asked how come I was asleep already." In fact I had been mad at him for waking me.

"Maybe it's Brian," Ryan suggested.

"Brian?" Steve asked. "Why him?"

"I've seen them arguing at work. But then, I guess it could be anyone. Jason seemed to be at odds with everyone."

We lay like that for a short while, and then Steve said, "I don't know about you guys, but I'm pooped. I think I'll call it a day and hit the road."

After Steve left, we climbed into bed.

Ryan was still sleeping when I awoke the next morning. I was still a little apprehensive about the previous night, so I made sure not to disturb him when I climbed out of bed. The main reason I didn't want him awake was because I was going to see Chris, and I didn't want him to give me a rough time.

Later on, when Chris and I were sitting drinking coffee, Detective Jerry Mack dropped in to talk with Chris. "I'd really like to talk to you on your own, Chris," he said.

"It's okay, Tyler is my best friend, and I don't want him to leave."

"Tyler I have to ask you to keep this discussion confidential because we don't want this information to become public knowledge. It might hamper the investigation if it did."

"Sure, you have my word."

"Okay then. What I'm going to tell you is heavy, so maybe it's just as well that you stay. We think that Jason must have known the killer. It looks as though he let him in, and then when he turned around he was knocked unconscious. It looks as though he was sodomized while he was alive, and then he was repeatedly stabbed. He would probably have bled to death very quickly and wouldn't have felt anything. We also feel the killer knew him because of the vicious mutilations, which were all done post-mortem."

Chris let out a long wail then fell against me. I held him tightly as sobs shook his body. "Who would do such a terrible thing to him? He was so loving and kind, and he was always helping others," I said.

"How do you know he was raped?" Chris asked after a few moments.

"Well the person who raped him didn't use a condom. There was semen in his rectum, so we'll be able to get a DNA. As you know, Chris, there were three ampoules of Demerol found on your coffee table. We're still trying to find out where they came from. The trauma room drug count was correct last night and this morning, so we can't figure it out."

"Well it definitely wasn't Jason. He didn't do drugs. Whoever killed him must've brought the Demerol with them."

"But where would the Demerol come from?"

"Maybe someone did the old placebo thing," Chris volunteered.

"What's that?" Detective Mack asked.

"Staff on drugs have tried it before. When the doctor orders Demerol, they pocket the ampoule, and then inject sterile water into the patient. Of course, they can't do it all the time or they'd be found out."

I could see the light going on in the detective's eyes. "So that's how it's done. I'm glad I spoke to you. Maybe this will help. I better get back to work and spread the word."

They had given Chris the night off, so I stayed with him until five and then went home. There were three messages for me, one hand written, and two phone messages. The written message was from Ryan telling me that he had gone in to work. One of the telephone messages was from Ryan asking where the fuck I was, and the other was from Steve, asking me to call.

I decided not to call Ryan. I didn't feel like listening to him putting down Chris, but I did call Steve.

Steve answered on the first ring. "I'm glad you called. I need to talk to you urgently," he said. "Can we meet this afternoon? I don't want you to tell Ryan about this."

"I don't know, Steve. I'm not sure it's such a good idea."

"Please I have to talk to you. It's not what you think."

I thought for a while, and then said, "Okay, but it better not be here. I don't want Ryan to know. He can be real mean sometimes."

"Sure, I understand. Do you want to come over here?"

"No, I don't think so. Could we meet somewhere neutral?"

"How about Riverside Park?" Steve suggested.

"That sounds good. About six-thirty?"

"Yeah, that'll be fine." We arranged where in the park to meet, then Steve said, "See you there," and hung up.

I was sitting on a bench, watching a pair of Mallards, when Steve showed up. My heart gave an extra beat when I saw him. He looked even better than he had the night before. He took a seat next to me and kissed me on the cheek. My heart did a little flip. "I don't know where to start, Tyler, so I guess I better barrel right in. Do you remember last night?"

"I sure do," I interrupted. "It was great."

He smiled then continued. "It was, wasn't it? But that's not what I was going to say. Do you remember what Ryan said when we were talking about Jason? He said that he was home by eleven-thirty."

"Sure I remember. I told you he woke me up."

"Well that's not true, Tyler, I saw him in the parking lot at about eleven-forty when I was going home. He was with Jason, and they seemed to be having some kind of argument. If he hadn't made that statement, I wouldn't have given it a second thought. I've got a feeling he was somehow involved in Jason's death."

"You must be wrong. It couldn't have been him. He was at home."

"How do you know he was at home?" Steve asked.

"Well he was, because ... ." I couldn't finish because I knew I didn't really know. I hadn't looked at the clock. Ryan had woken me up and told me it was eleven-thirty. Had he been trying to establish an alibi?

"You're not sure are you?"

I shook my head, "No I'm not. But it's not possible. Ryan would never do anything like that. I've known him for two years. I would know if it was him."

"I've got a bad feeling about this, Tyler. What are we going to do?"

I thought for a while. Something was gnawing in the back of my mind. Something else had happened that didn't sit right. What was it? It had something to do with Ryan. Something he had said. Suddenly it came to me. "When the police interviewed you what did they tell you?"

"Not much. Only that Jason had been murdered. Why?"

"Did they say anything about drugs?"

"Drugs? Why would they say anything about drugs?" Steve asked.

I told him what the Detective had told me, and then I told him that Ryan knew about the drugs. Ryan could only have known about the drugs if he'd been at the scene of the murder.

"That's weird. I've had a funny feeling for a while about the sedation that I've prescribed. Some patients continued to have pain after their sedation. It always seemed to happen when Ryan was working with me."

"Oh, God. I can't believe this. Surely there must be some logical explanation. What about Brian?"

"I think that's a lot of hogwash. Jason was well liked by all the staff and patients. The only person I've ever seen him arguing with was Ryan."

"Oh shit, this is awful. What are we going to do?"

"I think we should talk to the police. We can't just ignore it," Steve said.

"But what if we're wrong? It would ruin him. I'm really scared, Steve. What if he does something to me?"

Steve put his arm around my shoulder, rubbed my neck, and kissed the top of my head. "I think you should go home and act as though everything is normal. Don't say anything. I'll speak to ... who did you say?"

"Detective Jerry Mack."

"You go home now and try to act normal. If you feel threatened in any way, just walk out of there and go to the police. Give me a call when you can."

"Before I go," I said, "I want to ask you something. It seemed as though you and Ryan were pretty familiar with each other last night. Had you slept with him before?"

"Yeah, I'm sorry. He's been over to my place quite a few times. That's how I knew he liked to get fucked."

I was nervous when I left Steve, but I was determined to find out if the two-timing asshole was guilty of murder. I knew that whatever happened, there was no way that I would be able to continue living with him. It would never be the same.

I made sure that I was in bed when Ryan got home. I didn't want to talk to him, scared that I would give myself away. I played dead when he climbed into bed, but when he started playing with my rear-end, I suddenly realized what I had to do. I pretended to respond to his advances, making sure he had a safe on, and then opened myself to him. I felt abused and hurt when he pounded into me, not seeming to care if I was enjoying myself. I was ready to scream when he finally climaxed in my chute.

When he pulled out, I rolled over and removed the safe. "I'll look after it," I volunteered.

"Thanks, sweetie," he said as he turned his back to me.

Asshole, I thought. *That's the last time you're getting into me.* I carefully carried the safe into the bathroom. I tied a knot in the safe, and then dropped it into an old pill bottle and put it in the refrigerator. I pulled a blanket out of the closet and then settled down on the sofa. It took a long time before I finally drifted off to sleep.

The next morning, I was out of the apartment by eight. I went straight to Central Police Headquarters and asked for Detective Mack. They said he would be in at nine, so I sat waiting and worrying.

When he came through the door, he looked at me in surprise. "Aren't you Chris's friend?"

I nodded. "I need to speak to you. It's urgent."

"Come on up to my office," he said.

I could hardly contain myself when we were eventually seated at his desk. "Did Steve talk with you yesterday?"

"You're the one," he said. "I didn't realize it was you when he told me about Ryan. You're actually his lover?"

"Yes ... you have a problem with that?"

"No not at all. I couldn't care less, I'm just surprised ... that's all."

"Good, because I've brought you a gift."

"A gift?" he said.

"Yeah," I said handing him the bottle, "I thought you might like to run a DNA test on this."

He looked in the bottle, and then opened his mouth in surprise. "What the ... it's a condom. Has it got Ryan's semen in it?"

"Yeah, a big load. Is it okay?"

"Sure. Thanks a lot. I'll get it tested right away. Where can I get in touch with you?"

"I'm not going back home. I think I'll move in with Chris for a while until things are settled."

"That sounds like a good idea. I'll be in touch as soon as I can, and don't say anything to Ryan. It could be dangerous."

I went home, and was packing a bag when Ryan awoke. "What're doing?" he asked.

"I've decided to spend a few days with Chris. He needs me."

"I don't want you to go. What about me? I need you, too."

"I don't care. He needs me, and I'm going."

I was scared that he would try and stop me, but he must have seen something in my eyes because he just let me go.

The next few days seemed to drag on endlessly. Ryan phoned a few times, but Chris always managed to convince him I wasn't home. Steve phoned every day, and we chatted for long periods. It was three days after I had seen Detective Mack when he showed up at the door.

"There's no easy way to say this," he began. "You and Steve were right, Tyler. The semen that you brought in proves without a doubt that Ryan was the killer."

"Oh, God, no," Chris wailed. "Why would he do such a thing?"

"We think that Jason must have seen Ryan stealing the drugs, and that he threatened Ryan with exposure. Ryan couldn't let that happen, so he killed him and then planted the Demerol in your apartment. As we speak, he is being arrested and charged with murder."

My mind was in a whirl. How could I have been so blind? He'd used and abused me all the time we were together, and yet I had still stayed with him and believed in him.

After Detective Mack left, Chris and I talked for a long time. I was scared that he would blame me, but he didn't. I phoned Steve and gave him the news. We had both been on edge since we had spoken to the police, but could now relax. Steve asked me if he could see me sometime, and I said yes, not realizing that love would flourish out of my despair.

The chiming of the mantel clock brought me back to the present. I placed the anniversary card on the table and carried the phone back to the bedroom. I was looking forward to the night, wondering what new and wonderful things Steve would have in store for me.

THE DAY JOHN IRVIN GOT MARRIED
By Ron Radle

Ron Radle has been published in a number of erotic anthologies in the past couple of years and is the author of two novels, *Two Sides of the Coin* and *Degrees of Passion*.

I cried.

Not at the ceremony itself. That would have made for a pretty picture, wouldn't it: a groomsman bursting into tears right along with the bride's maids and the bride's mother and the little old maid somewhere out in the church pews lamenting her own failed nuptials. No, but I cried a good bit before the actual wedding and afterwards because in actuality, I was more than one of John's groomsmen. I was, for several years, his lover.

We grew up together in the same small town in the upper middle portion of South Carolina, not all that far from Charlotte. Oh, it was years later before we ever bedded down with each other. In fact, the both of us were in college when that event first took place. But until then, we were as close a couple of boys could be and shared all the good and the bad associated with pre-adolescence and adolescence itself. All the scrapes and bumps of little league sports and tree house adventures, all the overblown heartache of teenybopper romance, all the irritation of school teachers whose incessant homework made it hard for us to practice those habits and pastimes we liked best: hunting, fishing, swimming, sports, going to the movies, listening to music, talking about girls. John grew up in the same town I did, but he was a little more country. That's because he spent a lot of time helping out his granddad on his farm in the rural part of the county. Me, I couldn't be bothered with the vicissitudes of farm life. I was too good for all that dirt and heat and stink of manure. As I became older, I turned into more of a, well, not a sissy exactly, but something close, I guess. Books interested me more along with good music and fine paintings and all the other preoccupations one would associate with an "intellectual."

John noticed this change in me and wasn't exactly comfortable with it. He was afraid I'd get all slack and flabby and sickly, that I'd become some kind of shut-in, a hermit, and such a lifestyle would limit my lifespan. He invited me out a lot to his granddad's place in York County to see how the "other half" lived. But I never did get the hang of country living and working, although it was fun watching John himself enjoy it. And, it was easy to see why he was so popular with girls. He had a head of wild, unkempt dark hair, which he usually kept hidden with a John Deere cap. Clichés can only do justice to those blue eyes: piercing, penetrating, and darkly crystalline. His smile was sexy-goofy, owing to the unevenness of a couple of his front teeth, a "problem" (not really, at least not to me) he would eventually remedy with the aid of braces. And his body. That cinched it. His arms and chest especially well-defined not only from weight-lifting but also from the outdoors work he did for his granddaddy. The weightlifting built the muscles; the farm work molded them and gave them a kind of natural definition you wouldn't find in a professional bodybuilder. Nice butt, too. Curved and firm. Women like nice butts. And they're not alone in that admiration. It was a special pleasure for me to watch John doing farm work shirtless, although I was careful never to let him see me watching him.

I dated, too, at least for the first couple of years of high school. But by the time I was a senior, it no longer interested me. I gave it up. I didn't even go to the senior prom. This worried John some, too. His last words to me after graduation were "I'm going to find somebody for you, buddy, if I have to raise hell and high water to do it."

Well, he didn't have to find anyone for me. I'd already found someone. John Irvin.

John left York County and went to school in the further eastern part of the state, not too far from Clemson University. He liked Clemson and wanted to go to school there, but he didn't have the grades. So he settled for a private religious school nearby. I went to a well-known university there in the county in the county's largest town and majored in English. John and I maintained a fairly close contact with each other those first few months of college, but then things between us grew distant. He became a connoisseur of the party life and let his grades drop. I wasn't a complete bookworm in college. I did have some fun. But I was no John Irvin, that's for sure.

We had a real reunion that summer after our first year in school. Again John went to work for his granddaddy in the fields. And I tagged along occasionally. John's body, on shirtless display for me, had grown even more beautiful, it seemed. He hadn't gotten the beer belly I thought might come from so much drinking. When I discreetly commented on his muscle tone, he said he had been making a lot of use of the school gym.

The summer wasn't all work though. We managed to take up our favorite pastimes together, one of them being fishing. John's granddaddy's property was bounded on the north side by a beautiful, clear lake that stretched more than a quarter of a mile and was, in the sunshine, as green as a muscadine grape skin. We took off early in the morning one day for the lake weighed down with our poles and bait and tackle boxes. We packed a little lunch, too, and John brought along something extra, a cooler of ice-cold beers. We sat all day long with poles in the water, going over old times – old for a pair of nineteen year olds, that is. After a while his talk consisted mainly of the girls he had met at school, the ones he wanted to bang and the couple he had. I tuned that out fairly quickly. It made me too jealous to hear of his sexual conquests, modest as they were. I was jealous, of course, of the girls. And before we knew it, the sun had slipped west in the sky and left the lake bank in semi-darkness. The lake itself had begun to turn black. Beside each of us lay about half a dozen empty beer bottles, and that buzz, along with the good, cool breeze off the water, gave John Irvin an inspiration.

"Let's go skinny dipping," he said to me, that uneven grin brighter than anything else around at the moment.

"What?" I asked. My heart raced fast. My stomach drew into a knot.

"We've never done it before. At least I haven't. Have you?"

I shook my head. Cautious me, all I could do was think of the danger of going into the water after having consumed so much beer. When I mentioned this to John, he sort of laughed and stood.

"That's your problem, bro. You play it too safe. You don't really live."

He walked off from me, shedding first his shirt, stepping out of his canvas sneakers, then shucking down his jeans and white jockey briefs at the same time. There stood revealed, in more than just my fantasies now, his perfectly shaped ass. It hovered in front of me just a moment like a pair of muscular moons. I swallowed hard at seeing it, my mouth going moist.

"John!" I hollered out, as much from desire as from concern for his safety.

The water splashed. "Get in here!" he called. "The water feels so good."

I stood and began to undress, wanting to but not wanting, confused almost to the point of tears and a little bit drunk, too, I suppose. But soon I was naked and heading for the water, heading for that dark circle John was making with the motions of his arms and legs. We would die, I was sure of it, but we would die together. I would die with the man I loved more than just about anything else in the world.

Except we didn't. We lived. We left the water together and dropped down into the grass, the full moon now riding our skin and making it bone-pale. We laughed at the insanity of what we'd just done and lay back in the grass to recount it. John did anyway. I spent my time eying his nudity, taking in as much as I could while I could before we got dressed. His thick hair was matted to his head. His ridged muscles were bejeweled by water droplets. His dick lay curled in the curve of his right thigh. It was hard then to gauge how big it was. And of course it was soft right then. But it didn't matter. It belonged to John Irvin. That was enough. I hurt with how much I wanted him right then, and I had to be careful that my desire didn't show too much in the most obvious place, so I lay kind of at an angle so my crotch was shielded.

We didn't say anything for a long time, and I don't know what happened, but I must have drifted off to sleep. Too much beer, too much thrashing in the water, too much general exhaustion. I wasn't sure if I was dreaming or not, but when I opened my eyes, I heard this regular noise beside me, this quiet and steady beat of something being rubbed, maybe sanded down. There was labored breathing, too. I looked to my right. John Irvin was there, eyes open, staring down at himself, his mouth slightly parted. I looked further. He had hold of his dick and was jacking it with a lot of concentration and determination. I made some kind of noise, involuntarily. John looked over at me.

"Hey, buddy," he said then looked back down at his prick. "You caught me." I tried to laugh but couldn't. "I don't know what it is, but I'm just about the horniest son of a bitch there is. You know? Just thinking about pussy so much. Licking it. Having my fingers in it. Putting my dick in it. I guess it's just part of being young. Are you like that, too?"

He looked back at me for an answer, but I was watching how his hand manipulated his meat. Just from a crude estimation, it looked like he packed a good seven inches, at least hard. I licked my lips and heard myself answer at last, "No, not really."

"No? Oh yeah. You're too busy studying and reading books and all to think about sex. Man, I don't know what I'm going to do with you. I've tried to be a good example to you!" He laughed and let his dick go. "Guess I best stop that for right now. I'm embarrassing you. I can take care of it later."

"No!" I yelled, almost desperately. "Please don't stop!"

He eyed me in the dark with concern. "You all right? Hey, what's the matter?"

No doubt the desperation sounded in my voice, the hurt, the want, the attempt to suppress all of it. And he saw the tears in my eyes, too.

"What's the matter?" he repeated.

And I came out with it, figuring all consequences be damned. I couldn't hold it in any longer. "I want you!"

"Hey!"

And that's when everything spilled out of me in one gush – the fact I was gay, of course, but also the torch I'd been carrying around for him for so long, not just sexually but emotionally, too. He was the finest, sweetest, most handsome man I'd ever known and ever expected to know. The fact couldn't be changed. Nothing could be helped. It was what it was.

Of course, I expected him to spit on me and curse me and dress and leave me for good, but he didn't. He sat on his elbow and stared down at me. Even in the growing dusk, I could see the confusion in his face, and all I could do was shrug.

He lay back down and stared up at the sky. "And it would make you feel better if you could suck my dick?" he asked finally.

My throat went dry, but I tried to answer anyway. "I don't know, John. Some, I guess."

"'Cause that's all I could give you. I couldn't love you. Not that way. Like a brother, yeah. Like a friend. But not like that."

"I know. That's why it hurts so."

After a few minutes his hand went back to his crotch and he picked up his limp dick and began to stroke it again. His eyes were closed. No doubt he was thinking about some girl he'd fucked or would like to. I watched his hand move up and down the length of his cock and felt my own prick stirring to life once more. He was shaking, his whole body; with his other hand he cupped his nuts then slid it slowly up his torso to one of his small, pointed nipples, which he rubbed. When a few minutes had lapsed, John looked at me and said, in a voice shaking from the pleasure he gave himself, "You better come get this before the lid pops off it."

I hesitated just a moment then slowly pushed down the grass on my elbow till I was parallel with his crotch. He let his dick go. It stood straight up in the air but threatened to drop to his belly until I grabbed hold of it and stroked it as he had done. But there had to be more contact than this. More than just a handjob. It had to be more intimate. It would be my only chance. So I pressed the prick to my face and ran it round my lips, letting my tongue out to taste the top, which was already salty with precum. I ran my tongue around the head slowly, flicking it at the front where the head was divided, and pressing my tongue into the piss slit. Then in one gulp, I had it in my whole mouth and was sucking away. I wasn't the most experienced cocksucker. Indeed John's made about the third dick I had ever had in my mouth, but what one lacks in experience he can make up for in sheer love, and I bounced my face up and down John's dick tirelessly, let him hit the back of my throat, somehow withstanding the gags such a motion gave me. My hand rotated at the base of his dick, and with my other hand, I played with and tickled his balls.

I could look up and see that John wasn't watching me. He had his head back and his eyes closed, and all of a sudden, he called out, "Oh that's so damn good, Elizabeth! Oh yes, Becky, keep sucking me just like that! Don't stop, Mallory. Oh that's right. Tickle my balls, Alicia." He was trying to remain straight while having a gay experience. The roll call of names almost made me laugh, but I was too intent on loving his dick to be distracted. At one point, I attempted to disturb this illusion. I let go of his prick and asked, "Is it good, John? Is it good?" He nodded quickly without looking at me, as though he didn't want to acknowledge the fact he was being blown by another man.

I brought him to climax with my hand, jerking as hard as I could. He never winced or cried out, so obviously he could take it. My middle finger in particular really rubbed hard against the underside of his dick head, and in just a few moments he did groan. He bucked his hips. He laid his hand over mine, and then came the explosion of cum, three hot gobs of it one after the other filling his hand and mine. Then the both of us slowed down and cooled down, and things came to a rest. He resumed natural breathing and looked at me, smiling.

"Did that help?"

I nodded wordlessly.

"I'm sorry, buddy, but I just can't do the same to you. It's just not in me, you know, to suck another dude's dick."

"It's all right, John. You've done enough. You've done more than enough."

"But I want you to get off, too. So play with yourself. I won't watch if you don't want me to."

"But I do! I want you to watch. I want you to talk me through it. Oh please, John, do that."

So while I stroked myself to climax, John said very dirty things, mainly about pussy and tits and all, but as long as he was part of it, as long as I could picture him fucking that pussy or sucking those tits, it helped move me along to orgasm. Of course what I really wanted to picture was him and me engaged in a naked embrace, both of us hot and hard and determined as hell to be rid of all our lust, jacking each other, kissing, sucking, fucking, doing our damnedest to exorcise the demon. Thinking that way turned on the burner in my balls. I could feel the cum climbing my dick. It reached the head. I cried out his name and fired the sperm into the air.

"That a boy!" John said beside me. "That's a champ!"

We didn't speak of the incident on our way home, and I was convinced beyond doubt that I had just lost my best friend. So it came as quite a surprise when John called me a few days later and invited me back to the lake. Of course I accepted the invitation, and that whole long, lazy day the coolish green air was charged with sexual electricity. We both knew, without expressing the fact in words that sex would occur between us again. And sure enough, as the sun sank behind the pine trees to our west, John jumped up from the grass and proposed a skinny dip in the water. I didn't protest this time. We undressed together and went together into the water. We splashed about and horsed around as any other pair of young men would do. But when we emerged back onto the bank and lay down (this time on towels; we brought towels), we knew we would cross the line from friendship into something else. John lay back. So did I. He coughed after a while. That was a signal. I cleared my throat and said, "May I, John? Please?"

He said nothing else but gestured vaguely to his crotch. I wasted no time getting down there or in taking his cock into my mouth and hardening it with my tireless sucking and licking. He was stiff as stone in no time. But I didn't want him to come just yet. I wanted to show him something else, just how far I'd go in my devotion to him.

"Turn over," I told him, taking his dick out of my mouth and catching my breath.

"What?" he asked. "Why?"

"Just do it," I answered, urging him onto his belly.

He complied reluctantly. His ass glowed in the growing dark. Its flesh was firm but pliant, almost spongy. I spread the cheeks.

"Hey, wait a minute, Ronnie!" John protested, but I kept him on his stomach. "I'm not into any anal shit. I let you blow me, okay ... What's that? What are you doing? Is that your ...? Oh my God! I've never had anybody do that before. It's nasty and hot at the same time. Fuck!"

My tongue gingerly probed the outskirts of his puckering pink asshole. Then I attempted to plunge my tongue into his ass as far as it would go. I ended up just sucking at the hole and licking it. At the same time, since John was lying partway on his side, I had hold of his hard dick and was jacking it like crazy. He let out a moan and soon filled my hand with his jism. I used it to get myself off.

There was one last trip to the lake that summer, and again we knew it would result in sex.

"I suppose," John said, naked from the water and drying off on his towel, "it would make you feel good if I fucked you."

A lump held in my throat. But I could still answer him. "Yes it would, John. Very much. I would love for you to fuck me."

We used no lube and no condoms. It was the first time I had been fucked, but I didn't tell him that. I didn't want to scare him off. I positioned myself on my hands and knees and offered my butt up to him. He pushed gently into me, but it still hurt like hell. It was agony, in fact, and I came this close to asking him to stop. It hurt like hell for several minutes until he established a regular rhythm inside me. Then it wasn't so bad. And before he was done, it felt good. He seemed to be bumping into my prostate with the head of his dick. He held my hips and rammed me. He breathed hard. Now and then whimpers of pleasure escaped him, while below, I bit my lip, hoping at the same time that it would end soon and that it would never end. But of course it did end. He gasped and pulled out of me and showered his semen all over my back and ass. Then with force he turned me over and did something he had not done up to that time: he laid his hand on my prick and got me off with about a dozen strong jerks.

It was the last such meeting between us. We didn't see much more of each other that summer. And when school began a month or later, we didn't see each other at all. John was a drifter by nature and extremely restless. He could not stay in one place for long. He ended up leaving the private Baptist school and attending several other universities in the area, all without much academic success. He was more interested in sports and women. (This analysis I got from John's mother, Betty.) I remained in college and got my degree in four years and began a career as a local newspaper journalist. I returned home. It wasn't the best place in the world, but it was one I knew and felt comfortable in. And that's pretty much how the intervening years passed.

Then came the phone call. John's voice called my name through the receiver with the same energy as he had done everything else. It was three years after our last time at the lake, when John had fucked me. It was something I thought about every day and jacked off to. And there had been no abatement of my love for him.

"What's up, buddy?" he asked me.

I was almost too astonished to answer, as I'd really come to think I'd never hear from him again. "I thought you'd dropped off the face of the earth," I said.

"Oh no, Ronnie. I'm still hanging in and hanging on. Just not quite the wild man I used to be."

"Is that right?"

"Yep. Someone has tamed me."

My mouth went dry, but still I said, "Oh yeah?"

"Yep. Pretty little girl named Jennifer." And without my prodding, he told me about Jennifer: how he'd met her at the last school he attended, Limestone in Gaffney, how she was a radiology major, how she had two children, a boy and a girl, from a previous marriage. All that. I heard the words but didn't process them very clearly. This was like a final blow, a final nail in the metaphorical coffin that was my love and hope for John Irvin, that somehow he'd see the light and come over to my side and let me love him the way he ought to be loved, by a man, with all the depth and fearlessness and ferocity one man brings to another in the act of love.

"And guess what? Now this is the part you're not going to believe."

"What's that?" I asked, not adding that I didn't believe any of it or didn't want to.

"We're getting married."

I let the statement stand without comment. Several moments lapsed.

"Ronnie, did you hear me? Jennifer and I are getting married."

"I did hear it, yes, John. Congratulations."

"Me! Getting married! It's the craziest damn thing!"

"You're right. Hard to believe."

"And of course, I want my best friend in the world to be a groomsman."

Again I left him a while in silence.

"Ronnie, did you hear me? I want you to be part of the ceremony. As a groomsman."

"Yes, I heard you, John. Of course I'll do it. Yes, I'll be happy to do it."

What else could I tell him? I couldn't turn him down. After all, he was the man I loved.

FOR THE LOVE OF MARRIAGE
By Aiden Lovely

Aiden Lovely resides in New Hampshire. Lovely is a freelance writer that has written many stories. Lovely's work has appeared in many anthologies.

"Never give up" was a slogan Storie once saw on a bumper sticker but somehow devoted his life to the meaning most of the time. When push came to shove, he would do anything to get what he wanted. A description like that made him seem like an impatient brat, but honestly his personality was much gentler. He wasn't in the business of wanting frivolous things like one night-stands or expensive status symbols; he already had the man he wanted, and he worked very hard to get him. But, he was on the brink of giving up on one matter. Marriage.

Storie sat in a small cushioned seat with his legs crossed at the ankles in a dim lit mom and pop pizzeria. The aroma from the brick oven, melted cheese and fresh sauce loomed before him as he rested his crossed arms on the table. He wasn't sure if he were just in a bad mood because of his situation or if it were because his boyfriend was late again.

His situation wasn't life-threatening but it sure felt that way; and he knew no matter how he considered his options, he was being selfish. Storie wanted to tie the knot now that gay marriage was recently legalized in New York, but his partner felt differently. His focus was interrupted when he heard the employee flirt on and on about droning things with nervous laughter after every word. He didn't have to glance over to know why, he just assumed it was that guy – also known as his boyfriend, but called "that guy" in his mind when he was upset. And just as he imagined that guy was sporting the same charming smile that captured so many hearts. It was that same beaming grin that made Storie fall in love with him, but at this moment, made Storie feel so possessive. Plopping down in the seat across from him was "that guy" looking as handsome as ever and smelling so expensive. That guy was Vincent. His looks were deceiving at times, and he was often referred to as poker-face. He always had that stern look when he stared at the disgruntled Storie.

"Try not to look so grim," he said.

"It's your fault." Storie didn't bother to lift his head when he spoke. To think it was that stern expression on Vincent's face that used to provoke a nervous shuddering in his chest long before he had the gumption to confess his feelings. They had been a couple for a little more than three years, so Storie kept the past to the past. This particular pizzeria held a lot of memories for the two, including their first date, so they made it a routine to dine here when time allowed.

Storie folded his slice in the middle of the greasy crust and pulled the hot cheese off with his teeth. In the sudden silence, he glanced at Vincent. He saw the exhaustion in Vincent's face – the deep set bags and the blank stare. They hadn't screwed in a while. As time pressed on, all those sporadic sexual adventures they participated in such as barebacking in the dark alley near their apartment or the dangerous road head Storie gave Vincent when they drove for long hours had all unconsciously came to a halt. What was going on? When he thought about it, Vincent had been working extremely hard to take care of all the finances. But what bothered him more than Vincent's refusal to marry was that they hadn't made love in so long that even just giving Vincent a quickie couldn't rekindle their passion.

The days were they would dine at fancy restaurants had died more than a year ago, and even with Vincent sitting across from him, Storie felt as if he were eating alone. Maybe this lifestyle was preventing Vincent from even considering marriage more than his own beliefs.

Vincent leaned back, his arms folded, "What? Is this about the marriage thing again? Look, I told you we don't need marriage to signify anything. Marriage is just ..."

"A senseless routine used to promote heterosexual gender roles in society blah blah blah," Storie quickly interrupted. His voice droned on and ended with a sigh.

"Ok. I understand. You're angry."

"No, Vince, you don't understand," Storie withdrew from the table and pulled his parka on with a huff. To think this was supposed to be their happy date. Where had their passion gone? Storie wanted to ask, but he imagined if he did, he'd get a sarcastic answer. The outside smelt of autumn and the chilly winds pulled at their clothes.

Suddenly, Vincent's deep voice broke the silence, "I don't want to argue."

Storie was quiet. It was something that they seemed to do too much of lately. He felt his phone vibrate in his pocket, but he ignored it since his boyfriend was next to him.

Storie remained quiet because he knew anything he said had the possibility of turning into an argument. He glanced at the vacant alley as if he remembered the exact spot where his bare body had lain on the pavement with an out of breath Vincent above him. Why did their relationship have to change? He didn't bother to bring up the memory because something like that could never happen again.

Their silence continued as they reached the entrance of the apartment. He hung his parka on the coat rack next to Vincent's and then sat in the nearest chair to slip his shoes off.

Vincent massaged Storie's shoulders, "I'm going to bed," he said and then softly kissed Storie's cheek.

It was true that he missed Vincent's touch, but there was so much more he wanted. He gazed into Vincent's eyes and placed one hand on Vincent's face.

127

"Vincent," he said even though he already had his boyfriend's full attention. Although this may not have been the right time, he couldn't resist his confronting feelings.

"It's been three years; don't you think it's time for a serious commitment?"

Before Vincent could respond, Storie pressed his lips against Vincent's and after a moment, he slowly pulled away.

"Vincent, I love you. I love you so much. When I'm in your arms, I feel safe – I want to spend the rest of my days with you. If you can't say the same for me, then let's stop playing this game."

"You're still babbling about marriage? I don't have to give you a ring to prove I love you. Marriage isn't just about an expensive ring."

"It's not about the ring; it's about belonging to you and having a ring is a symbol that I'm yours. Why can't you understand?"

"Look. Storie; it's been three years, and I've loved you all those years, but lately, I don't know what to think about you. Maybe you don't love me as much as you think you do."

He wrapped his arms around Vincent, "Vince, please."

Vincent pushed his arms off, "I'm too exhausted for this right now."

Storie didn't say anything more. He watched Vincent walk away.

He felt bad, but now that Vincent was out of sight, he listened to his voicemails once again. He felt too guilty listening to them while Vincent was near. He had three messages, and he knew who they were from. When the unfamiliar phone number showed on his screen earlier, he just had a feeling not to answer. He pressed the phone to his ear and heard the heavy voice. He recognized it instantly. He knew the calls wouldn't stop until he answered at least one of them. Each message was the same; all begging him to call, saying it was urgent, and they needed to catch up on things. It wouldn't have been so bad if catching up on things wasn't intended as a desperate attempt to rekindle something that was lost more than three years ago. He was hesitating, but after taking a deep breath, his finger gently tapped the call back on his phone.

"Hello? Storie?" the man answered within two rings. Storie was reluctant to speak. He held his breath, thinking he should just hang up, but he didn't want to do that either.

"Hi," Storie said in a small voice.

"I'm surprised you answered my messages. How are you?"

"Pierre. Why have you been calling me lately?" he asked. While it was true that he felt he shouldn't have called at all, his temptation to see this now known stranger again was guiding his actions.

"Like I said in my message, I'm back in New York. I wanted to see you again. Catch up on life. Please Storie, don't hang up."

"Life is good. I am happily in love with Vincent. I love Vincent," Storie said, "Goodbye."

"No. Please. Storie, I'm not trying to pull whatever you think I am. Just meet me tomorrow for coffee, nothing crazy, just coffee. You can bring Vincent, too."

Storie paused for a moment. As much as he was curious of how Pierre was doing, he felt he should also tell him to stop in person since that was the polite thing to do for a guy who made love to him for an entire year.

"Storie?"

"Ok. I have to go now." He instantly hung up. He didn't want to hear the words, "good night." It would only intensify the feelings swelling up in his chest. Not Pierre. Anyone, but Pierre. And about bringing Vincent along, Storie would never.

That offer had been a lie to calm his suspicion. It was best not to tell Vincent about his planned rendezvous with Pierre. The last thing Vincent needed was to be stressed out over something Storie caused.

The doors of the café opened with a faint jiggle from the golden bells tied to the handle. The soft jazz music put him in a somewhat drowsy like state. He looked for Pierre but had no trouble finding him. Pierre always shined compared to others. He was the young blond man in the navy blue sweater, little moose design in the corner and a tartan blue blend collar peeking out from around his neck. Even wearing leather moccasins, he still looked out of place in this setting.

"It's nice to see you again without Vincent," Pierre greeted.

Without Vincent, Storie muttered in his head, what was that implying?

He focused all his attention on the melting whipped cream decorated with cinnamon in his cup. While he dodged Pierre's attempt at the *faire la bise*, he knew there was more to this greeting than just wanting to catch up.

"So, I'm guessing Vincent doesn't know about this. Am I right?" Pierre said. It was trick questions like that, which made Storie want to bolt out the door. They both knew if Vincent would have known, he would've been in the sourest mood possible. After all, if it weren't for Pierre studying abroad in France, Storie and Pierre would still be a couple. Pierre was the ex-boyfriend with the regretful parting and the last person Storie wanted to see when he was enduring a droning lifestyle.

"Yeah, he knows. We tell each other everything," Storie said and took a sip.

"I know when you're lying. I've known you and Vincent since college. If Vincent knew, he wouldn't have let you come."

Storie didn't say anything. Pierre then pressed his hand against Storie's hand. Storie looked up at him, his body already trembling from the touch. He wanted to say don't touch me, get away from me – stop messing with my head, but all of those commands would just make Pierre seduce him more. He expected to never see Pierre again, so he hid all the feelings he had too early to move on to Vincent. But he loved Vincent with all his heart. The rekindling feelings must have been intensified because the relationship Vincent and he shared was no longer satisfying the yearning in his trousers.

"I would've married you by now." Pierre massaged Storie's hand, "Your skin is so soft."

"I should go now."

"No. Storie. Running away isn't going to solve this. I tried that myself and look at where it's got me, heartbroken and alone," he said and then pressed Storie's hand against his beating heart, "I feel the same way I did for you then that I do now."

He gave Storie's skin a light peck, "Just come back to me. He's not gonna marry you."

A look of terror and regret washed over Storie's face. When he pulled his hand away, the spot where Pierre had planted a kiss was a tinted red.

"I really have to go now."

"Will I see you again?"

He let the words fall off his ears. He stood up, pushed in his chair and walked out.

When he returned home, the sun was slowly fading out of the sky. He shut the door behind him and removed any guilty expression from his face. He didn't deny that seeing Pierre so hungry for him bothered him more than cursing himself for going in the first place. Pierre's words hurt him. Maybe it was because even he believed that Vincent wasn't going to marry him. While it remained true that he didn't have to marry to stay in a committed relationship and most people got married to flash their rings, but for Storie, it was different. It was just his way of feeling even more committed to his partner. Whether marriage would rekindle their relationship or not, he just wanted Vincent to consider his feelings.

Vincent sat with his tie undone and his dress socks showing on the couch. His face looked somewhat grim. His arms were folded as his growl of a voice startled Storie, "Where were you?"

"Oh." Storie pressed his hand on his chest, "Vince, you scared me."

"Where were you?" Vincent repeated, "It's not like you to just leave like that."

"Sorry, I went to get something to eat. I would've picked you up something, but I assumed you already ate," Storie didn't look at him when he spoke. He sat on the nearest chair and slipped out of his boat shoes.

"Oh. It's just not like you to disappear. Usually you call or leave a note."

"I was with Pierre," Storie blurted out, staring at the floor. He couldn't live with himself if he didn't tell Vincent. Besides, if Vincent would have found out without him confessing that would only push Vincent further away.

"Pierre?" After a pause, Vincent spoke in a cold tone, "Oh. Him. It's been a while."

"I'm sorry," Storie quickly said.

"What did he want?" Vincent's calm words poured out as his face twisted in disgust.

"Why won't you marry me?"

"Where did that come from?"

"It's just a question. Why won't you marry me? Is it because you're not serious about me? Am I not good enough for you?"

"What are you taking about? After three years together, you have to question how I feel?"

"Well, I don't know what you feel for me anymore. You haven't touched me in a while."

"Yes, I have."

"Not like you used to. When we were first together, we couldn't keep our hands off each other. Is it because I bore you now?"

"You're ridiculous," Vincent said and a sigh followed, "You're still going on with that marriage babble. I told you; we don't have to get married to be together."

"I know we don't have to but I want to. Why can't you understand?"

"No. Why can't you understand? You expect me to change for you, but you won't change for me."

"Vince, you're being ridiculous. You're beliefs are ridiculous." After Storie said that, Vincent walked off into the bedroom.

"You're a jerk." Storie shouted from the other room. He didn't believe his own words, but he said them anyway. Pierre would have married him as soon as same-sex marriage was legal. Did that mean Pierre loved him more or did Pierre just feel the same about a commitment? A few hours passed, and neither of them spoke.

Storie turned the faucet, and the hot water stopped flowing out. He submerged his body in the water until it made a meniscus around his neck. A relaxing bath was what he needed. He would have asked Vincent to join him as a form of apology, but Vincent was already sleeping. Just thinking about the way Pierre hands used to feel crawling up his skin made his penis beg to be touched. It was a long time ago, but his body remembered the way Pierre made him glow. Even if he fell in love with Pierre all over again, he could never give up Vincent. Time had diminished their attraction, but nothing could ever rid him of his love for Vincent. It was difficult because he once felt this way for Pierre as well. He stroked his penis underwater until he felt the muscle grow firm. He was masturbating more than ever with so much pent-up. As his penis became a fleshy red color, his phone rang. It wasn't smart to have the phone in the bathroom, but like most people he felt a strange insecurity if it weren't by his side. He saw the number and felt awkward answering while he was naked and wet.

"Hello?"

"Ah. Storie. I didn't think you would answer … I'm sorry about what I said earlier."

"I really have to go."

"I know it's late, but I couldn't stop kicking myself for what I said to you."

"I'm hanging up now."

"Please. Storie. Can we talk? I really need to tell you something. It's urgent. Meet me outside in ten minutes."

Storie was silent on the line. Urgent or not, it was none of his business. It was this rekindled attachment to Pierre that made him agree to it.

Storie waited outside in a fleece jacket with nothing but his bare chest underneath. He was going to make this quick. Pierre's blue Pontiac pulled up next to him.

"Hi," Storie greeted in a dry voice.

"Get in. It's too chilly to stand outside and talk."

Storie sat in the passenger seat, staring at him with pensive eyes.

"I'm just gonna come out and say this. I was supposed to tell you earlier." Pierre looked away, but Storie saw his strangely sad expression reflected on the window pane.

"Seeing you opened up a wound. I knew I shouldn't have, but I had to see you before I leave."

"Leave?"

"Yeah. I'm leaving for Paris next week. The next time my feet touch the streets of New York, I'll be a famous fashion designer."

Storie fell silent. Neither of them spoke for a moment, and then Storie said very quietly, staring at the dashboard, "Pierre ... I already said goodbye to you once before like this, so why are you doing this again to me? Out of the blue you come – just when I am in rut."

"I thought you would want to know. I didn't mean to hurt you back then."

Even Storie was surprised with the tears streaming down his cheeks. He was reliving their departure all over again. His voice was reduced to sobs. Pierre drove his face closer with half opened lips and pressed them on Storie's. Storie became paralyzed at the warm touch. A strong shuddering controlled his body. He didn't want to give in, but he was unconsciously succumbing to the dominating man. A small cry weaseled from between his lips as Pierre's tongue filled his mouth. He felt the warm soft muscle roll over his tongue. As Pierre's tongue lashed out, a thin trail of saliva crawled from the corner of Storie's mouth. A jolting feeling filled his body. He was shocked by his docile reaction.

"I love you," Pierre quickly said when their lips parted. A faint dizziness crowded Storie's mind. He wanted to push Pierre away. Pierre always had a way of seducing him that he couldn't resist. Pierre's tongue slid down his neck. His teeth bit the zipper and unfastened it until Storie's bare chest was revealed. The powerless Storie looked at him as the words fell from Pierre's mouth, "I'm not gonna stop until I devour every inch of you."

With that said, he planted tiny kisses all over Storie's neck, leaving the skin red wherever his lips had touched. The truth was he wanted Pierre's penis deep inside him. He wiggled his hips, embarrassed that Pierre aroused him so much with just his tongue. He flinched when Pierre's tongue caressed his sensitive buds that were a bright pink color. The warmness gathered on his skin and his nipples became so hard. He wanted to say stop, but even if he did, Pierre wouldn't. With Pierre's hand slipped into his pants, Storie attempted to gain control over himself. His member was throbbing for a release the more Pierre hand stroked it. He was going to lose himself further if this continued. His body was already drowning out any control.

"Pierre. We have to stop," he mumbled.

"You can tell Vincent, I forced you."

"No," Storie struggled to move. Pierre's mouth covered his collarbone in light red marks. Pierre's hard member brushed up against Storie's thigh. When Pierre pulled back to undress the struggling man, Storie's hand collided with the persistent Pierre's face. Storie's chest heaved up and down as all of his thin body was on display.

"I can't believe you."

"What about you? You want me," the irritated Pierre said as he regained his posture.

"I'm going now," he said. He pulled on the door handle. He violently flinched when he felt Pierre's hand touch his shoulder.

"I'm sorry. I went too far. I lost control," Pierre said. He then revealed a plane ticket from his jacket pocket, "A one way ticket to France. Take it," he shoved it into the puzzled Storie's hand, "think of it as my proposal."

Storie didn't feel right the next day. He kept running his fingers along the edges of the ticket. One way to France. A chance to revisit the past. But then there was, of course the love of his life, Vincent.

He wore a turtle neck sweater to hide any marks. Vincent sat on the bed with his arms folded and a sour gaze locked on him. He sat on the floor with his back pressed against the bed.

"I'm sorry," he said with this being the third time he apologized.

"You know, you we're very discreet about meeting with him last night," Vincent said.

"I didn't mean to be." Storie had told Vincent everything as soon as Vincent came home from work. There was no way he could keep this a secret, but he didn't say anything about the ticket.

"I'm sure you can imagine how I feel right now." Vincent's voice was cold. Storie didn't flinch when he felt the new warmth of Vincent's hand rest on his shoulder. Vincent pulled him closer by the arm, "The thought of his hands on you drives me crazy. I feel if I saw him now, I'd kill him."

"Vincent ..." Storie's words drowned out.

"The thought of you being with him makes me sick." Vincent's grip tightened. He was keeping up a good charade of remaining calm. He pressed his damp lips on Storie's and held him. His hot breath tickled Storie's skin. Goose-bumps sprang on Storie's body as their tongues wove together. He tasted coffee on Vincent's lips.

He then pulled away, but Vincent pulled him closer.

"Vincent ... wait," he said with his voice pouring out in chunks, "My phone is vibrating."

Storie pressed his phone to his ear, "Hello?"

"I have to see you again."

Judging by Storie's terrified facial expression, Vincent roared, "Hang up on him."

"I can't Vincent. Please."

Vincent grabbed the phone from Storie's hand. Pressing it to his ear, he said, "I forbid Storie to ever see you again. He's mine." Although Vincent couldn't forbid Storie from doing anything, he said it anyway.

"I won't let you influence his decision. I proposed to him last night."

Vincent dropped the phone. He looked at Storie, "Is this true? He proposed to you?"

Storie looked down, "It wasn't a traditional proposal." The words weaseled out of his mouth, "He asked me to go Paris with him, and I don't know what to do. I could let him go again, but then what will I have? A dying relationship. It's not your fault, but I can't live like this. You're always at work, and it can't be helped but I have needs, too."

"What the hell is wrong with you?" Vincent said as he shook Storie' shoulders.

"I don't know how you feel about me anymore," Storie said. He regained himself and picked up the phone. Indeed, he was confused but the sacrifice was just too great. He jumped at the spur of moment, "Pierre, can you come get me? I want to discuss things."

Vincent sat in disbelief. Storie stood up. He assumed Pierre was probably on his way already because that was how impatient Pierre was at times. A choice like this was something Storie had dealt with once before, but it hurt all the same. Pierre would've have married him already – something Vincent wouldn't do. He didn't look at Vincent. He didn't even close the door behind him.

The cold air of the outside had no feeling on his skin. He walked a little ways past the alley where he and Vincent had once made love. He didn't know what he wanted right now.

138

When the Pontiac pulled beside him, he felt a jolt of reality in his chest. Suddenly, nervousness rendered him paralyzed. He paused, hesitant to even touch the car door. Maybe it was because if he got into that car, he'd never see Vincent again.

Pierre stepped out of the car. He slipped his hand around Storie's waist and kissed him. The spot from where their lips touched tingled. He looked back, but Pierre grabbed his chin and directed his face toward him. This was it. He could find out what he missed out on a few years ago.

Before he could go any further with Pierre, he noticed Vincent storming down the sidewalk. He knew Vincent would come, but somewhere in his mind he was trying to prepare himself for what if Vincent didn't come.

"Let's go before he catches up. Don't let him persuade you. He's not gonna marry you. I will."

Storie snatched his hand away from Pierre, "No, I want to hear what Vincent has to say."

When Vincent reached Storie, he didn't bother to speak; instead he lashed out at Pierre, grabbing him by the cuff of his shirt and raising his fist. Storie grabbed Vincent by the waist and tried to pull him back, but Vincent's strength was far more powerful.

"Vincent, please. Stop," Storie said.

"I'm going to kill him."

"Hit me," Pierre instigated, "It won't change Storie's mind. He wants me."

"You know nothing about Storie," Vincent said. He usually could keep his cool even when pressed, but when things involved Storie, not even he could control himself. He roughly released Pierre with his fist still threatening the guy, and faced Storie, "I love you."

"Vincent ..." Storie said.

Vincent turned toward Pierre, "Storie belongs me. I'll screw him right in front of you as his punishment for even thinking about going to France with you."

"What?" Storie was almost horrified at the sudden words. Pierre was shocked, too. Before Storie could protest, Vincent had already pushed him on his back in the nearby alley. His body was limp from the surprise of it all.

When Vincent ripped off his clothes like a beast, he was no longer in disbelief. He lay with his legs spread apart, and his pale body was too warm to feel the coldness of the ground. Neither of them cared to see if Pierre was still watching. Storie imagined that Pierre probably hurried off in defeat. He couldn't think much when Vincent was capturing his mind, body and soul.

Vincent's sweaty body was above him. The first kiss was soft and sweet. His lips pressed against Storie's in a jab like motion, but once Storie's lips were half open, he shoved his blazing tongue inside. The muscles coiled, and his tongue tickled the roof of Storie's mouth. When he pulled away, a thin string of saliva broke and lay on his chin.

"It's been a while since I kissed you like this," he said in the lewdest way possible. Storie wanted to say anything, but when he attempted words, Vincent's tongue lashed out at his. Filling his mouth, he could only manage to let little moans escape through his breaths. Since Vincent was so close, the scent of his cologne and sweat was intensified.

Unconsciously, Storie's finger darted to Vincent's hard-on, still bulging through the denim. He wanted it badly and that was all the invitation Vincent needed. The noise of the zipper revived a strong happiness in Storie, drawing his lips to a smile. Just looking at his face from this view overwhelmed him with emotion. His swollen cock was an indication.

Vincent didn't hesitate. He pressed the tip of his stiff penis against Storie's anus. Storie was so tight; it was always like this, but right now seemed like he was tighter than usual. Storie cried out. He wiggled his hips in both pain and pleasure. And even though Vincent hadn't used his member on him yet, Storie already felt as if he were about to explode. Each inch crawled inside the shuddering Storie as he moaned. His body was squeezing the shaft so viciously that he heard Vincent groan as well, "Oh god ... you're so tight,"

Instead of hurling a complaint like "it's been so long since you screwed me," Storie struggled to breathe.

"Relax," Vincent's voice was a husky whisper. He began thrusting at a quick rhythm. Storie released a frenzy of short moans as his anus stretched to fully accommodate the thick rod. His hips bucked as Vincent's meat was buried deep inside him. His mounds of flesh scrapped back and forth on the ground as Vincent diligently thrust inside. Feeling the warmth of Vincent's lips pressed against his again created a kiss tenderer than any other they had shared in the past. As a wave of bittersweet pleasure flooded his body, even with Vincent's mouth on his, moans still struggled to escape. Vincent caressed Storie's body. Fingers excited him so easily.

His body rocked back and forth. He couldn't hold back any longer. A sweet fluid ran down his shaft and spilled on his thigh. When he managed to look at Vincent apologetically for releasing so soon, he noticed Vincent had no intention of stopping there. He was determined to make Storie come twice.

Beads of sweat ran down his forehead. He didn't bother to wipe them. The jagged noise of their friction echoed off the walls of the alley and the air seemed so hot. Storie bit his bottom lip. His fingers grappled at the ground until his hands clinched into fists. Vincent pushed in deeper, slamming his tool against the hot walls of Storie. All that remained exposed was Vincent's balls. The next climax was coming soon. Vincent's pace quickened. The intense pleasure made Storie feel so weak. He bucked his hips, loving the deep penetration. Vincent's penis twitched, and he gave one last thrust. Storie's cock was impatient. He already came, but his penis was begging for another release. Vincent jerked back, released a violent groan and flooded Storie's body with his milk. Simultaneously, Storie's juices gushed out, circling his navel. He breathed heavily, his chest bouncing up and down and his eyes closed. Vincent slouched over on him.

"I can't believe I screwed you outside."

"Yeah," Storie said. He forgot where he was for a little while.

"Pierre's gone."

"Oh," Storie said and then giggled a little.

"What are you giggling about?"

"You. I can't believe you screwed me in front of him. Jeez – Vincent, sometimes I really don't know who you are," Storie said with an exhausted smile. He then kissed his boyfriend and wrapped his limp arms loosely around Vincent's shoulders.

"Were you really going to go?" Vincent said.

"Huh?"

"You know, go with Pierre?"

Storie didn't say anything. He couldn't judge himself because at the time, he felt helpless. The two were silent for a moment.

"I don't have your ring yet, and I know this is a little sudden but ... will you marry me?"

"Vincent ..." the name spilled from between Storie's lips. He gazed into his soon to be husband's eyes and kissed him. It was a moment like this that made Storie fall in love with him again and again.

It was 10:00 am, which was a little too early for Storie, but today was different. He was happy in a bittersweet way. He was at the airport with the ticket to France in hand. The edges were slightly bent because he had been fidgeting with it as he waited. As planned, he spotted Pierre dressed in a trench coat and holding luggage.

"I didn't expect to see you here. You're not a morning person."

"Yeah I didn't expect to be here."

When the nervous chit-chat died, they found themselves just staring into each other eyes. Then Pierre interrupted, "I have to get going."

"Oh. Yeah. I just wanted to give you this."

He handed Pierre the ticket. Pierre hesitated at first but then accepted it.

"Maybe I could invite you to my wedding, some day. It'll be fun."

Pierre smiled at him. It was a fake smile, somewhat more provoking than the Mona Lisa.

"Goodbye, Storie," he said.

When Pierre quickly walked away, Storie remained standing there. He watched Pierre until he was out of sight. He looked down at the silver ring with the small white diamond in the center on his finger. He exited with a sharp breath. As he stepped toward the car, he heard Vincent from the window, "Hurry up, it's going to rain soon."

"I'm coming."

Storie looked up at the sky and said quietly to himself, "Goodbye Pierre and thank you for rekindling us." He then smiled and ran toward the man with whom he was going to spend the rest of his days.

DAVID V. GOLIATH
By Fox Lee

Fox Lee is a writer of gay erotica and horror (as Natalie L. Sin). In addition to writing, she enjoys way too much coffee and is the proud owner of a "pushorkie." Visit her at: www.facebook.com/natalie.sin.39

My cellphone rang on the way to the bar. I answered, knowing it would be Bryan, one of my best friends and the man behind that night's blind date. My romantic life was in a dry spell, and according to Bryan, if I didn't go on a date soon I would forget how. I told him he was an asshole, and stole a bottle of his Jack Daniels.

"Hello, Bryan," I said. "Are you checking up on me?"

"Yes. Are you on your way?"

"Yes. Did you tell him to keep an eye out for a guy that looks like he just got back from a rock concert?"

"Yes, because heaven forbid you dress up for a date."

"It's a clean shirt."

"David, you make a very good living. Do you think you could maybe put on a polo shirt once in a while?"

"No. Anything else?"

"Do you even own a tie?"

"I mean do I need to know anything else for this date?"

"Well ..."

I stopped in my tracks. I knew all along Bryan was holding something back, and I wanted to know what it was before I stepped into the bar and inflicted my reaction on some poor guy who didn't know what was coming.

"I'm going to find out in less than five minutes," I said. "You might was well tell me."

"Billy isn't exactly your type. Physically."

"Jesus Christ, did you set me up with a bear?"

He snorted. "You think I would waste a bear on you?"

"You can't fuck them all, Bryan."

"I can try. And he's not a bear. I met him in a chatroom for Rockabilly fans, back in college."

I could handle a rockabilly. My heart belonged to eighties' rock, but I had a healthy respect for its ancestors. But music taste wasn't physical, so I pressed on Bryan harder.

"Send me a picture. Now."

"Fine. Hold on."

Thank goodness for smart phones, I thought. Even if Bryan didn't have a picture of the guy, he could grab one from online and send it.

"There, Bryan said. "It's on its way."

The picture arrived, and I groaned my disapproval into the phone. Billy was my age, tall and fit with broad shoulders.

"He's taller than me," I said.

"Oh boo fucking hoo. Poor baby doesn't get to date a delicate little flower."

"They aren't delicate little flowers."

Bryan and I had the opposite taste in men. He liked bears, the hairier the better, while I stuck to Asians like myself. I liked them slender and boyish, unlike myself, and preferably a little younger. Bryan said it made me a dirty old man, I argued that you can't be a dirty old man in your thirties.

"You owe me for this," I said as I neared the bar. "Big time."

"Be nice. Billy is a really good guy."

"That doesn't mean I'm going to suck his dick."

I hung up on Bryan, and tucked the phone into my pocket after switching it to vibrate. Bad date or not, I believed in being a gentleman. The alpha male, if you will. The latter of which being a bit difficult when you were dating a Japanese giant.

It was worse in person. Even before he stood up, I could tell Billy was at least six and a half feet tall. He looked down at me, his eyes focused more on my belt than my face. I thought he was sizing me up, until I saw that his ears were bright red. He was nervous, more than I had ever seen someone before. The ears led me to the hair, which was styled like a nineteen-fifties greaser. I added "Fonzie" to the Japanese giant title, and took a seat next to him at the bar.

"So you're David," he said.

"Yes." I signaled the bartender, and ordered a whiskey neat. Billy had a beer, which he toyed with while he spoke.

"I've really been looking forward to meeting you," he said.

He still wouldn't look at me. He would look at parts of me, at nearby objects on the bar, but never at me. I felt a twinge and cautioned my heart to watch itself. I didn't care how goofy he was, I wasn't dating Japanese Fonzie Giant. My whiskey came, placed absent-mindedly by the bartender to my far left, and I brushed Billy's hand when I reached for it. His beer bottle shot across the bar, fell on its side, and rolled onto the floor where it crashed on the bartender's side. Billy stared at it, wide eyed, then at me. The bartender came over, his eyes shooting daggers between us.

"My bad," I told him. "I have a nervous tic."

"Be more careful," the guy snapped.

He stomped off to get a broom and dustpan, and I gave him the finger as soon as his back was turned.

147

"Let's go sit at a table, so I don't have look at that asshole." I put my arm around Billy's waist, and led him to a booth by the window. "I'll tell the hostess where we are and get some menus."

I had slipped into the role of "guy in charge," something that delighted, then eventually pissed off, nearly every guy I ever dated. I believed people were equal in a relationship, but for me it was like dancing. More often than not, someone had to lead.

"You didn't have to cover for me," Billy said, when I came back.

"He would have bitched at you."

"No one ever bitches at you?"

"Not for long."

We looked over the menus in silence and ordered without exchanging notes on what we would get to eat like people normally do on a date. After the waitress left, I prayed Billy would say something, anything, to keep the date from circling any further down the drain.

"Have you ever been to Japan?" He asked. "I was born there, in Tokyo, it's a great place to visit."

My body sagged in relief. "I've been all over Japan, Tokyo's my favorite, especially Shibuya."

Billy grinned, the first genuine smile I had seen on him. "Do you know any Japanese?"

I grinned back and told him to show me his dick, in perfect Tokyo-style Japanese. Billy's arm jerked, and his glass met its untimely end on the restaurant floor.

"I'm sorry," he said to the waitress who ran over. "I'm so sorry!"

"It's OK, sweety," She patted him on the arm like he was a little kid. "Do you want me to bring you another?"

"Yes, please."

I was mortified. Not at him, but at myself.

"I'm sorry," I said. "I didn't really mean what I said, I was just showing off."

"It's OK. It's just a little surprising when you hear it in your own language. I'm not a prude or anything."

"I believe you."

"How do you know Japanese so well?"

I usually explained my ability with one sentence, I have a Japanese stepmother, but Billy looked so lost, and somehow small, on his side of the booth that I went with the long version.

"Once upon a time my dad got his girlfriend pregnant," I said. "He was happy, she was not. They had to get married, at least that's what her family said, which they did. She had the baby six months later, and disappeared a few days after that. My dad got over her, what he couldn't get over was the thought of me growing up without a mother." I drank my whiskey, and let the beginning of the story settle in Billy's head. He nodded, and I went on. "Meanwhile, in Japan, there was a woman who got really sick as a teenager. She got better, but the doctors told her she would never be able to have children. One day, she met a guy from Thailand who was in Japan on business. He flirted with her, badly, but she agreed to go out to dinner with him because he had the kindest eyes she had ever seen. That's the part of the story where I throw up a little."

"It's sweet," Billy said. "And they got married?"

"That same year. I was still young, so she's the only mother I ever had. She never thought of me as a stepson, and made sure I knew the 'other side' of my family. Which meant Japanese language lessons and yearly trips to her home city. And that is how I can say filthy things to people in Japanese."

"That's what I always wanted. A really memorable love story, I mean." Billy said.

"No luck yet?"

"I've only had one serious relationship, and they wouldn't exactly make a movie out of it."

"You've only dated one guy?"

I blurted it out without thinking. Billy looked down and shrugged.

"I've dated other guys, but nothing stuck. My ex said that dating me was like bait and switch."

The food arrived, sparing Billy from the indignity of having to elaborate. I steered the conversation back to Japan, and Japanese food, then to music. Billy seemed content for me to take the lead, and brightened up over the course of the meal. By the time I asked for the check, I felt sure that no more glass would shatter that evening. I walked him to his car, intent on saying goodbye for the first and last time. I hugged him, gave him the "glad we met" pat on the back and stepped away. Billy looked deflated, which made me feel like a piece of shit. I told myself it was weird that he was that invested after one dinner, and I had nothing to feel guilty about.

"Can I ask you a question?" He asked. "Is it really that big a deal, the way I look?"

My inside's froze, and my mouth filled with cotton. I made a mental note to kill Bryan, when I got a chance.

"It's OK," Billy said. "You like what you like. I just hoped that if we met, I could get you to make an exception. Two years wasted, huh?"

The cotton melted, and slid down my throat. I took a step closer. "Two years?"

"Fuck," Billy sighed. "Can you pretend you didn't hear that?"

"Not really," I said. "Let's take a drive."

I nodded toward the driver's side, and got into the passenger's.

"Where am I going?" Billy asked.

"You're dropping me off at my apartment. On the way, you can explain what you meant by two years."

Billy left the parking lot, and I told him which turn to take to get to my place.

"You can start now," I said.

"Bryan keeps a picture of the two of you in his apartment, he keeps pictures of lots of his friends, but you were the one I noticed. I asked him to introduce me, but he said it wasn't a good idea. It took two years to get him to feel sorry enough for me to set us up."

"Why didn't you just contact me yourself? Look up my number on his phone, or find out my email address?"

"I couldn't. I'm not good at that."

"You can annoy Bryan for two years, but you can't call me on the phone?"

"I can't make the first move. It's too scary. I know that must make me sound like a loser, but that's just the way I am."

I wanted to mount him. I wanted to pull his pants down around his ankles, twist him backwards on the seat, and make him scream my name. The problem was that he was still driving, and my condoms were back in the apartment. As soon as he got to my building and parked, I snatched the keys out of the ignition and beckoned him to follow me.

I managed to wait until we were in the elevator to push him against the wall and shove my tongue down his throat. Billy whimpered, an honest to god helpless whimper, and hung on to me like he was afraid the bottom was going to drop out of the elevator. My hand went down the front of his pants, where it was greeted by at least seven rock hard inches. I unwrapped them inside my apartment, putting aside giving Billy the grand tour for later. He fell backwards onto my couch, his knees spread wide and his ankles bound together by his jeans and underwear. I took my shirt off, and tossed it to the side.

"Tell me when you're going to come," I said. "I want to watch."

"What changed?" He asked. "I don't want to look a gift horse in the mouse or anything, but ..."

Instead of answering, I sucked his cock into my mouth and flicked it with the tip of my tongue. Billy whimpered again, entirely at my mercy, and suddenly I didn't give two shits how broad his shoulders were. I tugged his balls, lightly, and bobbed on his thick shaft. He stroked my hair and panted my name. As the spaces between "Davids" decreased, he yelled that he was coming, and I let his cock pop out of my mouth and aimed it at my chest. When he was done and opened his eyes, there was a river running down my stomach toward my own throbbing organ.

"Come here, baby," I said. "Clean up your mess."

Billy dropped to his knees and bent me backwards over the coffee table. His tongue started above my navel, and worked its way up slowly, savoring every drop. He lingered on my nipples, sucking and biting until there were tiny sharp peaks aching for more.

"Get in bed," I told him. "On your hands and knees."

"Do you want the rest of my clothes off?"

"God, yes!"

I waited for him to undress, before taking my own clothes off and getting the condoms and lube. I crawled up on the bed behind him, where I took time to appreciate the view. Billy's ass was virtually hairless, and rounded in a way that begged to be fucked. I lubed up a finger, and teased his hole. Billy sucked in his breath, then groaned as I kissed the base of his spine.

"You like that?" I asked. "You want to be finger fucked?"

"Yes." Billy pressed the side of his face into the pillow. "So much."

I slipped one finger into him, then two. Billy took them easily, and his insides wrapped my thrusting digits like a glove. I slapped his ass, and told him to fuck back. Billy did as he was told, moving his hips in time with my fingers until his cock was swollen and red.

"All right," I said. "Let's see how much dick it takes to get a big boy like you off."

I took him in a single thrust, making sure to lube my dick well first. I pulled out just as fast, stopped at the tip and went into him again. Rinse and repeat I said to myself, as I took Billy's ass like a jackhammer. I was capable of more nuance, even tenderness, but at that moment all I wanted to do was make him come hard enough to make up for two years of waiting. My balls bitch-slapped him with every stroke, to which Billy said thank you, over and over again.

"It's so good," he moaned. "Your cock is so good."

"What?" I asked. "First time taking it from behind?"

"Yes," he said. "Don't stop."

I could't believe it, how could anyone look at an ass like that and not want their dick in it?

"Come on Billy," I said. "Show Davy boy how hard you can come."

One more slap, and Billy shot his load across my mattress. I came a few seconds later. By then his body was so sweaty my hands almost slipped when I grabbed his hips to drive myself in deeper. After I spent my load, I saw spots, and slumped out of Billy and onto my side. I closed my eyes, for just a second, and woke up an hour later. Billy had a towel down on his side of the bed; he was fast asleep and facing toward the window. I got up, and went to find my cell phone.

"Hey Bryan. I can't come for lunch tomorrow, I have plans."

"What plans?"

"Fuck you, what plans. I just called to let you know, I have to get back to bed."

"In bed already, that was a great date." Bryan sighed. "Look, were you at least nice to him?"

"Ask him yourself, you stuffy old lady."

I hung up, happy with the knowledge that my parting comment would piss Bryan off to no end. When I got back in bed, Billy woke up, and looked at me with bleary eyes.

"Do you want me to get going?" He asked.

"No, I want you to stay here."

He turned into me, and I put my arms around him. He smelled good, and I liked how warm and solid his body was inside my embrace.

"Was it OK?" He asked. "Being with someone like me?"

"Tall?"

"I'm not the big man in bed. They always expect me to be."

"Just because you're over six feet tall, doesn't mean I expect you to throw me over your shoulder and have your way with me. In fact, that would kind of be a deal breaker."

"Is that why you date little guys?"

"If you think size has anything to do with how passive someone is, I have a few exes you can meet. One of them cursed me out for wanting to pay for too many dates. He said if I felt that way about dating, I should stick to women. I date skinny guys because they're fucking hot as hell."

"So I'm not a deal breaker?"

"You're hot as hell." I rested my forehead against his, and looked into his eyes. "You want to hear another story?"

"Can I hear the one about your mother and father again?"

"I want to tell you a different one." I swallowed hard. I could feel my heart punching my chest. "I'm going to tell you about how I met the man I'm going to marry."

# # # # #

"You aren't wearing a tie." Bryan frowned.

"Neither is your date," I said.

"He's not a groom!"

"Are you ever happy?" I asked. "Can't you just go be smug about the fact that you played matchmaker?"

"You look like you're going to a funeral."

"And Billy looks like he's going to try and call James Dean back from the grave."

Bryan shook his head and led me out to the front of the temple, where a Buddhist priest was waiting to marry me and Billy in a Eastern/Western fusion ceremony. It was our way of making sure everyone we invited felt included, instead of being forced to attend a "cultural experience."

"I called the catering company," Bryan whispered. "They still won't switch to plastic glasses."

I wanted to complain, but instead, I started laughing, harder and harder, until I saw Billy come down the aisle. That shut me up, and I had to lock my knees to keep from hitting the ground. I relaxed them, as he got closer, and ran to meet him halfway.

"David!" Bryan yelled. "Get back here, you kiss him after the ceremony! After!"

I ignored him. When we pulled apart, Billy smiled at me.

"You showed up."

"Cute," I said. "Hold onto my hand. Don't let go until it's over."

Billy's smile faltered. "Are you scared?"

"Yes," I said, too low for anyone but him to hear. "Not of marrying you, I don't know what the fuck I'm scared of; just hold my hand and tell me one thing."

Billy grabbed my hand and squeezed. "What?"

"Are you sure you can put up with me for the rest of your life?"

"Don't worry. Bryan tried to convince me you were a terrible idea when I first asked to meet you."

"And you really want to marry me?"

Billy kissed me, and I had to lock my knees again.

"Yes," he said. "Now lead the way."

THE KEEP
By Jay Starre

Residing on English Bay in Vancouver, Canada, Jay Starre has pumped out steamy gay fiction for dozens of anthologies and has written two gay erotic novels. Contact Jay Starre on Facebook.

The day was warm but a breeze off the ocean wafted up to the high tower on the eastern wall of the Keep to soothe and cool him. Ricardo tenderly bathed the unconscious young man's beautiful face with a wet cloth. As he gazed down at the closed eyes he wondered when they would open again – or if they would open again.

He recalled the beauty of those eyes, even when glazed in delirium. It had been only the previous morning when he had looked into them for the first time. They were blue, but with a lovely ring of gold around the pupil that was quite entrancing. At the gate to his Keep, the youth had fallen into his arms, babbling desperately in a foreign tongue that he recognized as some odd dialect of the English language.

He had collapsed, then still staring up into Ricardo's eyes with a desperate but hopeful plea, had slipped into unconsciousness. He was still in that condition now.

Ricardo had insisted on carrying him up the stairs to this quiet tower room rather than leave the duty to his servants. He had insisted on watching over the youth as well, even changing him out of his disheveled and sweat-soaked clothing and bathing him.

Slender, but with the supple muscle of an active person, the youth was quite tanned over most of his body except for the area from his slim waist down to his lower thigh just above the knee. It was a little unusual, as if he'd been laboring outdoors with only a pair of knee-length breeches to protect himself from the bright Sicilian sun. A fisherman? A dock laborer?

Whatever might be his profession or station, he had been dressed in simple trousers, tunic and boots with neither cap nor cape nor purse. No weapon either. It was certainly a mystery.

His guards and servants had been horrified when he decided to tend to the stranger personally rather than leave it to them. Abdul, the Castellan of the Keep and his Master-at-Arms, had been adamant. "You are a Duke! This is beneath you!"

He had to laugh at that. At the tender age of twenty, a Duke he may be, but he had no Dukedom to speak of. His Uncle inhabited the family Castle in the north near the capital Palermo while he languished here at this dismal and isolated Keep on the southeast coast. For his own safety, supposedly, but for all intents and purposes a prisoner.

Politics. He was not much good at them yet. If he was to survive, he knew he would have to get better. But for now, he had this handsome young man to think of.

A dimple in his chin cried out for a light kiss. The cheeks were unshaven and a very light beard of soft ginger graced the narrow profile. His nose was not much, especially when compared to a great Italian one like his own. The eyes – ah how he wished to see them open again!

He rose quickly, suddenly wishing to escape the desperate longing welling up in his breast. He strode to the open window and placed his hands on the smooth stone sill and gripped tightly, thus able to still their trembling. The view out the window was calming. Far below, a stretch of white sand gleamed under a spring sun. The azure Mediterranean waters lapped gently at the strand. He turned his gaze to the south where he looked down upon one of the Keep's courtyards. A trio of tall palms swayed in the light breeze. A small fountain splashed. Beyond that walled yard, the southern wall of the Keep fell to meet the slope below.

Grape vines marched in tidy rows downward to the plain at the foot of the walled retreat.

He assessed his emotions, something he had been taught to do by one of his tutors, the Byzantine monk Dimitri. What upset him so about the languishing stranger behind him? The lovely youth was pitiable, of course, and that did distress him. He hoped for his recovery, as he would for anyone in that sad state. But, he hoped more than a little, much more. The young man's beauty was certainly a factor in this powerful hope Ricardo entertained, but there was more. Somehow, he felt a kinship with the man. A kinship that was as powerful as what he would feel for a family member. Even more than that. Even more.

And he must admit to himself a greater truth. He felt himself to be in the same situation as this helpless youth. He was not quite awake, not engaged in his life as a vigorous youth should be. He was somehow dreaming, much as the red-headed young man behind him must now be doing.

With a sigh, he turned and made his way back to the slumbering stranger. He sat again at his side and took up the wet cloth to bathe his sweat-soaked brow. So sad!

Then, spontaneously but quite naturally, he bent and kissed the dimple in that smooth chin. He blushed at the powerfully sensual delight he experienced from the simple gesture. Vividly, he recalled the youth's throbbing erection earlier that morning when he had been bathed. His own cock rose to the occasion, increasing the blush on his smooth amber cheeks.

"Where am I?"

Ricardo shot upright. He spoke! And in Italian!

"You are at the Keep of the Palm and the Vine. I am Duke Ricardo di Genoista, at your service. You have been gravely ill. How do you feel?"

He had attempted to speak clearly and slowly, regardless of the fact his pulse raced and his face remained crimson.

"I feel ... all right. A little tired, stiff perhaps. May I ask, what is the date? And who did you say you were?"

The youth rose without aid to a sitting position. Ricardo was glad to see that. He smiled encouragingly and spoke again as clearly as possible. "It is the fifth day of April in the year of Our Lord 1130. I am the Duke Ricardo di Genoista of Palermo. You are my guest, although I hadn't thought to invite you. Do you not recall arriving here two days ago? You were delirious. And may I ask your name?"

"I am Matthew ... Matthew Brock. I don't recall arriving here. I don't recall ... much of anything. That is strange."

The look on his face was pitiable. Confused, frightened, then eager as he gazed directly into Ricardo's eyes in an obvious plea for answers.

"I'm afraid I cannot tell you anything. You arrived on foot, with no horse, no companions, and with merely the clothes on your back. Are you a Norman? You certainly have the look of one."

"A Norman? I'm not sure what you mean. This is very odd. I can't recall anything. Nothing. Except ... you look familiar. And your voice ... it seems I've heard it before."

Ricardo's blush of embarrassment returned. He had spoken to the youth while he tended to him, imagining it might somehow help him recover. Perhaps he had heard!

"Well. You must rest some more. Your memory will return once you have recovered more fully. May I offer you some watered wine? Perhaps something to eat?"

A smile flickered across the freckled countenance briefly. It was a quirky and engaging smile, with the left corner of the pink lip curled higher than other. It did not last more than a moment.

"A Duke serves me? Isn't that unusual? But yes, I am thirsty! And hungry, I believe. I would also like to get up and walk around a bit. Test my legs, if I may."

He was very polite. Ricardo helped him to his feet and kept an arm around his waist as he took a few steps toward the nearby window. "I think I'm fine. You don't need to hold me up, Your Majesty."

That quirky grin returned briefly as they exchanged a quick glance and then both burst out laughing.

"You may call me Ricardo, although Your Majesty does have a nice ring to it."

They had reached the window. Matthew was leaning over the sill and peering at the view with great interest. "Where is this Keep? It looks tropical, or Mediterranean."

"We are on the island of Sicily. That is indeed the Mediterranean Sea below. You don't recall coming to Sicily? Or perhaps living here somewhere nearby?"

The young red-head gazed out at the sandy shore below quietly. A puzzled expression gave way to one of resignation. "No, I don't recall where I've been before waking just now." He turned away from the view and faced Ricardo. "The only thing that seems familiar is you."

The Duke blushed again, a common fault his uncle had reprimanded him for many a time. "Well, let's hope it's a pleasant familiarity."

"Yes, definitely." The grin flashed then disappeared.

The baggy wool robe he wore hid his body from neck to ankle, but Ricardo recalled with sudden clarity the slim form beneath, which he had bathed only a few hours earlier. His cock rose beneath his trousers and throbbed. What was the matter with him? He was obsessed! Or bewitched!

"I have some duties to attend to, Matthew. If you are able, please come down for supper later. Will you be all right for the time being?"

"Yes, to supper and to being all right. I am pretty hungry, and I feel pretty good. I'll just take turns resting and walking about the room until supper. Thank you for your kindness, Your Dukeness."

He smiled and attempted a bow. They both laughed again and on that note, Ricardo left, still chuckling.

That first evening at supper, Ricardo dressed for the occasion. He wasn't entirely sure why since he hadn't been doing so as a habit. They had few guests, all of whom were hand-picked by his uncle. His presence at the Keep was a closely guarded secret.

He wore a long robe belted at the waist, of deep brown brocade and heavy enough to fend off the cold of the early spring evenings. It was a robe favored at the Court of their King Roger II who himself preferred many of the Moorish customs of his predecessors.

A thick chain mail necklace of woven gold and silver surrounded his neck and fell to his breast. He was bare-headed, and his thick raven hair fell in waves to hover just below his ears. The gold around his neck set off the golden sheen in his lovely eyes.

Matthew arrived in a robe provided out of Ricardo's own closet. Although the two were very different in build, Matthew lean and almost slight while Ricardo was husky and broad, they were of equal height. The Duke's gown fit his mysterious guest well enough. It was of soft green and trimmed with a rich crimson. Matthew's hair was free and although washed and brushed, fell in a tangle of small curls about the top of his head in a reddish-brown tousle. It had been cut short against his scalp around his ears and the back of his head, which was quite unusual.

The table was set simply with their everyday plate and utensils. Ricardo cared little for expensive or showy things. The food though was quite the opposite. His family was very wealthy and could afford the best of fare. He liked to eat and in this was not stingy.

Roasted fowl and rabbit, caught by either his men or himself, accompanied succulent pork and beef cuts. Dried fruits cooked in local honey and baked breads redolent of herbs joined early spring salads from nearby peasants' gardens. He paid them well for their trouble.

Wine from the Keep's own cellars was mixed with cool water from the Keep's spring.

A dozen candles flickered brightly on the heavy oak table while a fire crackled in the stone hearth beside it. Only Ricardo and Matthew dined. Everyone else at the Keep was considered a servant and thus delegated to the kitchen for their meals.

"Do you eat alone usually? That must be a little boring, I'd think."

"Ah, yes. Boring it would be if I didn't have many good books to entertain myself with. I usually read at supper."

"Not tonight, though?"

"You may entertain me, if you wish."

"How? Would you have me dance? Or sing? Or perhaps play the lyre?"

Spontaneously, the red-head stepped away from the table and took up the lyre that leaned against the stones on the left of the hearth. He had no idea why he did it, other than perhaps because of the flush of exhilaration he felt merely upon finding himself alive and well enough to walk about and relish the thought of a meal.

He sat, a wan smile on his face, propped the instrument on his knee then began to strum it with the bow. After a few awkward notes, a melody emerged. Lively and quite strange, too.

"I have never heard the like," Ricardo admitted with a grin.

"I have no idea where I learned to play, nor where I've heard this song. But I like it. Does it stink?"

Ricardo threw back his head and laughed out loud. "No, but the meal will if we leave it too long. Come, dine with me."

They shared glances and smiles as they ate and drank, Ricardo as intrigued as ever by the stranger and Matthew equally intrigued by the very handsome Duke he found himself with at table.

In silent agreement, they avoided the topic of Matthew's mysterious memory loss. Disregarding the strangeness of the situation, Ricardo chose to treat the young red-head as he would any male guest. "Tomorrow we will ride if you are feeling well enough. The fresh air will do you good. At least they always say that, don't they?"

"I would like that. I believe I'm feeling quite well even now, although I am growing a little sleepy. It must be the wine."

Ricardo rose and offered Matthew a hand. "Come then, I will make sure you can negotiate the stairs to your chamber."

Matthew offered his quirky smile as he, too, stood and took the Duke's hand. There was a moment where they locked eyes as their hands clasped, but both looked away quickly. Still, neither made a move to release that firm handclasp until Matthew was inside his tower room and seated on his bed.

"Good night, friend. Sleep well," Ricardo murmured as he took his leave.

"You as well. And thank you," Matthew called out.

Ricardo was reluctant to leave him on his own, but could think of no rational excuse to remain. On his way to his own chambers, he almost turned around and went back to offer Matthew a place on the floor beside his hearth. But that seemed foolishly overprotective, and he decided against it.

He awoke to his servant's hand on his shoulder. "Master. The stranger is possessed. He is crying out in tongues. The devil has taken hold of him!"

"Hush, Mahmet. I will come. Give me my robe!"

Regardless of his admonition to the quaking Arab servant, Ricardo experienced a small shudder of dread as he contemplated the possibility of Satan in his Keep, or of a demon possessing his sweet guest who was alone and defenseless in his tower room.

Yet he did not hesitate as he raced up stairs and across corridors to reach Matthew in his apparent distress. He found the youth tossing and turning in his bed and crying out. He was not alone at least. A servant girl, the Italian Teresa, stood nearby wringing her hands and afraid to approach.

"He is speaking English. There is no demon here. Leave us."

Ricardo stepped up to the bed and immediately reached out to the writhing youth. The moment his hand settled on Matthew's arm, the red-head ceased his tossing and came awake. He sat up abruptly and let out a huge groan.

"Ricardo! I'm back here! I was dreaming I was in Los Angeles in a hospital room. Someone was beside me holding my hand. I couldn't see him even though I tried so hard."

The young Duke was somewhat confused by Matthew's statement. He had no idea where Los Angeles was, but wondered if he was speaking of the angels, or if the place he called a hospital was an abbey of The Hospitallers, the order of Knights who tended to the sick and infirm.

"Come. I think it best you sleep in my chambers. It will save me the effort of running back and forth in the middle of the night."

It seemed it was the perfect thing to say. Matthew offered no resistance or made no complaint as he rose to follow the Duke to his rooms. Ricardo's servants quickly, and nervously, made up a pallet with blankets beside the hearth and only a half dozen yards from their Master's bed.

Matthew went right to sleep without a word. Ricardo remained awake for a short time gazing at the red-head on his pallet by the light of the flickering fire. He wished sorely to bring the young man into his bed and wrap his arms around him to protect him from those disturbing dreams. He fell asleep imagining that tender scenario.

He awoke to sunlight flooding the room from the windows in the eastern wall that faced the sea. Matthew was up and adding some faggots to the fire. "You are awake. Did you sleep well? I didn't hear you ... calling out or anything."

Matthew turned to face Ricardo. He nodded and smiled briefly. "I slept soundly. Perhaps your room is enchanted. Thank you. I am a nuisance, I think."

"Nonsense! I really am glad you are here, regardless of the mystery you offer. Shall we ask the servants to bring us a meal?"

They ate in the room, a fine repast of boiled eggs and warm crusty bread with slices of cooked ham. Nothing was said of the night before. When a servant came to clear away the remains of their breakfast, Ricardo commanded him to fetch the lyre Matthew had been playing the previous evening.

"I would have you play again. In payment for all the disturbance you bring to my otherwise placid prison."

Matthew cocked his head and gave Ricardo a curious look, but chose not to question his odd statement. The young

Duke had said nothing of his own circumstances. Matthew had enough to worry about.

The young red-head sat on a stool in the far corner beneath the open window in the warmth of the morning sun and took up the instrument when it arrived. He began to play with a subdued focus. It was magical. Ricardo was reminded of a bard he had once heard at King Roger's Court who hailed from the wild hinterlands of Scotland in the British Isles. It was lively but poignant, mysterious and rich with the beat of the sea and the winds.

He was pulled from contemplating the lovely youth and his entrancing music by the arrival of the Keep's Castellan. This was expected as the Master-at-Arms regularly reported to the Duke at this time.

Abdul, made his report with quiet solemnity. Erect and lean in his flowing robe of navy blue and emerald, his piercing olive eyes gazed out from under ink-black brows above a hawk nose that swooped down to thin lips and a wide mouth. A dark headdress hid his hair. He looked altogether terrifying to the watching Matthew.

"I have news from Palermo. Your uncle once again commands you to remain here at the Keep. He believes that once the current campaigns in southern Italy have come to some conclusion, either for or against King Roger, it may be safe enough for your return to the capital. Perhaps in the autumn, Lord."

"Ah, perhaps in the autumn. Last autumn, Uncle promised I would be welcome back in the spring, and it is now spring. Come, Abdul, what is the truth of it? You have received messages from others not so cozy with Uncle. I would know it all."

Abdul turned his fierce but contained gaze upon Matthew. The young red-head gazed back at him directly while continuing to play.

167

"Your young friend. Would it be better if he was not bothered with such matters?"

On the spur of the moment, Ricardo made a decision contrary to his previous reasoning. "No. It would be better if he was bothered with such matters. I would seek his advice as well as yours."

"Are you certain, Lord? He is a stranger here. His story of memory loss is far from plausible, and he has the look of a Norman about him. He could be a spy sent by enemies of your family. Comely and congenial, one could easily be taken in by his seeming innocence."

Matthew rose, his freckled complexion flushed. "I am no liar, Master Abdul, but I understand your concern and have no quarrel with it. I'll leave."

Ricardo raised both hands, one toward each of the two men. "Truce, please. I, too, understand your concerns, Abdul. But I trust Matthew. As I trust you. Please continue. And Matthew, please remain."

Abdul bowed to his Lord, then turned and bowed to Matthew. It was an unequivocal statement of absolute obedience. He continued speaking. "Lord, I have heard that your uncle, Prince Donaldo of Salerno, and your cousin Count Silvestri of Melfi are secretly conspiring against King Roger. Your Uncle Pietro in Palermo attempts to straddle both horses until he senses a clear winner of this race. Lord Pietro simply does not trust you in Palermo where you might also hear these rumors and perhaps impetuously decide to choose the King over family. He truly does feel you to be safer here at the Keep, but also sees himself as safer without you in Palermo at Court."

"Just so. Thank you for your honesty as usual. You may go."

The tall Moor bowed and departed without another word. Ricardo paced the room with his hands behind his back in quiet contemplation while Matthew took up the lyre again. Finally, he paused before the seated red-head. "What do you think, my friend?"

"More important, I would assume, what do you want?"

Ricardo bust out laughing, then lay a hand on the red-head's shoulder and answered. "Want? I was the son of a duke before I was a duke. All my life I was offered whatever I wanted. Fine food, fine horses, fine books, fine whores if I'd been so inclined. But all these things were of the same sort, material and ephemeral. I was never asked what I wanted to do with my life. Now, it seems you are asking me this. And I suppose I should have an answer, yet I fear I do not. Not now, not yet."

"Give it some time, Ricardo. Should we ride today? I'm eager to try it. Hopefully I won't look the fool."

Ricardo had to wonder. Had Matthew never ridden a horse? Stranger and stranger.

It was clear this was the case when they were in the stables on the ground floor of the Keep and confronted with the time to mount their steeds. Laughing, Matthew had to ask for direction, which Ricardo gladly offered. It was all very novel and great fun as the young Duke became the instructor to his naïve guest.

He chose the gentlest of his geldings for the novice rider, which certainly helped prevent any disasters. The horse was utterly placid and followed Ricardo's more boisterous mare with no quarrel. All Matthew had to do was maintain his seat in the saddle.

He did that surprisingly well after the first few minutes of awkwardness. Looking back at the red-head, Ricardo noted how he observed and then mimicked the Duke's own movements and manners. Even if he had never mounted a horse before, he was undoubtedly an experienced athlete of some sort. Guessing this to be the case, Ricardo decided to further test his new friend's mysterious abilities.

"How about some swordplay? Would this also be a practice you have never enjoyed?"

They had just ridden up the slope of a small knoll overlooking the sea. The morning was cool yet with the dew of a chilly spring night still moistening the grass in the shadier spots. There was no breeze to speak of and only a few birds chirped in the bushes. It was very quiet.

"What is this place? What are these ruins?"

Matthew gazed about in wonder as he took in their surroundings, too much in awe of the deserted majesty of the place to respond to Ricardo's joking challenge. It was a ruin of some sort, obviously. Tall columns marched in a pair of broken rows on either side of them while a number of other columns were scattered around the area in jumbled disarray. It looked as if it had once been some kind of Greek temple or palace.

"I have been told that more than fifteen hundred years ago, the Greeks themselves built this temple when they settled Sicily. Since then, the Romans came and conquered, then the Byzantines who were themselves somewhat Greek, then the Muslim Arabs, and now the Normans, and we Italians. Isn't it inspiring to see the handiwork of the ancients, even in this tumbled down state?"

Matthew's look changed from awe to puzzled confusion. "Fifteen hundred years ago. How strange. I feel somehow as if those centuries are nothing but moments. Another thousand years from now, where will I be?"

Recognizing the anguish beneath the murmured words, Ricardo chose then to repeat his earlier challenge. "Come, Matthew. Let's dismount. I'm eager to test your fighting skills."

Ricardo had moved up close so that their horses were side-by-side. As he spoke he reached out and placed a hand on Matthew's shoulder. The moment he touched him, the red-head seemed to come out of his inward withdrawal.

"Yes. Why not? I wondered why you burdened me with this scabbard when we dressed this morning."

Ricardo had actually enjoyed dressing his guest before they set out earlier. He offered him clothes from his own closet, breeches, tunic, boots and cloak, and yes a sword belt with scabbard and weapon. This was how he himself would dress when preparing for a ride outside the safety of the Keep, and it seemed proper to also dress Matthew in that manner.

They dismounted and tethered their horses to one of the remaining upright columns before Ricardo began to teach his young guest the art of swordplay. Removing their cloaks, they squared off in tunic and breeches under the bright morning sun in the midst of the tumbled Greek ruins.

It was enjoyable and mysteriously intriguing for both young men. Matthew's first efforts were laughable and neither minded making a joke of it. But the red-head's enthusiasm quickly made up for his awkwardness. Before long, they were leaping and hopping about from grassy field to atop fallen columns and back again. Again, it was obvious to Ricardo that Matthew was an experienced athlete, quite light on his feet and accustomed to agile leaps and bounds. It was almost as if he was a trained dancer or tumbler.

He was also reckless. Their swords clanged loudly as they chased one another about the ruins, laughing and shouting dares. It was up to Ricardo to prevent any injury, which was a challenge with the wild fervor of his inexperienced partner to contend with.

Matthew halted in his leaping enthusiasm only long enough to tear off his tunic and thus go shirt-less in the Sicilian sunshine. Ricardo followed suit. Now the pair showed

171

off their differing body types as the slim and lean red-head battled the husky and powerful Duke.

Ricardo was hard-put not to get distracted by the glorious sight of those slender muscles rippling and the smooth tanned flesh awash in sweat. But with Matthew's wild abandon to attend to he was forced to pay close attention to their sport or risk accident. Nonetheless, his cock reared up stiff and eager beneath his trousers.

"Truce, friend! We have worked up a good lather, and I believe it is time to get wet and cool off," Ricardo called out as Matthew leaped off a nearby pile of rubble directly toward him.

"Truce, then! Are we going for a swim? I don't see a stream nearby," Matthew replied as he landed lightly beside Ricardo and smiled brightly.

"Come," the Duke answered with his own smile.

In the lee of the north side of the ruin there was a small depression in the slope. An ancient stone stairway led them down to a wall of rock and an obvious shrine. Just above head height, a carved image jutted from the wall. The time-pitted head of a Greek God with flowing locks of stone hair boasted a yawning mouth that spouted a flow of spring water to gush downward.

Laughing, Ricardo dropped his sword to the grass and stepped up to the little waterfall. Bending over, he thrust his bare head and naked upper body beneath the flow. A rush of pleasant cold washed over him. He let out a yelp of glee as he shook his head back and forth under the flow and then leaned forward to press his hands against the wet stone while the water ran down over his upturned face.

He heard Matthew laughing behind him. He was absolutely certain the reckless youth would be more than willing to join him in the cold shower. He turned around to invite him in and was shocked to find the red-head in the act of tearing off his trousers. His sword and boots were already discarded on the grass beside Ricardo's sword.

"Here I come!"

And he was there beside him, totally naked. Ricardo fell back slightly, open-mouthed and momentarily uncertain. The rush of cold had gone to his head, and he felt totally exhilarated. It seemed as if his vision was suddenly marvelously acute. The youth beside him shone with glowing clarity.

His slim body was half-tan and half porcelain-pale. His crotch and bottom were almost translucent, a light bush of fair hair at the base of his pink cock and balls, and none whatsoever across the round fullness of his ass. The pale cheeks glistened ivory as the water from the spout cascaded down over them.

There was nothing to do but follow his reckless friend's lead, otherwise his boots and trousers were about to get soaked as Matthew vigorously splashed about in the flowing waterfall. Disregarding the tell-tale betrayal of his rearing cock, he kicked off his boots and hopped out of his trousers.

Matthew turned in time to catch a glimpse of that stiff prick as Ricardo slipped into the waterfall beside him. His crooked grin seemed slightly wicked as he pulled the Duke against him and forced him under the gusher.

They wrestled playfully under the spout, pushing and pulling in and out of the water. They found themselves in a sort of embrace as they struggled, and once more gazing into each other's eyes.

It took all of Ricardo's resolve not to press his lips against his young friend's and thrust his stiff cock into his smooth belly. Matthew seemed oblivious to the erotic tension and continued to wrestle with the naked Duke, forcing his face under the waterfall and laughing as he did.

"Truce," Ricardo sputtered as he pulled away.

"Truce," Matthew agreed, though neither released their grip on each other's arms and shoulders immediately.

"I am famished. Shall we return to the Keep for a meal? I feel fairly certain you have enjoyed enough fresh air for the day!"

"Of course. Thank you. What a fine morning it's been!"

Ricardo's cock had remained stiff even under the cold shower, and as they dressed he dared glance at Matthew's crotch to take note of the thrilling fact his pink member had swollen upright as well.

Both aglow from the scrappy sword-play and invigorating shower, they rode back to the Keep engaged in merry conversation. But when the stone walls of the Keep reared up before them, Ricardo's mood dampened.

Matthew noticed. "I'm sorry for your situation, Ricardo. I know you feel as if you are imprisoned, but I have to confess when I gaze at these daunting walls, I feel comforted. Only because you live within them, and I'm blessed to share that prison."

Ricardo was touched, and a little chastened. Although he was concerned for his guest's welfare, he seemed unable to resist lascivious thoughts from rearing up to cloud that concern. He also had to admit he feared Matthew's recovery might mean the handsome youth no longer had need of him.

That night they returned to that theme briefly before falling asleep. Ricardo lay in his high bed and Matthew on the floor beside the hearth. Wooden steps that led up to the Duke's bed were covered in rich Arabic carpets and the pillars that held up the curtains were elaborately carved in Arabic script as was the huge base board and head board. Forest green wool curtains surrounded it. They were pulled open where they faced Matthew on his pallet.

"Your dreams trouble you, Matthew. And I know you wish to remember your past. But you seem more content than I would in your situation. Why is that?"

"Ah, if you must know the truth. It is because of you. I am happy just be near you. You make up for all the rest."

Ricardo felt suddenly breathless. The urge to invite the sweet young stranger into his bed was almost irresistible. But, he believed this was a selfish desire. Matthew was very vulnerable. He had no friends, no life that he could recall, only Ricardo. The young Duke would not betray the trust that had blossomed between them. He would not.

"I am happy to hear it. I am happy to be near you as well. The bars of my prison are less tiresome with you by my side. Good night, my friend. If you dream tonight, may you dream of a pleasant past."

"Thank you. Your concern is a real help. I hope I don't disturb you again tonight."

But he did. Once more the hapless youth called out in the night in his barbarous English and only ceased his thrashing and crying out when Ricardo came to lay a hand on him.

Matthew's troubled gaze dissolved into a brief but trusting smile before he slipped back into quiet sleep. Ricardo knelt beside him for some time as the embers in the hearth lit the youth's soft face in an angelic glow. Finally, he returned to his bed.

The disturbed nights were repeated over the next week. Matthew claimed he could recall nothing of the nightmares, or of his past, and put up a good front in pretending it didn't matter to him. And Ricardo put up a good front pretending he did not lust after the slim red-head's vigorous body every waking hour.

Exercise seemed to be a balm they both enjoyed. They rode out into the countryside daily.

This particular day they rode north into a deserted countryside where Ricardo knew they would be alone. He wasn't entirely certain of his motivations.

By mid-afternoon, they came to a meadow that was broad and empty, splashed with a plethora of sun-gold wild flowers and boasting only a solitary olive tree in its center. Ricardo felt a sudden stab of empathetic loneliness at the sight of that gnarled and ancient tree. Ever since his father had died, he had been without love of any sort. He turned in the saddle and glanced at the youth cantering just behind. A flush of excitement suffused his handsome face while that crooked smile of his brightened the solemn and lost expression he sometimes favored. He certainly had taken to riding, even though he'd claimed that he'd never ridden before – that he could recall.

Ricardo reined in from a canter just ahead of that lone olive tree. He pulled his horse to a halt and leaped from the saddle all in one graceful movement. Matthew reined in his own steed with considerably less expertise but did manage to come to a halt beside the young Duke with laughing breathlessness. He dismounted and tethered his horse to a branch beside Ricardo's.

All at once it seemed eerily quiet. The horses were still breathing hard, and so were the two young men. A few insects buzzed around the nearby patches of golden flowers. A raven's lone caw floated in the distance.

The day was very warm, more noticeable now that they had come to a halt. The breeze off the sea was muted by the low hills between them and the shore. The sun was high and the only shade was beneath the twisted branches of the olive. They stood close, smiling at each other, neither speaking.

Ricardo's hand came out to gently settle on Matthew's shoulder. The intent was friendly affection, but when the red-head let out a huge sigh, a release of breath that was seemed much more than it appeared on the surface, the young Duke felt himself all at once trembling, but oddly calm at the same time.

All his misgivings about his passion for the youth's beautiful body dissolved as one of Matthew's hands came up to gently squeeze his own where it lay upon the red-head's shoulder.

"It is time. May I kiss you?" As ever, the young Duke was scrupulously polite. Matthew couldn't help but laugh.

"I wondered if you would ever ask," he replied as he snorted back his laughter.

Happily encouraged by Matthew's boisterous response, he smiled in return as he leaned in and kissed the pink lips to silence that laughter. The moment their lips touched, they fell into each other's arms with a desperate abandon.

They tore each other's clothes off while still kissing, their tongues diving between each other's lips, and their breath coming in snorts and gasps. When they had finally shed everything and stood on the soft spring grass beneath the dappled shade of that ancient olive, they broke apart for a moment to gaze at each other in total wonder.

Then, wordlessly they came together again in a frenzy of desire. They seized each other's stiff pricks and pumped them as they kissed again. Ricardo's free hand came around to cup and squeeze a round cheek of Matthew's ass, and the red-head followed his lead to roam a hand over the hefty expanse of the Duke's full bottom.

A total lack of inhibition on either of their parts elevated their explorations to a free-for-all of joyful thrusting and heaving against each other. They pumped each other's cocks and dove into each other's deep ass-cracks. Fingers found holes to stroke and probe.

They broke their sloppy kiss once more to seamlessly slide into a new position. Matthew turned around to lean forward and place his hands on the gnarled bole of the olive and spread his bare feet wide apart while Ricardo knelt in the grass behind him and reached out for his beautiful ass.

The smooth cheeks were flushed slightly pink from the Duke's vigorous handling, and as he spread them wide, he could see the puckered hole was flushed, too. He moaned loudly as he gawked at the gorgeous sight of that naked body, presented for his use with feet spread and ass jutting backwards.

Although Matthew was slim, his shoulders were broad and his back tapered down to the small waist before the compact globes of his ass reared outward in pale glory. He wriggled them with enticing lasciviousness as the Duke pulled the sweet cheeks open.

Ricardo buried his face between those lovely mounds and attacked the wrinkled slot. He tasted male musk and sweat, slithering his tongue between the quivering anal lips and deep into the warm pit beyond. He sucked on it, stabbed at it, and licked it all over. He could not get enough of it, and Matthew wriggled back into that wet attack with corresponding greed.

The kneeling Duke reached one hand around to seize Matthew's rearing pole. The curved rod was quite lengthy with a tapered head and a rigidness to it that testified to his desire. As Ricardo delved into his sweet asshole, that column of male meat jerked and throbbed in his hand.

He pulled away from his feast with a smack and a slurp. The pink hole was swollen and dripping with saliva. It was ready for cock. He rose on shaky legs and moved in to plant his prick where his face had just been. He spit down over the fat pole, dark purple now and throbbing with desire. Matthew reached back with one hand and added more spit to the gooey mess already there. Ricardo spit again, and again. Matthew wriggled against the stiffness and whispered his need.

"Do it, Ricardo. I need you in me. I need you in me more than anything else in the world."

His golden eyes moist with tears of joy, he obeyed the red-head's command. He aimed for the pink hole and began to press against it. Both of them gasped as blunt cock-head immediately slipped past quivering sphincter and slithered inward.

Quivering heat enveloped his prick. Snug but accommodating anal muscle welcomed him. Matthew groaned as he pushed backwards and swallowed up half of Ricardo's thick meat in one slow gulp.

The Duke leaned forward and found Matthew's face as the young red-head turned his head and met him. They kissed again, slowly and deeply as that fat prick steadily burrowed home. It seemed as if they were made for each other as balls met ass and they became one.

Ricardo held himself within the quivering cavern as they both caught their breath around a steamy kiss, then began to withdraw. Slowly he pulled almost all the way out, then just as slowly he pushed back in. Matthew's quaking hole took him in with clinging warmth then released him with yielding ease. In and out, slowly at first, then more rapidly, then with a grunting and slamming excitement that had them both on the brink of orgasm.

Matthew forestalled their climax by pulling forward and disengaging. Ricardo groaned and shuddered as his stiff cock slid from the torrid anal slot it had been plundering. He had little time to catch his breath as the red-head laughingly turned to grasp his waist and drag him down to the soft grass. He knelt between the bigger youth's thighs and pushed them up and back.

With that quirky grin brightening his face and lovely blue-gold eyes boring into Ricardo's, he dropped down to return the Duke's earlier favor. He began licking his hefty ass. Ricardo moaned and reared as wet tongue slid up and down his parted ass-crevice. When that tongue settled on his hole and began to suck and probe, he shook from head to toe.

His big ass jerked wildly as Matthew slapped it playfully and continued to lick and suck on his tender hole. He grabbed his own bare feet and held them up as the red-head sucked his hole inside out with a greedy fervor that matched his own earlier enthusiasm for eating ass.

His big body flopped and quivered as the slimmer red-head licked his ass and slapped and massaged his husky ass mounds. Ricardo felt his asshole quivering open for the tickling lips and digging tongue and knew he was quite ready for a deeper probing.

Matthew slid a finger between the snapping ass-lips and wriggled it in circles as he added more spit to the dripping maw. Another finger soon followed. Ricardo heaved upward, grunting like a gored boar between wild fits of choked laughter.

The slim red-head pulled out of the young Duke's wet ass-crack and crawled atop him. Without hesitating, he thrust his cock into the steamy-moist pit he had just eaten and fingered. Ricardo gripped his shoulders and pulled him down into a fierce embrace as his feet thrashed in the air and he took cock to the root.

Already heated up to a feverish pitch, the pair rutted like beasts as Matthew slammed down into Ricardo's spit-wet asshole with relentless enthusiasm. They kissed again, wrapped tightly in each other's arms as the fuck grew wilder and wilder.

Matthew's round white bottom rose and fell as he drove his cock into Ricardo's willing hole. Ricardo's feet bobbed in the air as he took it without a hitch. His burly arms held Matthew close as he heaved himself up off the grass to meet every deep thrust he was offered.

Naked in the redolent spring grass in the shade of the ancient olive's gnarled branches, they lost complete track of time. Matthew pounded Ricardo's ass relentlessly until once more they approached their release.

But neither was yet prepared for an end to the vigorous play. Ricardo, certainly the more powerful of the pair, abruptly turned the tables on his red-headed friend by rolling them over so that he was now on top. At first he merely rode the slimmer youth's stiff cock, driving his beefy bottom down over it. Then he rose off the slim cock with a groan and moved back to kneel between Matthew's lean thighs. Grasping the backs of his knees, he pushed them forward until they pressed against the smooth chest.

He fucked deeply and steadily, every thrust of his huge prick eliciting a satisfying grunt as Matthew writhed beneath him. This time neither could hold back. The red-head's stiff pink tool erupted over his smooth belly in a geyser of creamy spunk. Ricardo felt the walls of his hole pulse and squeeze and knew he was done for, too.

He pulled out with a gasp and added his spew to Matthew's. Then he collapsed on the grass beside him. Naked and satiated, they lay quietly, thigh pressed to thigh and hands clasped. Ricardo wished the afternoon would last forever just as it was, and nothing of the world be allowed to intrude.

Staring up at the branches of the lonely olive tree, Ricardo pondered that thought. The tree was truly old. It could be hundreds of years old, as many of its kind were. It seemed appropriate to be basking in the timelessness of its age and praying for time to cease.

They eventually dressed and mounted. They took their time riding back to the Keep, and it was nearly dark by the time they reached it. Abdul was a little irritated by their long absence and had prepared a search party in case it was required. Ricardo thanked him effusively for his concern, which did much to assuage his foul mood.

That night Ricardo invited Matthew into his bed. They lay naked side-by-side but neither made a move to instigate another round of sexual games. Although they had enjoyed a thoroughly satisfying round of those games earlier in the afternoon, they were both virile young men and could easily have mustered up the vigor for more of the same.

But their need was for more than sexual gratification on the first night of sharing that bed. Tender caresses and gentle fondling soothed and satisfied their shared woes. They were both content to merely bask in each other's warmth. They fell asleep entangled in thighs and arms.

Ricardo awoke alone. Suddenly breathless and full of fear, he sat up and called out. "Matthew?"

"I'm here. I've been dreaming."

The slender young man stood beside the hearth. He had added a few small faggots, and the glow illuminated his naked body in an ethereal shimmer. Ricardo couldn't help the small moan of desire that nearly overwhelmed him.

"Come back to bed. Tell me all, if you wish."

Matthew returned, although he seemed reluctant until after he mounted the steps, then he slipped into the Duke's embrace with a sigh and began to speak.

Ricardo did not understand a great deal of it. There were words he found entirely unfathomable sprinkled amidst a story that seemed entirely implausible. Yet there was no denying Matthew's honest attempt at telling it.

"I dreamed of another life. A life I believe is mine, as much as this one. I am exactly the same as I am here, but in another place far from here and in another time far from now. Almost a thousand years in the future, in a land called America far across the Atlantic Ocean in a city called Los Angeles by another ocean called the Pacific.

"I am a champion competitive skate board trick rider. I play guitar in a band. I live a reckless life of pure adrenaline with little thought to consequence. That's why I chose to ride my skate board down a busy street instead of in the skate park, and that is why I was hit by a car and ended up in the hospital. I am there now, unconscious and dreaming, on the cusp of living or dying."

With only the flickering light of the distant hearth to illuminate his quiet features, Matthew rolled over onto his side to face Ricardo. "You are there beside me. You were there when I was hit by that car and you saved my life. Now, a thousand years from now, you remain at my side in the hospital, talking to me as I slumber, holding my hand as I struggle to come awake. It is you who holds my fate in your hands."

Ricardo's tears blurred his vision. He could hardly comprehend the strangeness of the story, but he could not deny the strangeness of Matthew's appearance at the Keep out of nowhere and all the other oddities of his circumstances.

"How? And why, Matthew?"

"I don't know. But I believe some things to be true now. I believe we are kindred spirits. I believe that once in a lifetime something momentous, even miraculous can occur that will change everything. Often it is the chance for love, in all its manifestations. What does love do best? Elevate both who love. This is what you have shown me, Ricardo, what love feels like and what love does."

Ricardo could not answer. He gathered the strange red-head in his burly arms and held him close. They fell asleep clinging to one another.

In the morning, they agreed to forgo delving any deeper into the meaning of it all and enjoy the day instead. They rode out as was their custom with no particular destination in mind. They found themselves on a bluff overlooking the sea. A brisk and salty breeze softened the heat of the afternoon.

"Shall we practice our swordplay again? I intend on becoming your bodyguard as payment for all your hospitality."

Ricardo burst out laughing. "My bodyguard? Well, perhaps. Your enthusiasm certainly works to your advantage, regardless of your lack of training and finesse."

Matthew pulled off his tunic and faced his bigger adversary with a grin. Ricardo followed his lead, and they were now both half-naked. A thrill of sensual pleasure added momentum to their engagement. Swords clashing, they chased each other about the small clearing with a precipitous bluff on one side and a copse of oak on the other.

As they battled, Ricardo couldn't help thinking of their conversation of the night before. Whether the youth was a lunatic, possessed, or merely an angel come down from heaven, he remained utterly beautiful and miraculously entrancing. More so, they seemed the perfect foil for one another. Matthew was sometimes reckless while Ricardo was sometimes indecisive. Proving him right, Matthew pushed him dangerously close to the edge of the cliff. The red-head laughed in his face as the burly young Duke pressed him back.

"Good work, friend! If only we could continue as now forever more," Ricardo called out between gasps for breath.

"You prefer to ride and exercise and practice swordplay over Court politics, I can see. But is that all you really want?"

The shouted challenge was followed by a grinning riposte, awkward but effective. Ricardo danced back and parried, shouting back his response. "My uncle believes me too naïve for politics. I have trouble arguing with that."

"Ah, my friend. You are smart and capable and shrewder than you believe. You are the Duke. Not your uncle. Either be the Duke, or not," Matthew reminded him with a smirk and a smash of his sword.

With that challenge echoing in the air, a sudden quiet descended, almost like a thunderclap it was so noticeable. The stiff breeze ceased. The cawing of the sea gulls circling over the bluff was abruptly silenced. They both halted in mid-stroke and stared at each other breathlessly.

The earth rocked violently. Both were knocked off their feet. Ricardo shouted. "Earthquake! Lie flat!"

It was not enough. The ground beneath him began to give way. A tear in the earth opened, and he felt terror grip him. If he tumbled to the sea below he would die, and he would lose Matthew!

Hands seized his shoulder and dragged him forward. Just in time. The bluff behind him collapsed, and he was left sprawled out on the edge of the precipice. Matthew held him.

#####

Matthew awoke in his hospital bed in Los Angeles. Bright California spring light flooded in from the window beside him. Basking in its glow, a young man in the uniform of a paramedic sat in a chair gazing down at him.

"You're awake. I'm so glad," the young man murmured quietly.

Matthew looked up at the handsome face he knew so well. Thick black hair swept back from his high forehead. Dark brows arched over lovely golden eyes. The long nose descended to hover over the wide mouth smiling so generously.

"Ricardo. You saved my life. Thank you."

"It's my job to save lives. But how did you know my name? Or that I saved you?" The look of wonder on his face was purely angelic. When he blushed brightly, Matthew had to smile.

"I just know. I also know you've been here at my side every day since the accident, on your lunch breaks like now and after work. You've been talking to me. And you've been holding my hand. You have saved my life again."

The conviction in his voice was unmistakable. Ricardo couldn't help laughing. "Your sudden recovery seems a little on the miraculous side. Take care not to get too ahead of yourself!"

"I won't. My reckless days are over. Or at least tempered. I'm going to rest a little with my eyes closed. But I won't go anywhere – I'm not going to die. Can you hold my hand?"

His quirky smile brought out an answering smile from the seated paramedic. He reached out and gripped Matthew's hand. "Promise?"

"I promise." And he meant it.

# # # # #

Ricardo rolled them over several times while the earth continued to shudder beneath them. They settled in the grass a dozen yards from the collapsed cliff. It was over almost as soon as it had begun.

"You saved my life," he gasped out as he gazed down at Matthew beneath him.

"I believe I did," he replied with a smirk.

They were both half-naked and covered in sweat, dirt and bits of grass. In sheer relief, they embraced and kissed, rolling again so that Matthew ended up on top. Ricardo found himself staring up at a halo of gold around the red-head's shining face. He truly looked like an angel.

His decision was made. "If I go to Palermo will you accompany me? As my bodyguard, of course, and as my friend."

"I will go with you wherever you want. I am yours. For a thousand years if you want."

"Promise?"

"I do."

THE GARDEN ISLE
By Jay Starre

A big hard dick and a willing hungry asshole- for me that had always been the basic criteria for a good relationship. Crude, yes, but I'd never been a flowers and poetry kind of dude. Love and romance? That was for movies and dreamers. I considered myself down-to-earth and never, ever walked around with my head in the clouds.

As far as sex goes, I wasn't really into the kinky stuff but had few inhibitions along the elemental lines of cock and ass play. I enjoyed sex. A lot. Again for me, that uninhibited viewpoint was a basic requirement of partnering up with another guy.

My first two real relationships fit within those parameters nicely.

Jamie's cock was perennially stiff, and he put it to good use massaging my hungry ass as often as I wanted it. Young and hung and not all that smart, he served up fancy French food in a downtown San Francisco restaurant. He banged my butt on week nights after his shifts for almost a year before we both tired of it. No drama and no regrets. We parted amicably enough and even got together once in a while over the next year for some wild repeat fucks.

Donovan was an entirely different story. His cock was plenty big enough, for sure, and he knew how to use it. His ass was damn sweet, too, and he offered it up for my use on a regular basis. There was no problem in the sexual arena. We were both versatile; we both liked to fuck and get fucked.

We moved in together. My townhouse in the Castro was big enough for two, and he paid rent, which helped me with the outrageous mortgage. We got along fine. His job at an upscale men's clothing store was relatively stress-free, and my career as a free-lance writer was breezing along without a hitch. All might have been perfect.

Except that my "love" for Donovan revolved entirely around his very sexy body and the need to possess and control his big hard dick and willing hungry asshole. I became obsessed, without really understanding how it came about.

In the Castro, good-looking and available men abound. We couldn't even stroll the streets without being cruised; going out became a nightmare for me. Donovan was blond and blue-eyed, and he had the sexiest bubble-butt imaginable. He was sociable, and I was less so. I was not the one that got chatted up at the bars or in the line-up at the grocery store. It was always Donovan.

He explained it to me. "Guys think you're arrogant. You're so quiet and serious; you look like Rock Hudson, and you're tall and muscular with killer blue eyes and that sexy, wavy black hair. No one dares approach you."

Maybe so, but there wasn't much I could do about any of that. Dudes drooled over him, and I just couldn't stand it.

My 30th birthday loomed on the horizon. I was unhappy. I fucked Donovan's very sweet ass hard and thoroughly, and he moaned and grunted sufficiently, but when I shot my load, I just felt even more desperate. I was sure he was getting it somewhere else with someone else.

Caressing those sweat-soaked mounds of just-fucked butt and wondering who else might have done the same or would do the same in the future when I wasn't keeping an eye on that gorgeous can suddenly got old.

"I'm going to Hawaii. For my birthday. By myself."

Surprise, surprise. To both of us. I just blurted that out and waited for the answer with pounding heart. The smooth white ass reared up slightly to wriggle against my stroking fingers.

"OK. I have to work over the holidays anyway. Big sale on."

Disappointment and exhilaration vied for control of my emotions. He didn't seem to care, and I wanted badly not to either. My hand moved away. It was the last time I touched that lovely round ass.

Kauai, the garden isle. I'd been toying with the idea of a visit ever since a couple of our buddies returned from there to report on its lush beauty. I had a ticket in hand the next morning and was on my way to the airport. Donovan offered to see me off, but I declined, although not without a pang of regret.

The long flight over the Pacific, the landing in Honolulu on Oahu, the transfer to the smaller plane for Kauai, the drive to my hotel in the small town of Waimea, all went by in a kind of blur. I slept through a lot of it, emotionally exhausted more than physically.

It didn't really hit me, where I was and how absolutely gorgeous the surroundings were, until I found myself shaking hands with the tour guide I'd hired before I left home.

"Aloha. Welcome to Hawaii, Scott. I'm Kyle."

"Thanks! And aloha to you, too," I replied. His firm handshake ended before I was quite ready for it. That initial physical contact sent a real live shiver through me.

I was here. It was now. Kyle was stunning.

He'd been recommended by my buddies. "He's hot, and he's sweet, and he'll run you ragged if you let him. He's gay, too, and single; or at least he was last month when we were there."

"In your email you said hiking was your favorite thing to do. Well, let's see if that's true. I've got a great one lined up for today. How soon can you be ready?"

As he spoke, the morning sun formed a golden halo around him. Everything seemed all at once brilliant, the azure sky, the lush greenery crowding the hotel entrance, his somewhat unruly mop of sandy-brown hair, and his golden eyes. And most of all his welcoming white smile.

"Uh, I should put on my hiking boots. And what should I bring? A pack? Snack? A water bottle? First aid kit?" I managed to joke.

"I have all that, except you should bring a water bottle along, too. And sun screen."

It was this first hike through Waimea Canyon with the spectacular volcanic mountains rearing on either side that clinched it for me. I didn't know Kyle at all then but discovered enough about him by the end of the day to completely alter my view of what life was all about.

It's the day I fell in love.

"At six million years, Kauai is the oldest of the Hawaiian Islands. Each of the islands in the chain has followed the same ancient scenario. They start out as a series of volcanic eruptions followed by continual erosion from the wickedly abundant rainfall."

He offered intermittent bits and bites of information as we hiked. All of it was fascinating. His voice was mesmerizing. Just ahead of me, his pumping butt beckoned, and it was a very sweet butt. He wore eye-catching and outrageously flowered shorts that clung to the firm cheeks. In San Francisco, I wouldn't be caught dead in something like that, but here in Hawaii, it was apparently normal every day wear. His T-shirt was a plain light blue, which actually matched the blue background in the colorful shorts. His small backpack was splashed with gigantic blooms as well, and even his hiking sandals were a vibrant gold and green.

Spectacular waterfalls. Towering volcanic hillsides of sheer and almost frightening dimensions. Emerald forest crowding the path. My mouth dropped open in awe at every turn. And there was always that pumping, flower-splashed ass to admire.

At that first hand-shake I found myself attracted to the Hawaiian guide in a very physical way. This was not unusual for me – it was almost always how I related to other guys. Personality took second place in my somewhat shallow view of men and what they offered.

But within the first hour of our new acquaintance, I found myself shifting gears. The stunning scenery, so fresh and alive and almost overpowering, had me feeling more aware than usual. Everything, including Kyle, seemed to vibrate with an ethereal beauty.

I listened to his softly spoken diatribe and was drawn into whatever he happened to offer up with enraptured interest. His voice was almost musical, subdued and unintrusive, and his topics were fascinating. He obviously took his guide duties seriously.

"All the rock you see around us, all of it, came from deep within the Earth. Spewed up by volcanoes, then heaved sideways by earthquakes, pushed up again, then covered with more lava. There are no dinosaur fossils to be found like in other places around the world. We stand on the Earth's guts, covered over by all this gorgeous vegetation of course."

I hadn't lied in my email when I stated hiking was my favorite pastime. I couldn't have been happier with the hours of walking, even though the paths were narrow and the incline often steep. I'd always found walking soothed me. So there was that to add to my keen pleasure in the day.

Combined with that interesting voice, my guide offered more than superficial friendliness. Whenever we halted for a break or to take in a view-point and faced each other, he looked me in the eyes with direct familiarity. His smile was quirky and genuine. The right corner of his upper lip curled fetchingly, and his white teeth flashed.

He was considerate. When a heavy mist rolled in and then became showers, he offered me a light rain slicker from his pack. Even though I refused it, I was grateful he'd thought to bring it along. The rain was hardly cold, and with the vigorous hiking, I found it refreshing on my bare head and limbs.

He regularly checked with me to see if I was tired. He brought out the lunch he'd thoughtfully packed, choosing an unbelievably stunning spot for a break. We sat on rocks beside a tumbling waterfall and ate the simple fare, mostly local fruit along with sandwiches. It stopped raining, the mist lifted, and the sun came back out. Everything sparkled.

"We can go on for another couple hours, if you're up to it. Or turn around if you've had enough. It's entirely up to you."

"Enough? How could a person ever get enough of this? I am in paradise."

"True. But don't be timid about calling it quits. I won't judge you," he replied with a chuckle.

Our decision to forge on was well-rewarded. Higher up and in a kind of cul-de-sac of soaring ridges, we came to a trio of waterfalls, one dropping down to a pool before spilling over into another precipitous cascade, then descending to a final pond at our feet.

It was incredible. I felt as if the earth was encasing me in its rocky arms and then showering me with its watery abundance. It was mystical.

Kyle crouched down at the lip of the pool and scooped up a double handful of the crystal clear water. "In Hawaii, we have a saying. Water is a blessing."

With a wink and a grin, he slurped it in. Looking down at his unruly mop of sandy-brown hair, his broad back and that solid butt, I couldn't help thinking how beautiful he was, not separate from the gorgeous surroundings, but a natural part of it.

I shivered, goose bumps rising on my forearms. It was something akin to sexual excitement, but not quite. Could it be spiritual? A complete pragmatist, this was definitely an unfamiliar arena for me.

The moment didn't really end either. I crouched down beside him and drank from the same pool, grinned back at him, and was for once in my life totally happy to be exactly where I was and unconcerned about what happened next.

When we rose and turned around to head back down the canyon, I was euphoric. The magic of the place and the magic of my guide had transfixed me. We arrived at the trail head just before dark. We'd been hiking for eight hours!

"Pretty good for your first day, Scott. I'll see you tomorrow morning around nine then?"

"Absolutely. Thanks so much for the awesome day, Kyle."

His parting smile left me feeling warm all over.

Even with the great lunch we'd had, I was starving. I gorged on the hotel buffet, stuffing in Hawaiian fruit til I managed to tear myself away and waddle to my room afterwards.

After that unbelievable day, there was one thing I just had to do. I'd been procrastinating on an important decision for what seemed like months. That indecision had been brutal on my sense of control over my life. I was somewhat of a control freak, to be honest.

I phoned Donovan.

"Hey, Donovan. How are you?"

"Fine, Scott. What's up? Are you having a good time? Oh and by the way, happy birthday. I haven't gotten you a present yet, but I'm looking."

We both laughed at that. He was the true procrastinator in our relationship.

"I've made a pretty big decision. I want us to split up. And I'd really like it if you could move out before I come home in two weeks. I know it's a lot to ask, and I understand if you can't swing it. But I'd appreciate it if you could. I'll pay your moving expenses."

I was known for my bluntness. I didn't expect Donovan to be shocked, and I was right.

"Hmmmn. I think I can do that for you. Daryl will let me room with him, I'm sure. But I gotta ask, are you mad at me? Did I do something to hurt you? Cuz, if I did, I'm sorry. I like you, Scott, and I'd hate for us not to remain friends."

Well, I was certainly the asshole in this case. He couldn't have been more accommodating and more reasonable. But that was the problem, in a way. He really didn't care that we were splitting up.

"Nothing you did, Donovan. I just want to move on. And we will be friends as long as you want a jerk like me for a friend."

He laughed, a familiar and easy sound that actually caused a little wrench on my heart-strings. I felt tears coming, and I hadn't cried about something for years.

"Thanks, Donovan. I'll talk to you again before I come back."

"No worries. Have a good vacation."

I did cry. It was sprinkling lightly outside my hotel window, and I stood on the balcony in the darkness and smelled the exotic fragrances of island flowers and the salt air while allowing my emotions to empty out of me.

San Francisco seemed a trillion miles away. But Donovan seemed close, and I couldn't help grieving over the end of what had been between us. I couldn't help feeling like I'd done something wrong too. Had I hurt him with my decision? Probably. Yet I had to admit he wouldn't let it bother him all that much. That hurt me, through no fault of his.

If he'd cried, like I was now, and begged me to reconsider, what would I have done? I honestly couldn't say. I realized that night, in that exotic paradise, that I had a lot to think about.

Kyle's knock on my door woke me the next morning. I'd slept in!

I was still half-asleep and rushed to let him in without bothering to dress. It was only after he came in and his eyes dropped to my crotch, I realized I had a morning boner still rearing its blunt head between us.

"Now that's a truly friendly, and big, Hawaiian welcome. Good morning to you, too."

"Damn! Sorry, Kyle. I'll get dressed. As you can see, I slept in. I'll be ready soon. Do we have time for breakfast somewhere?"

"Of course. Take your time. It's your vacation. And I'm getting a free porn show anyway. Nice butt, by the way."

I flushed bright pink and laughed self-consciously as I rummaged around for underwear and a pair of shorts. Still, I couldn't help being pleased at his comment. And speculate about his intentions. Did he have the hots for me? Like I did for him?

He was the first to allude to anything sexual, I thought afterwards, but in the context of me opening the door to him butt-naked, it could have been entirely innocent – and considerate. Meant to put me at ease, perhaps rather than hint at any inclinations on his part.

He had a car, and we drove to Hanalei Town in the valley of the same name.

"We're going to the last sugar plantation on the island. Once the government raised the minimum wage that spelled the end of sugarcane as an industry on the islands. The volcanic soil is very fertile though, and there are plenty of other crops still grown in the valley. Mainly taro, but also coffee, guava, mango, papaya, banana, kava, avocado, pineapple and star fruit."

"And macadamia nuts," I chimed in cheerfully. I'd already discovered a bountiful supply of the delicious nuts in the hotel lobby for sale and had been gorging on them while we drove.

The historic plantation was a more interesting visit than I'd have expected, mostly due to Kyle's vast knowledge of everything Hawaiian. He sprinkled his history with modern bits of info I couldn't help finding fascinating.

"Ranching has replaced sugarcane in many areas. And what's a ranch without horses? Are you up for a ride?"

This was his first surprise of the day. I hesitated before tossing caution to the wind and agreeing. "I've only ridden a horse twice, and both times the horse got the better of me," I admitted.

"I love it. An honest man for once. We'll make sure you get an obedient nag."

What was a holiday without new adventures? The horseback ride was totally unexpected and with Kyle's soothing manner to make it more than bearable, I had an amazing time.

The nag was gentle and accommodating. The trail was easy to negotiate, and the scenery spectacular. We passed by verdant fields of taro and pineapple, banana plantations, and open grasslands where cattle grazed before climbing to a lush tropical forest and then halting at a rocky outpoint where we could gaze out to sea.

Looking out from a cliff at an endless sea of sparkling blue, and a sky of utter softness in another hue of blue, I felt breathless against the power of all that vast space. I turned to see Kyle watching me. His crooked smile was as beautiful as the stunning view.

"You have a choice for tonight, Scott. After we get back from our ride, I can drive you to your hotel in Waimea Town or you can come with me to a luau here in Hanalei."

I hadn't fled San Francisco and flown halfway across the Pacific to spend my time doing the typical tourist stuff. I imagined a luau inhabited by plump vacationing Americans and camera-wielding Japanese with Hula dancers and an enormous stuffed pig roasting on the fire pit. But then I'd expected a sugarcane plantation to offer similarly mundane entertainment, and Kyle had made sure it hadn't.

I trusted him. "Luau. I'm hungry as heck anyway."

He laughed out loud. "You seem to be always hungry. How many pounds of macadamia nuts have you shoveled in so far today? And I've seen you gobble down three bananas and two whole mangos on top of that. It's a wonder you maintain such a fit physique. All that muscle needs fuel, I imagine."

I was thrilled that he'd noticed – my muscles, not that I was a hog. I'd always been a big eater but never been overweight. All the walking I've always done along with disciplined weight training seemed to keep off the pounds.

The luau that evening tested even my ability to sock it away. What a feast! And it was totally not what I expected. First of all, Kyle informed me we'd have to do some grocery shopping. "It's a potluck. We don't have the time to do any cooking, so fruit will have to do."

Did tourists bring their own food to a luau? I hadn't heard that. There was more I hadn't heard, it seemed. The quiet road we drove down just outside of Hanalei Town abruptly ended in a wall of tropical forest. A house, with wood siding and a sprawling porch, was set amidst the thick palms and ferns. At least a dozen cars and trucks were parked along the side of the road, and with no other residence nearby, it appeared they were all here for the luau.

"Hey Mom! I've brought Scott along."

197

A diminutive woman turned away from the small group she was chatting with just inside the front door. She smiled brightly as she came forward to clasp my hand in both her small ones. The resemblance between mother and son was apparent. Her long hair was thick and wavy and exactly the same shade of sandy-brown as her son's. Her eyes were golden and her smile just a little crooked. They even had the same slim nose.

"Aloha, Scott. Is Kyle treating you right? If he isn't, don't hesitate to let me know. I'm the boss, after all."

"She's not kidding," Kyle said as he pulled me away and further into the chaos of the busy house.

I had to ask. "You work for your mother?"

"My parents own the travel business. But my mother rules the roost, definitely. I take care of the gay clients."

"So you think I'm gay?" I joked.

"Uh, you hired me through Gaytravel.com. Besides, I've noticed the way you keep checking out my fat butt."

"Your butt isn't fat!"

We both laughed at my blurted effort at defense. Then, we were swallowed up in the festivities already in full swing. The back yard was where the luau itself took place, a wide expanse of green lawn with a fire pit boasting an enormous spitted pig garlanded with pineapple.

The crowd was a surprising mix. Even more surprising was the fact they were mostly Kyle's relatives. Some were even native Hawaiians. He explained the mystery.

"Luaus traditionally celebrate a wedding, or as in this case the first birthday of a child. It's my cousin's daughter's first birthday. Her husband will be glad to see he's not the only haole in attendance when he meets you."

I still didn't understand. I knew that haole was the Hawaiian term for white people.

"But aren't you a haole? And your mother? Your father?"

"Well, it's a matter of perspective," he said with a laugh.

He explained. On his mother's side, his grandmother was half-Hawaiian and half Portuguese. Her father, who had passed away, was a Swede. On his father's side, his grandfather was half Chinese and half Portuguese. His grandmother was Portuguese.

"The Portuguese, who came here in droves early on, worked with the Chinese in the fields, and some of them intermarried. Like my great-grandparents. And the Portuguese definitely do not consider themselves haole."

I had known Kyle's last name was Lee, but hadn't really connected that it was a Chinese name. I looked more closely at him in an effort to ferret out what ethnic features he'd inherited, and he grinned and winked as if he understood what I was doing.

He was so tan, I hadn't thought perhaps his skin was naturally a little darker than mine. And his eyes, now that I looked, were a little slanted, just a little. His thick brown hair was streaked lighter by hours in the sun, but probably would have been darker otherwise. Apparently, he was mostly Portuguese, and he looked it.

His relatives were a different matter. Hawaiians and Portuguese and a great-grandfather that walked with a cane and was without a doubt Chinese, it was quite a boisterous mix that seemed well-accustomed to one another. I was flattered that Kyle had asked me to join them.

We ate, and we ate, and we ate some more. There was even entertainment. A half dozen musicians, all relatives, played in shifts. I would never have chosen to listen to that type of music at home when I was relaxing, a lot of falsetto singing and the twanging ukulele, but that night I found it entrancing.

"Hawaiians didn't only invent surfing. They invented the steel guitar, too," Kyle informed me when his uncle stepped up to strum us a tune. His voice, deep and melodious, reminded me a little of Kyle's gentler conversational version.

And there was even a hula dancer. Kyle's cousin, the mother of the little girl whose birthday party it was, decked herself out in a grass skirt and a crown of flowers, then offered us an absolutely magical performance.

Her brown body, she was more Hawaiian than Portuguese, was voluptuous and smooth and her gently undulating movements and fluttering hands captivating. She smiled throughout, completely at ease as her family watched on.

"She dances for the tourists every weekend," Kyle whispered to me.

I had a few drinks, something I only do on occasion, and was feeling slightly tipsy when Kyle asked if I'd had enough. "It's getting late, and we have another early day tomorrow. More hiking! I don't mind driving if you want to return to your hotel in Waimea. I haven't had anything to drink. But we can stay here if you like."

"Here? Where?"

He grinned at me. "Not only do I work for my parents, I also live with them."

"Uh, so we'll be sleeping in your bedroom? Sign me up," I blurted out.

"Come on then. I have my own bungalow out back."

He led me down a jungle-lined trail to the small one-room bungalow he called home. "We have another three of these. My parents offer bed and breakfast to some of our clients."

The room was tidy but crowded. To my utter disappointment, two beds sat side-by-side along one wall. A small kitchen area and seating area lined the other wall, and a bathroom jutted off to one side. He made sure I knew where everything was in the bathroom, including a spare toothbrush, before he climbed into his own bed. I got a quick glance at his nearly naked body before he slipped under the covers. My hard-on hadn't subsided by the time I cleaned up and found myself standing beside the other bed.

The light from the single lamp still glowing would have betrayed me if Kyle hadn't reached over and turned it off. "Good night. I'll wake you in the morning."

"Thanks for the great day, Kyle. It was amazing."

He murmured a quiet reply I didn't quite catch as I stripped down to my own underwear and got into bed. With a stiff cock aching at my crotch, I was certain I wouldn't be getting to sleep any time soon. I was wrong.

Content to be exactly where I was, in Kyle's bedroom with him asleep only a few feet away, I passed out. Bright sunshine and his bright smile woke me the next morning.

Already showered, he was ready for the day. "We'll grab some breakfast before we go. Dad's a great cook."

His father was a great cook. Quiet and unassuming, he was the opposite of Kyle's mother. Taller than Kyle by a bit, he was very handsome and very hard-working. He had a formidable list of objectives tacked to a wall board beside the fridge. "Two new clients coming in on Saturday. Can you pick them up at the airport?"

"Yes sir," Kyle answered on the way out. He stopped to kiss his father on the cheek and pat his shoulder, a gesture of affection, which surprised me. His mother was nowhere to be seen.

"Mom's already out with clients. As you might have noticed, she drives me crazy, while my Dad is such a sweetheart you can't help but want to please him."

We drove to the north side of the island, the Na Pali Coast. Already I was struggling with the place names, most of them a jumble of vowels that seemed to slip off Kyle's tongue effortlessly but only left me confused.

If the names of the places we visited were hard to remember, the places themselves were more than memorable. If you think you've seen one precipitous mountainside, one gorgeous waterfall, or one stunning beach, then you've seen them all, Hawaii would prove you wrong.

Everything and every place seemed unique. We parked on the side of a meandering highway and embarked on a journey down a twisting trail that eventually led us to one of those stunning beaches.

Lovely white sand greeted us as we reached the bottom. It was raining lightly, which was totally normal for this side of the island. "The Na Pali Coast is one of the rainiest places on the planet," Kyle informed me.

Rain in Hawaii was not like rain in San Francisco, which could be dreary and oppressive. Unless the island was experiencing a typhoon, which did happen on occasion, the rainfall was warm and refreshing.

And Kyle knew what he was doing. This beach included a natural shelter under overhanging rock. We spread our blanket and ate our lunch while taking in the view protected from the elements.

The rain hadn't deterred us but apparently had kept others away. We were totally alone. Kyle's father had packed us a lunch from leftovers from the luau, and we ate it as we chatted. Then the sun came out.

It was breath-taking. A light breeze off the water blew away the clouds, and there was nothing but blue sky and blue ocean in front of us. The white sand stretched away on either side of us, book-ended by two similar outcroppings of volcanic rock topped by unruly crowns of palm.

Steam rose from the verdant Hawaiian forest that climbed the steep hills behind us. I was mesmerized by the alteration and taken by surprise when I noticed Kyle stripping at my side.

As we'd eaten, I couldn't help fantasizing about having some hot and wild sex with my gorgeous guide right then and there on that spectacular beach. I wasn't about to hit on him and risk spoiling the new friendship we'd forged so quickly. But I could dream without any harm coming of it.

Now, here he was suddenly getting naked. My cock responded instantly by getting hard as rock. He quickly dashed my soaring hopes. "I packed a swimsuit for you, too," he said with a grin.

I flushed and laughed. "Why how considerate," I mumbled while trying to tear my eyes from his naked body.

His skin was amazing. Flawlessly smooth and uniformly tan, there was only one area that hadn't seen much sun – a band of pale amber around his crotch and over the jutting mounds of his fantastic ass. His cock wasn't stiff like mine, but it was thick and seemed a little swollen as it bobbed at his waist. Too soon, he covered it up.

As I followed his example and stripped, I had to turn away in order to hide my raging boner only to hear him chuckle behind me.

"Don't worry about it. I've seen it before. Remember?"

"Oh yeah. That's right. Still, I don't want to offend you by waving it in your face."

"I take it as a compliment," he replied.

There was that about him. He just was so damn considerate. Whatever I did seemed OK with him.

The brilliant white sand was wet and warm under our bare feet as we headed for the water. After the misty rain, the day was almost too brilliant, especially with the white sand reflecting the afternoon sun and the foamy water sparkling with it.

The water was warm, too. I'd always loved the ocean and the salty taste of it. I wallowed in the gentle waves with Kyle at my side. We bobbed in the swell a little further out, then caught a wave in to the shore where we lay side-by-side on our backs and stared up at the endless sky.

Lying in the wet sand, surf tickled our bare feet and calves. The hot Hawaiian sun beat down on us. It was on exquisitely sensual experience, and I had no desire to move from there. Ever.

Eventually, I turned to look at Kyle. He was staring up at the sky, his eyes half-closed, but seemed to sense my gaze. His head turned, and he looked into my eyes. He smiled.

"Awesome, isn't it?"

He reached out, his hand already only inches from mine, and lay it over mine, entangling our fingers and squeezing gently.

If he hadn't done that, I probably wouldn't have kissed him. At least I don't think so. But that touch was so spontaneous and so tender, I couldn't help responding. I rose onto my side and leaned over him. Still gazing into his golden eyes, I dropped down to kiss those upturned, bowed lips.

He kissed me back, his hand squeezing mine, and his bare thigh pressing against my own. His mouth opened, and he welcomed my tongue. He took it in and sucked gently on it. It wasn't a sloppy or aggressive kiss on either of our parts, but it was open and uninhibited. I breathed in his breath, and he breathed in mine.

I couldn't recall a kiss that had ever lasted so long in all the myriad kisses of my past. For what seemed like an eternity, it was only that kiss, our lips touching and our tongues exploring, our hands entangled, and our thighs pressed against each other. There was no other movement toward something more, until finally my left hand slipped of its own accord from my hip where it lay quietly, to drop over his crotch.

I found his cock. It was stiff now and throbbing under his swim trunks. I gripped it through the material and slowly pumped it. The rigid plumpness of it had me moaning as our kiss became more intense.

His free hand settled on my chest. Gently but insistently, he pushed me away. I came up off his mouth with a gasp. Gazing down at him my eyes questioned although I found no words.

"That was lovely. Thank you. But let's not go there now."

"OK," I answered, unable not to smile back at him even though I was clearly being rejected.

It was very odd. Rather than feeling rebuffed, I felt the opposite. Perhaps it was because he continued to hold my hand as I lay back and returned to the idle sunbathing we'd been engaged in before that magical kiss.

I was not a patient type of dude, usually. If I wanted something, I worked for it doggedly and rarely wavered in my determination to get it. Yet here I was, accepting that kiss and hand-holding for what it was rather than doing my utmost to pursue an agenda of getting my guide naked and my cock up his ass.

Who the hell was this new person? I had no idea.

The timeless interlude eventually came to an end. Kyle rose, his hand gripping mine as he helped me up. "We'd better get hiking or risk being stranded in the dark."

"I wouldn't mind that," I admitted.

"Another time," he replied enigmatically.

We packed up and headed up the steep trail. Nothing changed, and everything changed. Kyle continued to offer up his informative chatter and considerate attention. I continued to check out his solid butt-cheeks and spring wood.

But now there was another element of familiarity between us. We'd kissed. I'd touched his cock, even if his swimsuit was between my hand and the heated flesh. There was no going back, even if there was no way forward – yet.

Again, I supposed I would have trouble sleeping that night, but didn't. The moment I lay down in my bed in the hotel, I fell into a deep and peaceful sleep.

I still had eleven more days on the island and was counting my lucky stars that I had booked Kyle for my entire stay on Kauai. I had him at my disposal every day, but not all day ever day. Sometimes he took out other clients in the morning, and sometimes in the afternoon or evening. But I saw him every day regardless.

It had been a little expensive booking a guide for all that time, but when I traveled, I believed in worrying less about the cost and more about the experience. Kyle was an experience worth every penny.

I had my laptop with me, a complete office in itself and managed to write regularly. I sent out three different fitness articles, four blurbs for a blogger acquaintance of mine, a travel story and even stayed up late one night pumping out a porn story for an editor friend who published anthologies of gay erotica.

I let Kyle surprise me every day with our itinerary. I surrendered control to him and was happy I did. He took good care of me. A different hike in a different but spectacular location, a swim in a pond below a waterfall, an afternoon sailing with a friend of his around the island, and even a dawn effort at surfing. I hadn't surfed since I was twenty.

We talked, mostly him, but I did open up more than usual. I found myself telling him things of which I rarely ever spoke. Like how my divorced mother and father seemed to despise each other and how hard it was for my younger twin brothers who still lived with my mother to handle the bitter battles over holidays and celebrations. I even told him about Donovan.

"So it's over now? I'm sorry. You haven't seemed too down about it. I would never have guessed."

The steamy island forest surrounded us as we hiked and talked. There was nowhere to hide from that question. "It's definitely over. And I'm not down about it. In fact, I am totally relieved. Awful, huh?"

"No, honest."

Not surprisingly, the days flew by. Before I knew it, it was our final day together. Kyle picked me up early, and we drove to one of the dozens of canyons that offered good hiking and great scenery.

"I think you'll really like this place. It'll be like we're the only two people on earth. Careful though, it's slippery. Keep one hand on my shoulder."

I wasn't sure what he was talking about. We'd halted beside a slender waterfall that dropped straight down from towering cliffs above on our right. On our left, a wall of more greenery blocked the view down.

He pulled aside the branches in our way and stepped down off the trail. Intrigued, I followed. The waterfall continued its downward plunge, but beside it a rocky trail headed in the same direction.

It was slippery, but he seemed familiar with the way, and I felt comfortable following with his shoulder to steady myself. Of course touching him or being touched by him always resulted in a throbbing hard-on, and by the time we reached to bottom, it was aching and leaking.

"Beautiful, isn't it? We can spread our blanket under that overhang."

I forgot momentarily about my boner as I found myself gawking at the amazing surroundings. We had arrived on a small beach. The sand was a rich ochre red while the lush emerald forest hung down over us in a semi-circle. Jumbled and broken volcanic rock bordered either side of the beach. The misty rainfall made it seem all the more close and hidden from the world. It was all ours for the day.

As he spread our blanket, he dropped his totally unexpected bombshell.

"My parents have been bugging me to open up an office in San Francisco. I am seriously considering it. Would you be interested in renting me a room?"

I was stunned. My mouth literally dropped open. I blurted out the first thing that came to mind. "Yes! Please thank god yes!"

He burst out laughing and pulled me into his arms. We hugged and laughed some more while I thought furiously.

Over the past two weeks, ever since that first hand-shake, I'd attempted not to think too much about the past or the future. I tried to focus instead on the moment and the time we had together. Of course I'd failed more often than not. I'd wondered if it was possible for me to move to Kauai to be with him; that is if he wanted me to. It was a bad time to sell my apartment, and with the way the market was, I'd probably lose my shirt. On the other hand I could work from anywhere if I wanted to. But I had grown up in San Francisco, and I had to admit however much I loved the beauty of Hawaii, I loved the urban hustle and bustle, too.

What did I want? Sex, like before in my relationships? Or something more? What was I willing to do for love? It was a moment of utter clarity. If I had the chance to be with Kyle, nothing else mattered. I realized what had been wrong with me before. I'd been homesick for a place I'd never been. I was looking for a home for my heart and Kyle was that home.

Yet I had to ask. "What do you like about me?"

"For one thing, you're quiet. I can talk and talk and you'll listen to every word I say. I like that! And you're honest. I feel like I know exactly how you feel when I'm with you and there's no guessing or pretending. I trust you. That's very important to me."

"And what about my body? Am I sexy?" In my mind, I was bursting to ask the obvious, "Do you want to fuck me? Do you want me to fuck you?"

He answered my unspoken question with his hands. Before I knew what was happening, he'd unbuttoned my fly and pulled down my shorts, while dropping to his knees at the same time. My hard-on bobbed in his face, and he grinned as he took it in his mouth and began to suck on it.

"Oh my god, oh my god, please don't stop. I love you, I fucking love you," I chanted as I thrust into his mouth and reached down to tangle my fingers in his thick, unruly, gorgeous hair.

He gurgled an incoherent reply as his lips caressed the head of my swollen rod, and his tongue swabbed the slit. My knees trembled, and I felt light-headed. I was gasping for breath, and he'd been sucking for less than a minute.

He was obviously just getting started. His hands, broad and calloused but so gentle, reached around to caress my bare ass. I felt burned, spreading my feet and opening the crack of my ass just in time for Kyle's fingers to slide in and find my asshole.

I grunted, again thrusting into that wet mouth as a fingertip stroked and then lightly probed. I could hardly believe it. The intimate intensity seemed all at once nearly overpowering. Kyle did not relent as he dropped down to engulf my entire cock, right to the root. His finger pushed past the ring of my sphincter and slid knuckle deep.

I shook from head to toe, staring down at his face full of my cock and squirming around the finger buried in my aching butt-hole. I was all his, trembling, moaning and absolutely, unequivocally in love.

He pulled off and looked up at me with spit on his lips and a crooked grin lighting up his face. "Let's lie down. I want to sit on your face while I suck your cock."

"Hell yeah! Anything, any damn thing you want!"

He rolled onto his back while unbuttoning his flowered shorts and pulling them off. I got a good look at his ass and the deep divide between his full cheeks. He was going to sit on my face! I couldn't help myself and tackled him.

Laughing and rolling on the blanket, we ended up head to crotch. Kyle did exactly as he'd promised by planting his knees on either side of my face and dropping down to smother me with his plump butt-cheeks. He dove for my cock at the same time and sucked it deep.

His enthusiasm was a kick-start for my own repressed desire. I'd been wanting to feel his body against mine, to touch and to taste him and to smell him. It was happening. I shoved my face into his crack and rooted around for his hole.

I spread those full cheeks with my hands and probed with my tongue. His skin was so warm and smooth I had to lick it all over. I tasted his salty sweat before I found the wrinkled rim of his pouting hole and began to stroke it furiously. I was incensed with the need to eat that hole, using my lips to clamp over it and my tongue to swipe the pouting entrance.

He wriggled over my face and groaned deep in his chest as he matched my wild strokes with bobbing lips and suctioning cheeks. When his asshole pushed outward in a gaping welcome I attacked with twisting stabs. His entire body jerked on top of me.

He grabbed the underside of my knees and pulled them up and back. Momentarily pulling off my cock, he spit on his fingers then drove them down into my exposed butt valley. Two spit-wet fingers wormed their way into me.

I flopped under him and arched my back to press upward into those fingers. He gulped down my cock again as his fingers pumped in and out of my slippery hole.

I ate his ass while my hands ran over the satin-smooth expanse of his spread butt. He had a really big ass, padded muscle that swelled out from his slim waist in twin mounds of lush flesh I just could not get enough of.

His cock and balls mashed against my chin and neck as he humped my face and bobbed over my cock. His spit dribbled down to coat my ass-crack and lube the fingers he stuffed into me.

It was a tableau of intimacy I could only have dreamed. He held nothing back. His asshole yawned open for my tongue. His fingers rooted deep in my asshole, twisting and rubbing and drilling. His lips and tongue roamed up and down my stiff shank and throbbing cock-head in a boisterous drive.

As it had day after day, the rain lost its battle with the sun, and the clouds parted. Sudden brilliance flooded our little cavern. Kyle's gorgeous butt blocked my view of the beach, but not that golden brightness now surrounding us.

Again, it was Kyle who called the shots. "Let's go out on the sand and fuck," he said after pulling his mouth off my cock.

"I'm all for that," I answered as he rose off my face. I got a good look at his pink butt-hole all wet with my spit and twitching. I groaned and bit my lip, keen to get my cock up it, if that was his plan, rather than his cock up my ass.

He'd come prepared. Naked and seemingly unabashed about it, he quickly rummaged through his pack to pull out a condoms and lube. I'd been ready to search for a condom in my wallet which I'd placed there hopefully after our first day of hiking, but he was too quick for me.

It was typically considerate of him to smile up at me with those lovely golden eyes and roll down the condom over my cock with gentle hands. I gasped as he massaged a copious smear of lube over it, then gawked with lust as he turned around and bent over for me.

"It's all yours. Fuck me good, Scott."

He placed both hands on his butt and spread the melon-cheeks wide. Once again I was staring at his flushed, pouting asshole. I lunged for it. Reaching to seize his slim waist, I rammed my well-lubed cock up his ass.

"Yeah! Fuck me hard!"

I'd eaten out that hole thoroughly, which was probably the reason it parted to easily to that powerful thrust. It felt snug enough, but then seemed to collapse inward and swallow me up. I was amazed and incensed. I just had to fuck that butt!

"Damn, Kyle! I've been wanting this ass for so goddamn long! You've been driving me crazy!"

"Now that you've got it, show me what you can do to it!!"

He meant it. He held himself in place by sheer willpower, his feet buried in the warm red sand and his knees locked. With his hands on his own sweet ass-cheeks, he held them open for my vigorous assault and grunted loudly with every slam of my hips against him.

The wet sand was already warm and the sun hot beating down on us. We both broke out in a wash of sweat. The beads of moisture glistened on his golden body. My cock slipped in and out effortlessly, faster and faster.

I slid a hand around his waist and found his cock. Fat and stiff, it drooled in my hand as I began to pump it. That had him slamming his ass back against me and grunting even more loudly.

I would never have fucked him so wildly if he hadn't asked me to, and so obviously wanted. It was not my usual style. I liked to take my time, until the very end when approaching orgasm transformed me into an animal.

He'd brought that animal out of me in the very first moment. It raged in both of us as the sun beat down on us and the waves rhythmically attacked the shore. The world was all ours and no one else's.

Orgasm came, but not before I fucked him down on his hands and knees in the sand, then on his back with his feet in the air. In that final position our mouths clamped together as my cock slammed deep into his sucking hole. It was the last straw, his ass wide open and welcoming, my cock encased in his quivering slot.

I came inside him, the condom protecting us. He shot a copious load between our slippery bellies. His tongue was in my mouth. His eyes were open, staring up into mine. With our chests pressed together, that shared climax was all at once mirrored in the matching rhythm of our beating hearts. It was a little miraculous.

"Next time, it'll be the other way around," he said after we came up for air.

I was ecstatic, not just at the thought of his cock up my ass, but at the notion there would be a next time. I was still leaving his gorgeous island the next day.

"Are you seriously thinking of coming to San Francisco? This was a great two weeks, but I have to admit I want more. And more. In fact, I want days and days and night after night of this. I want it for the rest of my life." I admitted.

"I'll be in San Francisco in a week. As long as you'll have me."

"Have you? Have you? You bet your sweet ass I'll have you!"

We rolled in the sand and wrestled our way down to the water. Splashing and laughing, we washed off the sweat and sand and cum.

"The day is still young, Scott. Then there's that ass of yours to fuck."

Promises, promises. Fortunately for me, Kyle proved capable of keeping his.

COURTESY OF THE HOTEL
By Derrick Della Giorgia

Derrick Della Giorgia was born in Italy and currently lives between Manhattan and Rome. His work has been published in several anthologies and literary magazines. Visit him at www.derrickdellagiorgia.com.

The island of Culebra, between Puerto Rico and the U.S. Virgin islands, was the most beautiful creation of rough nature Kootcho and I had ever seen, until we ran into Mario, the late-twenties Austrian at the reception at our hotel. The incandescent air that wrapped that paradise teased one's imagination, and I had already tried to put my hands on Kootcho's naked torso. "I wanna have you." I had whispered into his ear on the boat trip to the island, and he had told me to be patient for a little longer before "I take my bathing suite off, and I let you take care of my itch." It was our third year together, and we had decided to celebrate, dedicating to ourselves those seven days of pure sex and beach. I couldn't wait to take his white shorts off and lick all the salt off his asshole. After three years, my hormones reacted like the first time to his blond short curly hair, his blue eyes and his firm half Polish and half Hungarian body. I needed to see him with his legs spread open, and we still had to go through damn reception!

"Xavier. Look at the guy behind the desk," said Kootcho as he opened the door.

"Fuck." I replied. This six-four tall, dark hair, dark eyes man in a blue night suit waited for us with a polite smile on his face.

"Hello, welcome to FBZO Hotel, my name is Mario, how can I help you?" He quickly introduced himself with his cumbersome German accent and left the desk to help us with our luggage.

"Hello. We have a reservation under the name of Della Giorgia."

"We were waiting for you, Sir. Please, follow me." He put our bags in the elevator and waited for us to enter the little room where we would have been standing in our half-nakedness almost against his suit. Once in there, I gave him my back, hoping he would stare at my muscular tanned shoulders and my little hard ass teasing him from inside the synthetic black fabric of my shorts. My desire grew so strong that it upset my stomach, and I had to strategically place an arm below my waist to hide the uncontrollable erection that kept pushing between my legs.

Kootcho and I couldn't even look into each other's eyes, too concentrated to pretend we were indifferent to that confection of flesh. Mario walked us to the room and explained how everything worked, obtaining our undivided attention. His short hair cut, his impeccably shaven beard, his long white teeth, his pulpy lips, his slender wrists. Nothing went unnoticed.

As he closed the door, I put my hand on my cock, and I looked at Kootcho who simply mouthed "Fuck" again, without adding any more comments. Then I grabbed him from behind, and I started licking his salty neck, right under his left ear, as with my hands I pressed his tiny waist against my puffed out shorts.

"I wanna fuck your ass off you."

"Please, fucking get into my ass."

I bit his right deltoid, and without letting my teeth go, I pulled him to the window to enjoy the view and get that burning sun light on his smooth back. The spasms in my groin were unbearable and transmitted from the head of my cock to the very base in the vicinity of my asshole. I landed the palm of my left hand on his throat, and with my right hand, I wrapped my throbbing meat and stretched my balls, without taking my shorts off. Kootcho liked to feel the metal parts against his defenseless ass. I pulled down my foreskin in an attempt to release some pressure, and I crouched to eat my meal. When I finally rested my face in there, his hole was already spasmodically contracting and dilating: I pulled back to admire that beautiful ceremony and jumped into it again with my eyes closed, inhaling all his desire.

"Stick your tongue in there, please ..." He groaned, first desirous and then for the pleasure, when I finally licked and kissed and bit and sucked his meaty flower. The ring of flesh I was totally absorbed on, was smooth and wet and tasted like raw sugar on my tongue and my lips.

"Lay there, now!" Kootcho turned around spreading my saliva and his juice all over my face and threw me on the bed, my arms dangling from the side. "I wanna suck this horse tool." He admitted to me more than once that my cock size was among the primary reasons he had fallen in love with me. He had immediately loved to bury my burning eight fat inches down his young throat. He was only sixteen when I met him, already looking for an older companion to devote his blondness to. I was celebrating drinking age and his sister introduced me to him. Later, she confessed to me that Kootcho hadn't stopped describing my dark eyes and my European accent for a whole week, until we finally went on a date. My European accent never failed. That little trick had provided me with more than one unforgettable night, together with the story, which I had confectioned to perfection, of how my Spanish mother and my Italian father had met in Barcelona, fallen in love and moved together to New York. Guys couldn't resist my spicy personality and my perfect black eyebrows playing with my most intense looks.

"Slow down, I don't wanna come yet, not until I fuck that ass I was working on." He kept my foreskin as down as he could with both hands and sucked every drop my dick would anticipate. His body was amazing. Firm like a rock around his nipples, defined to perfection on his arms. The lines of his abs gently dug into his milk white skin and framed his sexy navel from where a delicate strip of blond hairs dove down. Watching his muscles contracting as he went down on my groin made it even harder to stop that white lava trapped in my balls. I forced his head down on me for the last time, and then I got him back against the window, in a way that my eyes could enjoy the turquoise water with the pale sand in the background and his naked body. I abandoned myself on my knees and started licking and swallowing all I could find on his inner thighs. With such voracity, that my head commenced to spin, and I only regained balance after I positioned my mouth on his sun-bathed hard cock. I navigated up and down, from his pulpy head down to his blond pubes, from his tight balls up to the entrance from where a gooy transparent honey was dispensed, until we both couldn't take it anymore and decided to come. I sat him on the window pane and lifted his legs up until I saw my hole. I positioned my hips against him and dove into his hot tight canal as I stroked his cock. He felt my pectorals and went down with his hands on my abs, chiselled by ten years of uninterrupted swimming lessons, until he couldn't take it anymore, and in an explosion of pleasure started pulling my thick black hair. He came right on my chest and abdomen and fed me his cum with his fingers making me burst my juice as deep inside him as I could reach.

"Do you wanna go swim?" He asked me.

"Sure." I wiped the sweat off my forehead.

On the beach, we thanked God we had already calmed our spirits, because the nakedness, the green of the palm trees, the sand running through our fingers, that odd silence pressed down by the heat, made us only want to take our bathing suit off and fuck in that paradise.

My piña colada was almost over, and it was 6:00 pm when Kootcho mentioned Mario again. "Xavier, I can't stop thinking of Mario. He is so hot. I have never wanted to go back to the hotel so much before." He laughed.

"Leave me alone. When he took us to the room in that elevator, for a second, I wondered what he would have done if I had grabbed his pouch."

"Ok, but not in the elevator, please! That was the only unsexy part to me." Kootcho had a serious phobia for elevators, and only under my non-stop insisting, he would accept to take one.

"Would you like to have a threesome?" I attempted, satisfying my fantasy.

"You don't even know if he's gay!"

"I think he likes us. Did you see how he was attentive to every movement when we got out?"

"I don't know. But I'll say a prayer."

We ran into the water and let the weakened waves massage our sore bodies. I felt the sand inside my bathing suit stimulating my balls and insinuating into my ass crack, and I got horny again. There was something magical on that island that provoked a sweet hunger. Even the live green vegetation developing not far from the beach seemed to invite to sex with all its wetness. A pure contrast to the salt drying on our skin, the sun cooking our brain and the smell of wild. I swam close to Kootcho, and I hugged him in the water, rubbing my body against his. He kissed me and closed his eyes as I caressed his smooth legs up and down underwater from his knees all the way up his white speedo.

"We should go back, change and go for dinner. Our fuck made me hungry. Come on, let's go say hi to Mario." He grabbed my hand and pulled me out of the water.

He was there. Hotter than before if that was possible.

"Hello again." We said almost simultaneously.

"How was the beach?" He asked with a smile, looking interested to know.

"Amazing, this whole island is amazing. I still can't believe this is true. It is like a dream. But you must be used to this." Kootcho picked up the conversation, being much better than I at entertaining people.

"No, no. I have only worked here for two months. I am from Austria. The island is still a beautiful mystery to me, too." His voice was so deep and masculine, and his politeness made every inch of his body so much more lickable than it was already.

"Oh, you are a fake local then!" We laughed at the stupid joke but happy as long as the conversation lasted. When he smiled, his cheeks went up a bit and made his secretive eyes even sexier.

"All right. See you later then." Our permanence in the hotel reception had a time limit considering we were wearing only our shorts (on purpose!) and our flip flops.

We entered the elevator despite Kootcho's disapproval, and I pushed the button for the fourth floor. I looked into Kootcho's eyes, and I mumbled "What I wouldn't do to that piece of man." At the same time a weird noise, one of those one heard at the mechanic, exploded all around the elevator, which went back to starting position. Lights off.

"What happened? What happened Xavier? What did you do? Open the doors!" Kootcho was panicking. Completely out of control.

"It's ok, don't worry. Everything is fine. Let me just press the button again. Must happen all the time." But no matter how many times I tried or which button I pressed, nothing happened.

"Press the alarm!" And he pressed it himself without waiting for me. He was panting and sweating profusely. He picked his iPod from his bag and put it on, then grabbed a muscle-relaxant from his pill box and swallowed it. Silence fell in the dark elevator. Only the alarm, outside. Suddenly, I realized that the elevator was way too small to host us for a long time. We both almost reached the six and a half foot roof, and our sweating bodies were eating up all the air.

"Hello?! Hello!" Mario was yelling from outside and knocking on the door.

"The elevator got stuck. We can't get out, please do something. Quickly." Kootcho hurried to explain and went back to his corner.

"Stay calm. It'll take only a second." We heard him running around and making a phone call, every passing second feeling like an eternity in that metal trap. I felt guilty. I had pushed Kootcho to take the elevator and was not at ease myself.

Luckily, Mario was fast enough, and after what might have been a handful of minutes, but felt like hours, he got us out of the elevator. Kootcho sat on the floor, against the wall and didn't move.

"Are you ok?" Mario asked him after a minute.

"I'm fine, I just need to calm down."

"Can I get you anything?" He put his big hand on Kootcho's naked shoulder and waited for an answer. The picture enthralled me to no end, my boyfriend shirtless on the floor in his wet shorts and that big Austrian hottie in his suit crouched next to him. That totally cancelled the elevator experience and ignited my crotch again.

"A cigarette, please."

He came back with a cigarette and waited with me for Kootcho to calm down. Mario told us he, too, was scared of elevators and for that reason he had done everything in his power to make that nightmare last as little as he could. At the age of twenty-seven, he said he could count on both his hands how many times he had taken an elevator. Probably stayed so fit because he used the stairs all the time, I thought.

When things calmed down, Mario offered us, for the inconvenience, to have a drink on their private terrace, courtesy of the hotel. He walked us up the stairs to the sixth floor, let us sit on the white couches and told us to wait there until he came back with the drinks.

"Wow, Kootcho. This is amazing." From up there, we could practically see most of the island: the beach where we had lain down, the few other sparse hotels, and the dense vegetation on the two hills behind us. Everything looked so much darker under the moon light, without all the liquid colors of the day. It was a pregnant darkness though, every corner unraveling more and more intricate details as we dedicated enough concentration to it. Somehow, the island amplified our body, transforming us into unfinished emotions.

"It's breathtaking."

"I want you." I caressed his abdomen still warm from all the sun he had taken and pushed the tips of my fingers into his speedo, enough to feel his humid pubes.

"Stop it. He's coming back!"

"So what ..."

We heard the Austrian's heavy steps up the stairs and stopped immediately. He came back with a bottle of vodka and every kind of juice.

"Would you like the lights on?"

"It's beautiful like this, thanks."

He positioned the tray on the table in front of the couch where we were sitting, and in doing so, he got so close to my right knee that it ended up an inch away from his crotch. I had my feet on the table. My blood was already all up in my head and down in my pants, and in a second of folly, instead of moving my leg away, I delicately pushed my knee into his pants, until I hit his leg first and then, while he was pouring the vodka and the juice into the glasses, his huge bulge. He didn't move away, but continued to pour, and the flowing of

222

liquids inspiring me even more, I slowly started to rub his balls. Still nothing. Only one glass left to go. I pushed further to make sure he understood it wasn't a mistake and put my hand behind his knee, distractedly. With my fingertips, I caressed the back of his leg, and then I finally felt his hard cock pushing against my knee. At that point, sure he liked our game, I grabbed his balls and cock with my hand, and I squeezed so much that he poured some juice out of the glass and on his hand. Kootcho blocked his arm midair and sucked the cranberry juice off his fingers, one by one.

"You are so fucking hot." I told him, and he started to smile.

We pulled him down on the couch and started kissing him on both sides. I pressed my lips against the scratchy beard that was slowly coming back, and Kootcho teased his ear, then we met on his lips and had our first three way kiss. He emitted the sexiest groans, as if he hadn't had sex in ages, or ever in his life, and buried his hands in our still wet shorts. I sighed deeply when he dipped his powerful middle finger into my asshole while with the rest of his hand squeezed my butt cheeks. I could taste the coffee he was drinking behind his desk down my throat, and watching the rhythmic movement of his hand up Kootcho's ass made the same treatment reserved to me even more irresistible. My only worry was how he was gonna fuck us both at the same time.

He took his jacket off while Kootcho unbuttoned his shirt, and I undid his pants, our breathing and the tropical birds in the back the only noises on the terrace. I unearthed a huge cut cock from his pants and inserted it in my mouth right away, not resisting another second to the pleasure of sucking that big boy. Kootcho took his speedo off and sat his ass on Mario's open mouth, feeding him like a famished baby. He took big mouthfuls of that offer and, when he could, pushed my head down on his dick making me feel it in my neck. At that point, I decided to take the initiative and spread my legs over his crotch, wetting my asshole with the thick pineapple juice he'd brought until he stroked my arm and pulled it away, finishing the work I had started, never neglecting the ass in his mouth. I sat on his obelisk, and after the first resistance, I took it in, altogether, happy only when I felt I was squashing his balls. He rode me with no manners, thrusting his hips inside of me and forcing me to hold on to his petrified chest in order not to fall off that pleasure machine. Once I got the rhythm, I joined him in Kootcho's ass and shared with him the juice, the salt and the sand that was trapped in the delicate folds of his skin. We exchanged ass, sand and saliva, and he never stopped pumping me.

"I wanna fuck this ass, too." He moaned into Kootcho's groin, and he spanked me to signal to me my dose was finished.

"Fuck me, Mario, please, fuck me as hard as you can," implored Kootcho.

I was still hungry, and as he entered the hole and started injecting Austrian energy into my boyfriend, I felt the urge to be in there with them, and I made my way.

"I wanna fuck you, too, Kootcho."

Our arms were intertwined, and in that nest of flesh, I attempted my crusade. I pushed my dick in between Mario's hard stick and Kootcho's already dilated fun door. With extreme patience, we managed to fit and performed what I considered the best fuck of my life for a long time. Our cocks were synchronized inside Kootcho's ass, and my balls kept banging on Mario's hardened testicles with every thrust. Kootcho couldn't resist the pressure inside anymore, and he came three consecutive times without even touching himself, forming a warm river that went down on Mario's chest and abdomen. Then Mario clutched with both his hands my ass and caused me to flood Kootcho's back, who in the meantime had lain down on him. Finally, it was the Austrian's turn. He extracted his sword from our lover's ass and positioned us both on the couch, like conquered preys. He stood in front of us in all his genuine power, cupping with his left hand his swollen sack and stroking his dark red head with his right until he shot his boiling juice on our faces and our chests, filling our mouths more than once.

All courtesy of the hotel.

That night was only the beginning though. The day after, we engraved bracelets with the letters: "KXM," which stand for Kootcho, Xavier and Mario. We discovered the sex we could share didn't have an end, and the love that came out of that made us feel even more complete. We all live in New York now, and our two-year poly-amorous relationship is strong and invincible. We even play with a fourth every once in a while!

OUR BAD BROMANCE
By R. W. Clinger

R. W. Clinger resides in Pittsburgh. He writes for STARbooks Press, and his naughty man-tales can be found in their numerous compilations. He can be reached by e-mail at <u>kenitorico@verizon.net</u>.

ONE – TAKE A RIDE (2013)

"You cute little bastard, get over here and kiss my face," Cooper "Coop" Diller said, winking at me and glinted with a smile. He was seated behind his laptop, half-concealed by the device, working. I could still make out his hairy chest, a perky nipple, and one or two of his perfectly sculpted abs. Coop was into taking care of his body, which meant he worked out about five times a week, ate a lot of vegetables, and obtained his eight required hours of sleep. Never had I seen an inner tube of fatty tissue around his middle.

"I want to kiss your cock instead of your face, if you want to know the truth."

Coop liked sex but not at our office. He shook his head and claimed in a playful manner, "I don't do dick."

"Yeah, right. Then how come you do my dick?"

"I rather like your dick, Mark."

"Good answer, guy," I replied and shared a laugh.

The air conditioner in the office of Our Bad Bromance was on the fritz, and we were both shirtless because of the impossible heat. If it were any day but Saturday, we would have toughed the heat, since the office had about thirty workers. Coop was certainly not the type of man to flaunt his good looks at our employees. In truth, both of us liked to be professional, and that's how we ran our business.

When the staff was away, though, we played. But not on that Saturday, unfortunately. In brief, Our Bad Bromance was a dating website for queers, which we established seven years ago. To date, we had almost three million clients worldwide. Each paid a monthly fee to use the site, which paid the bills and our thirty employees, including insurance plans. The reason we were working a Saturday was simple: we needed to update the website's services. By Monday morning, we wanted Our Bad Bromance site to be brighter, sexier, and beefed up with better security. Of course, we could accomplish our goal if Cooper and I stopped flirting with each other.

When did the hot guy across the room become my boyfriend? Since we were young bait in a Pittsburgh high school along one of the city's three rivers. Since Mr. DeBoir's gym glass and we had to climb that fifty foot rope to the gymnasium's ceiling. Since that sleepover when were eighteen and on the roof of his house, outside his bedroom window. Since sleepy-time in kindergarten. Since our mothers had us in strollers on Birch Street in Gibsonia, a suburb of Pittsburgh.

I studied his sexiness again, consuming it with lavish pleasure: six-two frame, 210 pounds of chiseled meat, chestnut brown hair, pool-blue eyes, a beefy hairy chest that was beautifully sculpted, and a puckered navel that I always liked to dip my nose into and give a good whiff. Coop was forty-two now. No longer a boy. More like a solid man who was completely mature. Once a lover boy and now my husband, who I immensely adored and wholly loved.

"Don't even give me that look, Markus Blue." He eyed me from head to toe, taking in my good looks: 180 pounds and suggestively fit at forty-two, five-eleven structure, smooth and freshly waxed chest, ab-lined stomach, blond hair, emerald green eyes, tiny crow's feet at the corners of my eyes, narrow treasure trail the color of honey, which fell into my tight khakis.

"What look is that?"

"A look that clearly states that you want to remove your jeans and take a ride on my middle."

I admit … I craved his nine-inch cut dong and how he indisputably (and rather roughly) used it on my bottom. Some queer men had a fondness for inflated rod and liked a good ride. I just happened to be one of those men, and Coop knew that.

"Who said I wanted to sink on your cock?"

"Trust me, we've been in our bad bromance for some years now, and I just know when you want a ride."

The irony of his comment was rather elementary: we didn't have a bad bromance together. In fact, our love affair with each other was almost three decades old and the complete opposite of bad. We never fought, never failed to run out of things to talk about, and never carried out affairs on each other. The sex between us was still XXX stuff, if the truth be told. I'm talking about Titanman, Chaos and Falcon naughty. I'm talking about the dirty games we would play together called Jock & Coach, Bad Cop & Burglar, Professor & Student, Master & Servant, Hustler & Client, and Hitchhiker & Driver. And even more naughty sex games: Shave Me, Tie Me Up, Spank My Bottom, Choker, and You've Been s Very Bad Bad Boy. Bottom line: no, our bromance wasn't bad at all, even with all the rough play. It was the bomb. The best. I couldn't have asked for better.

"There's no time to play with your crank, Mark."

Whatever. I relaxed in my office chair, spread my legs ever so slightly, unzipped my khakis, discovered no Aussiebums, Rufskins, or a cotton C-IN2, and pulled out my cut, eight-inch toy that he loved to play with like a little kid, or a dog with its bone. The power of a cock was unbelievable; both of us knew that. The poker was already hard between my legs, and I shook it to and fro like a flag, teasing him.

"Coop, why don't you humor me by getting on your knees and eating this slammer?"

"I wouldn't dare. That thing has been around the block. Put it away."

I gave the beef a stroke ... two strokes ... three strokes ... and felt a sting of euphoria shift northward through its length. Then a pearl-white bubble of ooze surfaced at its reddish, mushroom-shaped cap, which I removed with two fingertips and licked away with my outstretched tongue and endless hunger.

My sidekick adjusted himself. Obviously, he had grown a boner in his denim, which was a total turn-on for me. Sweat gathered on his forehead, shoulders, and hairy chest. He gulped saliva down the back of his throat and admitted, "You have me. Now what?"

"You don't give me many options."

"That's bullshit, Mark. I give you plenty of options the way you use me up like a whore."

"Just remember, you're the most attractive and sweetest whore on the planet."

He rubbed his denim-covered dick again and said, "Save it, pal. Don't shoot your cream. I want to play a sex game with you tonight after we accomplish this work."

I was surprised by his request, stopped jacking the beef at my center, and inquired with interest, "What kind of game are you talking about?"

"Find a Flag."

I laughed, raising an eyebrow at him. "Don't you mean Find a Fag?"

"I call it Flag and you call it Fag. It's the same thing no matter how you suck on it."

"Who cares what we call it. Both of us know it's a great game, which we haven't played for a very long time."

He agreed, grinning from ear to ear.

To play Find a Flag was every married guy's dream. Coop and I dressed up for a night on the town of bar-hopping. We usually went to The London Boy Bar, Brawny's, or Mechanical Interests. Together, we scouted a male patron who turned the both of us on. We bought the guy drinks. We danced the night away with him. Then we asked if we could bring him back to our apartment in the city, to which he always agreed.

Our pick was usually always the same: a redhead with shimmering green eyes, six-one frame, a beefy chest and arms, and was preferably a bottom. The man was always in his early twenties, innocent looking, and wasn't afraid of us.

What we did with him in our apartment was naughty by nature. Coop and I took turns banging the guy's throat with our tools. Then we blasted his ass for an hour or more. Safe sex was important to us so we always wore condoms. And after the dude was kicked out of our apartment, we showered. Never did we get his full name, address, cell number, or where he lived. Coop and I really didn't give a shit about those details. The man was simply a tool for us, pleasure discovered in our long-term relationship. A fag (or flag) that was found, used up, and nothing more.

"Don't even think of backing out of the game tonight now that you mentioned it," I scolded my lover. "I know how you work. You labor over the site all day, eat Chinese for dinner, and fall asleep."

"I do not."

"You do," I nagged, placing my cock away for the time being. "Don't get me all excited about something that isn't going to transpire tonight."

"We'll do it. I won't back out."

"Promise me, Coop."

"Cross my heart."

I held him to his word. He was caught, like always. Game on.

TWO – THE BROMANCE GAME (2003)

I moved to Pittsburgh and taught English at one of the public schools. The teaching job sucked, and I felt like a full-time baby-sitter; so much for that career and four-year degree being of much use. The job lasted me six months before I said fuck it and quit. When misery is found, make better; this is what I always say.

Two weeks later I started an office job at Mills & Tucker Insurance. I was an assistant's monkey boy. My duties entailed proofing insurance letters, filing, buying office supplies, making coffee, and ... frequently getting banged by my immediate supervisor over the Xerox copier.

The bottom-banger just happened to be Coop, my long-time crush; a rather pleasurable fringe benefit that came with the job.

It was typical sexual harassment in an office setting that was accomplished by Coop:

"Mr. Blue, can you please bend over and pick up my Waterman?"

"Mr. Blue, I think you've been working out ... Let me touch your bicep."

"Mr. Blue, we need to discuss your ass ... I mean tasks."

I put out on his desk, under his desk, against his city-view window, in his office chairs, against his walls, and just about every place I could put out. Most of the time we practiced baseball positions (catcher and pitcher) together opposed to reviewing insurance claims. Not that either of us gave a shit, though, since we found each other irresistible.

After six months underneath him, he gave me a raise and a new title: Extraordinaire Office Hump. I took it. What underling wouldn't?

# # # # #

How and why did I fall for a guy like Cooper Diller? He wasn't Hollywood good looking. He wasn't rich. He didn't drive a Bentley. And sometimes his shirts were horribly pressed. The man worked out a little too much, and he was a health nut. He liked to gossip and rarely visited his relatives. But ... none of those details prevented me from being his sex-toy, lunch-fuck, or officer-bangee. I liked him completely, not just for the sex. I could cry on his shoulder if I needed to. I could tell him dark secrets when there was no one else to tell. I could ...

There was a tinder box inside my apartment on Moss Street in South Side. Every single time he visited me, he placed a piece of scrap paper inside the box. One word was printed on each piece of paper: hug, kiss, suck, food, pat, jerk, mad, blow, hold, date, sleepover, beer, movies, eats, trip, and many others.

We played another game with each other; we always played games with each other.

The Bromance Game we called it.

The rules were simple: you removed a slip of paper from the tinder box; you read it; you did what was on the piece of paper to your partner. Coop was always my partner; no, let me restate that ... Coop was my only partner, just the way I wanted it.

If the small slip of paper said fuck, we fucked. If it said hold, we snuggled for the evening. If it said trip, we went gambling. If it said eat, we went out to dinner in Shadyside or Greentree. If it said blow, we did a sixty-niner on my bed or on the apartment's secondhand sofa.

The game never got old; the games still never get old.

2003. Bush was President of the free world, and it was the year when NASA launched the space shuttle Columbia, the United States planned to invade Iraq to capture Saddam Hussein, and Coop and I became monogamous with each other. Our relationship took off, exactly the way we knew it would. Serendipity at work. Real dates occurred. Ice skating. Movie dates. Walks in Frick Park. Boating on the Monongahela. Bar dates. Poker nights with his male pals. Roller derby. Penguins games. Gambling at The Mountaineer in West Virginia. Steelers games. Bicycling. Rock climbing. Shopping dates. Just about every date we could possibly share together, we did, and happily.

The sex on those dates was original by all means. Coop read John Patrick short stories and tried every position the queer author wrote about. Stories by Patrick became our sexual guide in and out of the bedroom. Heated sex between our bodies ensued for the next month, three months, six more months, and then …

"I have this idea, Mark."

"What kind of idea?"

We were at The Mortal Man Bar & Grill on Glenbury Street, drinking our asses off and trying to pick up a cute and well-built redhead to have a safe threesome with. The bar wasn't packed since it was only four o'clock in the afternoon. A few other queers lingered about the place, mostly drunken fags with broken hearts who were listening to The Stones on the overhead speakers.

"Spill it. What kind of idea?" My gaze scanned a musclehead with a bulging chest, lisp, ginger-colored hair, and almost-amber tinted eyes. The guy was drop dead gorgeous. I knew he was the one we would go home with and spend a few hours fucking.

"An on-line dating site for fags. What do you think?"

"That's a bad bromance ready to happen."

My boyfriend grinned from ear to ear again. "Exactly the opposite, my friend. I like that name. You'll be partners with me, right?"

Was he talking about a website-based business relationship or becoming his partner for life? Something told me he was talking about both.

"Our Bad Bromance," I said. "It has potential."

"You have potential," he admitted, kissed me on the lips, got me drunk, and took me home with the musclehead guy with red hair.

Kain was the guy's name that we picked up. He had a ten-inch cock that was cut, pierced nipples, and a sun tattoo on the nape of his back. That's really all I knew about him that first night. No last name. No age. No history. No phone number. A stranger for our needs. A find for us. A toy for that November night.

The erotic details with the play-thing were hardly forgettable. Kain begged for our cocks in his mouth and asshole. Coop was good with that and took over the guy's face. I was in charge of his tight and hairless ass. Together we worked him over while Kain was on his hands and knees. A video camera filmed the whole thing. Coop said he thought about uploading the hour-long flick to the Internet, but never did. Heatedly, we stared at each other while we banged the guy. As I plowed his bottom, Coop plowed his mouth. It was adult film making to the nth degree. Our labor of lust was unstoppable and prize-winning and ... glue that kept us together and sent our relationship to new heights – always.

Kain lived with us for about two months. Talk about an uber-alternative relationship back then. Three men under one roof and ... each other. Three men who showered side by side by side, and ate together, went clubbing together, and had sex with each other. The ultra-bromance. Our life of threesomehood.

We never asked Kain to leave; he did that on his own. He met a professor named Milton. An English guru from Pitt. They fell in love and ... I think they're still a couple today. In fact, I believe Kain obtained a doctorate in English and teaches at the university with his lover, in the same department. I wouldn't be surprised if the two weren't writing a gay mystery together, or something like that for queer readers. The perfect faggot couple. Queen bliss.

"Just the two of us," Coop said after Kain's tender goodbye.

"The way it ought to be."

"I'll miss him."

"Likewise."

"But it doesn't mean I fell in love with him."

"No way."

"That stuff is between you and me."

"What stuff?"

"The love stuff, Mark."

He totally caught me off guard, and I stared hard at him. "You love me?"

"Something like that."

I was drawn into his hulking arms and he kissed me. Thereafter, the conversation was soon lost because we had

236

guy-with-guy sex together for the rest of the evening and long into the night ... just the two of us.

THREE – QUICKIES (1993)

The world was such a small place, even in 1993. How old was I back then? Twenty-three? Twenty-four? Some irrational number that screamed I was young, fun, and filled with cum. Most of the guys I dated called me handsome and hard, a sex maniac, a porn star. Others simply liked me for my brain: he knows how to spell, and he's quite crafty with beads and glitter.

When Coop and I graduated from high school, we lost a few years together. But there were times when we saw each other, particularly in 1993 when *The Piano* and *Jurassic Park* ruled at the box office, when Meatloaf sang about doing anything for love, and Janet Jackson rocked the house with "That's the Way Love Goes," and people were reading *The Bridges of Madison County*, crying their asses off, and others were reading *Lasher* by Anne Rice. A blizzard froze over a quarter of the country that year, IBM took a huge loss, and Bill Clinton succeeded George H.W. Bush as the forty-second President. Rodney King testified that his civil rights were violated. Microsoft released Windows 3.11. President Clinton announced his "Don't Ask, Don't Tell" policy.

Was it a good year? Some would say yes. But honestly, I only thought it was good when I bumped into Coop, and we shared some heavy-duty quickies ...

#####

Winter:

I stood in the three-feet of snow that took over Pittsburgh in March. The gas tank in my Buick 88 was almost empty, and I was pumping fuel into it. The wind was biting, and the sky was nothing but a sheet of white frosting. Some thought it was the end of the world. Armageddon had finally discovered the human race. Others thought Jesus was going to slip out of heaven and rescue us from the damnation of the world's fury. I just thought it was a pretty wild snowstorm and nothing more.

I had stopped smoking weed, but I hadn't stopped drinking. No longer was I addicted to amphetamines; I read six hundred-page novels to keep my mind off the pills: *The Stand, War and Peace,* and *Gone With the Wind.* I was sleeping around a lot; I remember that like it was yesterday. I didn't have a boyfriend, I had sleepovers: Richard, Dodger, Phil, Hank, and Quall. I was underweight and needed to put some muscle on my body; all the sex I had didn't help. I was mostly tired and rarely ate.

Coop found me at Mercano's Fill-up. He snaked around one of the pumps and bloomed with a smile of intoxicated interest. As a hug ensued, he said, "I thought that was you."

"One hundred percent me."

We kissed in public, which could have gotten us killed back then. We stood in the freezing cold for the next ten minutes and talked about the last year: he was taking business classes at Pitt; I was ingesting drugs; he lived in an apartment in North Side, next to Three Rivers Stadium; I stayed with whomever I could.

"I live around the block. Do you want to come over and have a cup of cock?"

He said that. No shit. No lies. And I laughed.

"I meant coffee. Yeah ... coffee."

"Of course you did, Coop," I sarcastically replied and winked at him in a playful and agreeable nature.

We climbed into our cars, and I followed him to his apartment. Once inside, overlooking the blizzard, secluded in his one-bedroom place with the heat at full blast, our clothes came off, we bumped bodies together, and I spent the next twenty-four hours with him, mostly under his weight and flannel sheets.

#####

Spring: Early June.

I ended up at Coop's apartment on Sass Street, naked and snuggled between his legs. His nine-inch cock was pressed into the tunnel of my throat, and I toyed with his droopy balls. Slurps, moans, and grunts of erotic pleasure exited my mouth. Hip-thrusts from the guy gagged me, but I really didn't care much. My fingers discovered his hairy chest, rolled over his furred abs, tweaked his pert nipples, and touched the base of his smooth chin in a moderately sexy manner.

"Blow me," he whispered above me. "Don't stop."

I didn't stop ... at least not until he decided to come. What kind of afternoon fling was I if I had stopped blowing him before he burst his creamy and bittersweet load all over my face, which was exactly what I wanted him to accomplish?

Where was Coop's boyfriend during that springtime afternoon when the warm and cozy June sun splayed over our naked bodies? Jake, John, Jonas – whatever his name was – had a meeting in Oakland at Pitt. While the boyfriend was away, I played ... with Coop. Why not? Any horny young man like me would have, right?

He choked me with his cock. Something told me he wanted to, and laughed about it. Coop's fingertips dug into the back of my skull and he pushed my face over his sultry and alluring goods, which almost suffocated me, but in a good way, of course. "Suck the ooze out of me, guy," he called down and over my bare back. "Don't be shy."

I didn't eat any man's juice, not even Coop's. Yes, I had a lot of sex, but it was always safe. A blowjob was fine to carry out, but not a cum-lunch for my gut. Instead, my head bobbed up and down in an uproarious manner. I used my tongue on his pole, applied suction to the meat and ...

He huffed and puffed above me on the queen-size bed where he fucked his boyfriend of six months: Jake, John, Jonas – whatever his name was. Grunts of euphoria filled the room from his mouth. A long moan of passion echoed off the walls. Then he quickly pushed my head away and gushed a load on my right cheek and neck. Spew shot out of his hard pecker and drizzled my flesh. Warm, sticky churn glazed my skin, ending my blowjob on the bed with him, our afternoon quickie, and something that prompted my immediate escape from the apartment before his boyfriend returned home to enjoy some sloppy seconds with his dude.

Summer:

The day was steamy hot and all the city boys chose not to wear shirts. Beefy chests glowed in the summertime sun. Sweat rolled down and over carved abs. Treasure trails were coated in thin layers of masculine perspiration. Biceps gleamed with bronze tans. Navels were puckered and dribbled with enriching sunshine.

Jake, John, or Jonas was no longer Coop's boyfriend. Coop had another man attached to his right arm: Stone. A medium-size guy who looked exactly like Jesus. I bumped into the pair on the Birmingham Bridge, which crossed the Monongahela River. Coop and I almost ran into each other, grazing shoulders together. Stone almost took my face off because he obviously suffered from an anger management problem and felt that I was bothering his boyfriend.

"Coop, how are you?" I started the conversation, glowing with a smile.

He was apprehensive at first to answer me. Almost shy. It took me less than ten seconds to realize he was acting. "What's your name again?"

I told him.

"Yeah, that's right. I've been great, how are you?"

"Swell." Hard for him. Horny for him. Needing his cock in my throat again.

"How long has it been?"

Honestly, it was three days ago. I enjoyed a face fuck with him on Sass Street. Stone was out with a bunch of his buddies, and Coop stayed behind, so I could use his cock like a toy. "I can't remember."

"Stone, this is Mark Blue. We go way back."

I shook Stone's hand.

Unimpressed with me, he nodded his head. Then he asked, "Were you two boyfriends?"

Coop and I both shook our heads.

"Just wondering," Stone added and …

Almost ten hours later, when Stone went to see Green Day in concert at the Civic Arena, I ended up back at the apartment on Sass Street, between his boyfriend's legs, under his weight, and had Coop's condom-covered cock pressed into the deepest reaches of my bottom … until he shot his load in the plastic that separated our connected bodies in relentless lust.

FOUR – RED COWBOY (THIS EVENING)

We sit next to each other and eye up the hotties at Brawney's. It just happens to be military night at the bar and the place is wall-to-wall Marines and be-all-you-can-be men. Half of the male patrons are in green chamo. The other half are civilians who sport military buzz cuts that make them look like war heroes even if they aren't. Beefy men with Marine tattoos carry longneck bottles of beer. Navy guys are dressed in all white, but every dude in the place realizes that these men are not virgins. Lady Gaga plays on the jukebox. She sings something about Nebraska. The night is young, and no one sneaks into one of the corners for a blowjob. This will surely transpire as the night grows weary, though. In fact, the bathroom will probably be filled with queers by midnight, and an orgy will take place. The steamy bartenders clink glasses together with freshly poured cocktails. The bar is loaded with a bunch of queens, shoulder to shoulder.

We see Mr. Redhead seated at the bar between two military hunks that probably just came back from Afghanistan.

Red makes eye contact with my delicious husband.

Coop winks at him.

I raise my beer to the guy.

Before I know it, Red, with his six foot frame and Texas cowboy accent, makes his way up to our twosome.

Coop buys the steer a Rolling Rock, and I check the find out from head to toe, approving his cowboy build.

I ask if he has a military background. Red says he does and rattles off something to do with the Air Force.

Coop steps up to my side and holds me against him. He whispers in my ear, "This is the one we're taking home."

A laugh escapes my lips.

My sidekick winks at me. The look he shares with me says remarkable endearments: We are lovers forever. You and me, guy. Just the two of us. From boys to men. Let's get the game started and play with Red. Let's have fun tonight ... like we always do, of course.

LAST NIGHT ON SMITHFIELD STREET
By R. W. Clinger

ONE – SUNDAY MORNING

"You fell for me first," I said to Key. "Everything about you was glazed with fluffy emotions like those horrible Lifetime movies or harlequin books"

We circled each other in our bedroom like Walt Disney birds, preparing for brunch with the Queens of Willow Street, Vince and Kyle, our Sunday morning dates for the last gazillion years. Our preparation dance was a queer musical of sorts with a lot of primping, hair gel, hair removal, tucking, flattening, and poking. The only thing it was missing was a song out of *Hairspray*, I believed.

"Was Lifetime even around then, Robby?" Key asked at my right side. Both of us stood in front of the mirror in our *Architectural Digest*-styled bedroom. We were in nothing more than our boxer-briefs, aging together in a simple life: the real estate agent and the writer. He was still thin at forty-seven, but he didn't really look like a young Nicholas Cage anymore. I had gained a few pounds and was starting to look like my mother – God forbid! Key could eat the Bakery on Potomac and not gain a pound. I used Weight Watchers and gained twenty pounds. He still sported those sultry green eyes that melted me twenty years ago. I surmised often that they were magical: pools of intimacy, unrelenting dreams of spending his life with me, and tender. He still worked out. I liked to shop on-line. He remodeled the kitchen. I wrote another book: *Skin Artist*.

"Yes, Lifetime was around then. But Bravo wasn't ... nor was the Internet."

"They didn't have sexting or Ipads or Tom Toms."

"Or the term green."

"Lady Gaga was a baby and Bill Clinton was President."

"You mean Hillary. She ran the government back then. Balls to the wall, baby. Every queer wanted her to be the President."

"And then came Monica Lewinski ... literally."

"That delicious whore. I loved her. She knew how to treat a man."

"You know how to treat a man."

"You're just trying to get in my pants again."

"You know all my little, dirty secrets." He turned and faced me, wrapped his arms around my waist, drew our bare chests together, and kissed my neck.

I knew he wanted sex; he loved sex in the mornings. "Although your invitation to seduce me is flattering, we can't make love because we'll be late for brunch."

Key pulled his lips away from my neck, breathed in my skin, and said, "The Queens of Willow Street will understand."

I shook my head. "The Queens of Willow Street are bitches and will be pissed off. You never want to ruffle their feathers."

He left out a sigh of disappointment and pulled away from me. "In 1994, you would have jumped all over my invitation to boff me."

I rolled my eyes. "That's when I had a drinking problem."

"And cocaine."

"Yes, that, too."

"You stayed at my side ... even when I was being stupid."

"Stupid was sometimes sexy on you."

"You were my rock."

"I am still your rock."

His green eyes sparkled again; magic swirled in their coal-black pupils. "A quickie is in motion, Key."

"I love quickies," he admitted, went for my waist band, and fell to his knees, devouring my skin again.

TWO – THE QUEENS OF WILLOW STREET

Brunch was served at Pandora's Closet, a queer diner on Liberty Avenue in downtown Pittsburgh. The drive was short from our three-bedroom home in Brookline. Parking was free if you could find a meter.

Liberty Avenue was empty on Sunday mornings; young and old queers alike enjoyed sleeping in and skipping church. As usual, Pandora's had a line out the front door; some national television show recently visited it and called it something like tastefully simple. Key and I paid no attention to the line, walked around and through the mass, and entered; Vince and Kyle were always early for brunch and saved us a table.

"Hold up, Robby," my sidekick called from behind me. He grabbed my left elbow and tugged me to slow down.

I steered us to our regular table while taking in Pandora's Closet: a mix of Greek and Italian décor consisted of high-backed chairs, wide bar the color of sandstone, melancholic lighting; The Killers blasted down from the overhead sound system; reddish-turquoise blue tile was puzzled together under our feet. The place was wall to wall brunchers and every table was occupied. A heavy pork smell sprinkled with pepper and cilantro filled the diner. Sizzling eggs, chocolate chip waffles, and hollandaise sauce aromas also wafted about the premises. Morning-goers chatted with gleeful smiles at their tables. Some brunchers were suffering with hangovers and milked glasses of chilled water or steamy cups of Madagascar coffee while others were bright-eyed and bushy-tailed.

Vince waved from a window table. He was hulking, muscular, and still quite athletic at forty-three. He semi-stood and called out like Liza Minelli, "Darlings, over here!"

His lover, a Garth Stein look-alike male in his late forties, tugged on Vince's left arm and pulled him down to the table. Kyle snapped his fingers at Vince and sassily called upwards, "Sit, Vince … Down boy!"

To Vince's left was a third individual whom I had never seen before. As I sat across from the couple, I took in the young man's blond hair and sexy-blue eyes. The stranger's head of hair was a ball of curls, and his smile was impeccably white. I placed his medium-sized build at maybe twenty, delicious from inside-out, and rather alluring.

Key settled at my right side; he too took in the young stranger at brunch.

Vince called across the table, "Gentlemen, I'd like to introduce you to our new roommate, Greer Cartwell."

"Roommate?" my lover questioned with raised eyebrows and tongue-wagging interest.

Kyle admitted, "Yes. A friend of a friend's son. Greer is from Oklahoma. He's studying graphic design at the Art Institute on the Boulevard of the Allies."

I reached across the table with my right hand and introduced myself. Greer's handshake was very much like a cowboy's: hearty, clenching, and unwavering. Following my introduction, I turned my attention to Key and said, "This is my husband of seventeen years. His name is Key Bry."

Greer grinned, shaking Key's extended hand. In doing so, he chanted, "We both have strange first names."

"My real name is Keaton. All the queers at this table have always called me Key."

"Greer is my uncle's name. He died at a rodeo the week before I was born. A bucking stallion murdered him. My mom and dad thought it best to name me after him."

I nodded my head and thought: Oh my. How disheartening. That is not an upbeat fact to share on a Sunday morning during brunch.

Key nodded his head. He couldn't take his eyes off the blond ambition across from us. My husband licked his lips and seemed to drool over the boy.

With age, I learned to read Key's mind; an extended marriage allots for such telepathic tendencies. I knew he was thinking: He looks exactly like Robby seventeen years ago. He'll bed the boy before dusk.

My right elbow lunged into Key's ribs in a playful manner. Key made eye contact with me, wildly grinned, and winked at me.

Never did Key have an affair on me, and vice versa. We were always faithful to each other, through the good times together, and the bad. We shared basic rules: heavy flirting was allowed; an ass-grasp of a man's bulbous bottom never hurt anyone; kiss and tell regarding everything was essential; avoid a man's dick at all costs; always use our bottoms as exits, unless with each other. The rules worked, which kept our relationship valid, whole, and flourishing. Without such a design, Key being promiscuous and sexually needy, he would have devoured a dozen or more men during our years of partnership, which probably would have caused our love to fall apart and fully dissolve.

Had Key met with Greer during his stay in the city as a student, and the two shared intimate time together, I would have forgiven him. The boy was over half Key's age, seemed immature, and nothing less than a vat of masculine goo in a porn star's youthful body. Once Key banged the bottom's bottom, I was quite sure he would return to me. I was smart enough to know that I could not provide such a body for Key's one-night use, but I obtained other attributes that he found interesting. Things in a man-with-man marriage sagged, hair turned gray, and flesh was no longer supple and beautifully sun-beamed bronze. I was not twenty and Key knew it. There was no way in hell I could have sexually performed like Greer Cartwell, but that didn't mean I couldn't try. If he wanted me to balance my weight on one leg while he banged his nine-inch tool inside my rump, I was game. If he wanted me to hang from the ceiling and apply bites to my bottom, I wanted to be pleasurably bitten. Our sexual youth hadn't vanished completely. Extended evenings of sharing flesh-inside-flesh interludes were not over. Quickies seemed to work for the both of us, which were always heated, intense, and rather effective. Our sex now leaned toward more romance, emotional comfort, and less wham-bam-thank-you-Stan stuff. Sex in our forties was more passion-driven, enlightening, and just as fun as he would have shared with Greer, but in a different way. That's what I could do for my man; that was my intention on that Sunday morning brunch with the Queens of Willow Street and their blond and buoyant boy toy from Oklahoma.

THREE – GREER-REAR

What transpired after a round of strawberry-cream cheese filled muffins at our Pandora's Closet table? After many gawks and ganders at the blond Art Institute student, I was whisked away from the table. Following a long-winded tale of the young man's mid-west history, which consisted of an underage drinking fine, numerous boy-flings, and a summer camp just for cowboys, Key whispered into my left ear, "Come with me."

Translations in a marriage became quite easy after seventeen years of involvement with the same man. I knew when no meant yes, and I like it meant I really hate it. If he wanted to stay in for the night instead of attending one of Vince's festive cheese and wine parties, he took a long bubble bath. If he didn't want to have sex, he found a Rob Rosen book and started reading it. Key's activities were quite simple to decipher in the last few years. Not a single action could be translated without accuracy.

I knew come with me meant let me bang your rump in the men's room, Robby. So I followed him across Pandora's Closet, down a narrow, semi-dark hallway, and into the men's room.

He locked the door behind us. A fiery and heated kiss was shared, pants were dropped, ribbed plastic was applied to his nine inches of uncut dick, and I was bent over one of the American Standard sinks in a matter of seconds, obtaining the pounding of my life from my significant other.

Maybe he believed or interpreted that he wasn't ramming his cock into me. Instead, it was Greer-rear he was swinging to and fro with. Not that I minded, though. If the young and blond artist turned my husband on, I only benefited from it in the end, literally. The ride was swift and wild, heated and intense. Everything about it was fun, unplanned, and desired to the fullest.

As seven of his nine inches slipped into my rear, glided in and out, a question surfaced between my temples: When was the last time we had sex twice in one day? I couldn't remember. Maybe a decade before at Ross McDwindle's wedding; somewhere in an attic and then in a spare bedroom. Maybe longer. Whenever it was, it was simply incomparable to our motivated thrusting, grunting, and buildup of sweat that sealed us together as lovers inside Pandora's.

The bathroom romp was quick and unyielding. Our motion was erratic and relentless. Groans and grunts echoed off the walls. The east and west friction that we designed was breathtaking. Both of us seemed to have lost oxygen at the same time, but didn't stop our sexual antics among all the tile and stainless steel fixtures.

"Now," Key chanted behind me, bucking my bottom numerous times, ready to fire his load.

"Me, too," I announced, stroking my cock up and down, willing it to blow.

We came together, just like always. I covered the tile floor with my white ooze, and he filled the condom with his gunk. Clean-up was quick and rather uneventful. Afterwards, we kissed and fixed our clothes, rubbed wrinkles away, made sure our belts were fastened, and returned to our two friends and their boy toy, whom I wanted to personally thank for turning my husband's hormones on and making him bump his body against mine.

FOUR – THE GLOW FACTOR

"You two took forever. What were you doing in the bathroom with each other?" Kyle grinned from ear to ear, checking us out from head to toe, analyzing our every curve, expression, and whatnots.

"Absolutely nothing," my sidekick explained, attempting to sell his lie like a very bad car dealer.

"You're both glowing," Vince laughed.

The blond boy observed our chatter as if we were a play, enjoying its dialogue to the fullest. Wide eyes and reddish cheeks covered his boyishly adorable face.

"We don't glow anymore," I announced. "Men our age cannot glow. It's a proven fact in *GQ* ... or some magazine."

Both Kyle and his lover giggled like little girls at the window table. Key and I ignored them and sat at the table again. There, I wondered if men our age could glow. Did we still have that feature or not? I didn't know, and probably wouldn't ever find out the real answer to that question any time soon. I was beaming inside, though, overjoyed with the fast-fuck that was provided by my husband in Pandora's Closet's bathroom. My face was warm, as well as every other part of my body. I was thrilled that Key could still turn me on, just as he did when he was twenty-one ... -two ... -three and so-on. The lust had not dissipated throughout our shared years, even if a sexual catalyst such as the blond Oklahoma boy motivated my lover's libido, and sparked an interest in Key to bang my bottom in a public restroom. Life changed so quickly, and both of us knew we had to go with the flow to survive, together.

I admit, we all had too many mimosas in the next hour, excluding the boy, since he was far too young to drink in public. None of us should have climbed behind the wheels of our coupes, but we did. Legally, we were all drunk, and it was foolish to drive under such conditions. Men are fools, though, aren't they? Tool bags as some people call them. Since the beginning of time they have made the most horrible decisions. Men will always be foolish, I surmise, until the end of all our days.

Every Sunday morning/afternoon we usually stopped at Turn the Page Books on Brownsville. There, we scurried through the shelves of Tom Wolfe, Clive Barker, Sylvia Plath, John Patrick, and Jackie Collins. Key said he wasn't feeling well and politely decided for the both of us that we would go home; a nap was needed. On our short drive home, we both agreed that Greer would end up sleeping with Kyle and Vince by the end of his schooling. An affair among the three was surely going to ensue. Key said while turning on Pioneer, "It's how they keep their marriage together. They share things. I sort of get it. I pose no judgment regarding their companionship. Some couples like to share boys. Greer seems like a nice kid and will be fine with it. I don't think Kyle and Vince's relationship will deteriorate. The accommodation will probably help their marriage to stay afloat."

"Like Liam."

"Yes. Exactly like him."

Liam Hossentheim was an exchange student from Brussels. He lived with Kyle and Vince for a year. Pitt University paid the two a monthly fee to accommodate the young man's basic needs: food, board, and ... sex. The twenty-one-year-old college student had an affair with both men. No damage was done to their relationship, though. In fact, Key and I both agreed that Kyle and Vince's love for each other had matured, enhanced, and reached into a new level of intimacy because of the visiting student.

"What happened to Liam?" I inquired, noticing that my lover was driving very slowly, being cautious in his drunken state.

"I have no idea."

"He gave me the glow factor."

"Yes, I knew that. The man's amber-colored eyes seduced the both of us. He was beautiful in many ways."

"Do you think we will ever have a Liam or Greer in our lives?"

"Only time will tell."

"Would we break up? Would our marriage end?"

Key looked over at me, grinned, and whispered, "Hell no. Not in a thousand years."

I smiled, delighted with his answer, and responded, "Let's make it two thousand years."

FIVE – BOY-LOVE FOREVER

As Key took a Sunday afternoon nap I decided to write another chapter of my next gay mystery, *Skin Flick*. My office was rather small and compact: Netbook on a mahogany desk; two windows that overlooked city houses and Key's tomato and cucumber garden; Colt calendar on the wall telling me it was the end of August; Danish Modern reading chair; shelf of novels and nonfiction tomes. The floor was comprised of wooden boards recycled from an old Lancaster barn, splintery and a rather dull gray hue because of much use. Atop my desk was a picture of Key and me at Walt Disney World: suntanned, happy, and smiling. Beside the photograph sat a second photograph. In it, we both sported black tuxes accented in rose red, our commitment ceremony day, May 28. The photograph was taken a dozen years ago. Key had more hair, and I was thinner; partnership causes the most dramatic physical changes among men, but in a good way, of course.

I decided to put writing off for a few minutes. Inside my office was a tiny closet that was cluttered with stuff: a stack of hardback novels, rugby shirts, naughty DVDs, ancient manuscripts that were incomplete, and a photo album. I found the album, tugged it out of the mess, and sat in the reading chair with it on my lap. There, I opened the album to its first page and Keaton stared at me with a beaming smile: twenty-three years old, blond squirrel on the base of his chin, left eyebrow pierced, and a Celine Dion T-shirt, which cuddled his firm pecs. He looked sexy like a boy-bitch with a twinkle of mischievousness in his eyes.

The second photograph was of Key a few years later: inexpensive business suit, leather working satchel, Tom Cruise sunglasses, and a soul patch under his bottom lip. No longer did he sport the squirrel on his chin or the pierced eyebrow, maturing.

The next photograph was taken by Kyle and Lance's in-ground pool on the Fourth of July a few years ago. The day Lance fell into the pool, banged his head off the diving board, and almost drowned. The day Key decided to establish wills for the both of us and life insurance policies. The day it maybe hit him that we would live together for the rest of our lives as boys in love, middle-aged men in love, and older gentlemen in love.

I flipped to the next page and realized the five, smaller displayed photographs were out of sequence. Each was from

1992, the year Key and I met. A time when Paul Simon toured Africa, Jeffrey Dahmer was sentenced to life in prison, massive rioting over Rodney King transpired in Los Angeles, the Summer Olympics was held in Barcelona, Princess Di separated from Charles, and Taylor Lautner and Selena Gomez were born. The photographs were of downtown Pittsburgh: the Burmingham Bridge, Heinz Stadium, the Point, the Andy Warhol Museum, and the Kaufmann's Clock on the corners of Fifth and Smithfield.

My mind floated to that time and place when I had first met Keaton Bry, back to October 20, 1992, a Tuesday evening. Key and I met underneath the Kaufmann's Clock. The night was chilly with some wind. Oak and maple leaves blew around our feet. We stood waiting for the stop light to change, so we could cross Smithfield Street. Eye contact was made. Both of us carried out once-overs of each other. As he studied my thin build in green denim and a long-sleeved white cotton shirt over a sky-blue T-shirt, I gawked at his white-fringed cowboy boots, ass-gripping Levis, and red-and-brown plaid shirt. He sported a cowboy hat, but wasn't a cowboy. Something told me he was a city boy who just liked to dress as a cowboy. How strange. But I fell for his strangeness with ease.

"Hey," I said, very original, rather dull sounding.

"Back at you."

"It's getting cold. The snow will be here before we know it." I was horrible at picking up guys, maybe that's why I was single for two years before meeting Key.

He ignored my comment and pointed to the literature books in my right arm and hand, which were cupped against my chest. "You a student?"

"Point Park College. Just finished a class. Going home."

The light changed, but we didn't move. Key gave me another once-over, studying me from head to toe. "You eat dinner yet?"

I shook my head.

"You want to get some Mexican? I know of this place around the corner."

If the truth be told, I think I fell in love with him at that very second. The autumn wind blew against his blond eyebrows. His green eyes shined with interest to get to know and begin to understand me. A connection was designed within seconds on the street corner. I thought him cute, forward, smart, and tender. In due time, after a number of dates with him, a night of passion on his living room floor would transpire. I would learn that he was the greatest guy in the world: sensitive, brilliant with money, wanted to be a real estate agent, loved dogs, hated to read, enjoyed baking, and sort of had a Hollywood crush on Dean Cain. Thereafter, we would decide to try a long-term relationship together, a trip to Spain, gardening, purchasing a house together, owning a dog, buying a camp in the northern woods together, and share a commitment ceremony. Other things would transpire in the next seventeen years, some of which were not shiny and bright: bankruptcy of our business, cancer, an almost-fatal car wreck, and the death of his mother, which just about rocked our world to pieces. Great things would transpire also: together we survived cancer, novels and short stories were published, money was made, and the sex was unbelievable. That night on Smithfield Street changed our lives forever. Something magical in the autumn wind drew us together and cradled our bodies with the inexorable flux of time, an alignment between young men, boys then who would turn into men. Forever in love. Us. Today. Now.

"Mexican?" I questioned. "I like that."

He beamed a smile, lightly punched me in my right arm in a playful manner because the city was not as liberal then as it is today regarding two men kissing on a street corner. "Come with me, guy."

"I'm Robert," I said, following him, allowing him to lead me astray within the shadows of the city for the next seventeen years.

"Robby," he replied. "I like that. I'm Key. My real name is Keaton and ..."

#####

"Hey." Key popped his head into my office, awake from his nap.

I turned my head to the right and looked over my shoulder. He was wearing nothing more than a pair of coal-black boxer-briefs, his favorite underwear. Lustfully, I studied his thin chest, hard nipples, and the line of blond treasure trail that fell into his cotton material. "What's up?"

"What are you doing in here?"

He always asked me that. Why? I never knew, since I crafted words, sentences and paragraphs in that specific room and its small amount of space. "I was just looking through a photo album before I start to write. Remember that night on Smithfield Street?"

"Best night of my life. It feels like it was just last night to me. We stayed up talking until four o'clock in the morning. I didn't want you to leave, but you had to work in the morning. I hated to see you go. All I could think about the next day was you."

"I would have slept with you if you wanted me to."

"I liked you too much for that to happen. I waited to seduce you. Just when I thought it was right between us."

"Something tells me that you still like me."

He yanked down on the rim of his coal-black boxer-briefs and flashed me his deflated cock. Seconds passed, and he snapped the material's rim against his waist, concealing his goods yet again. "I like you just a little bit. My cock likes you a lot, though. I keep telling it not to get involved with you because it might fall in love with you."

"That would suck," I chanted, smiling from ear to ear because of his play.

He laughed. "You know a lot about sucking, don't you?"

"I do, but only with you."

"Faithful until the end."

"Of course."

"You want to come and finish my nap with me?" he asked, rubbing his stomach with his right palm.

I loved to nap, especially with him. "Only if I can spoon you. I get off on my limp cock touching your nice ass."

"I think we can arrange that," he replied, winked at me, and escaped to our bedroom where I would join him in just a few minutes.

THE EDITOR

MICKEY ERLACH is a full-time editor for STARbooks Press. He tries being Alpha, but his partner, Eric Summers, won't allow it.

ng any underwear. "Excuse me," I said, having a hard time looking

led by that bulge in his crotch. "but don't I know you?" "Maybe," h

of to   bout a m

n Ray   God, you

ser?   in?" he as

"Lik   s stronges

body   e on Gree

, he l   I ever sa

o to t   any ideas

king   ne same

coul   ery long t

d rac   ne swell.

with   e in store

go   behind s

see   in public

" he   vent to th

acy.   grabbed

rd. I

traci   t, so firm

it, ha

th my   bing dick

ng.   n cock, b

sound of unzipping filled the small space. I don't know who's hand

ut before I knew it, I had his rod in my hand, and mine was in his. "

o do?" he asked, his tone challenging. I knew exactly, and sank to